The Unabomber

and

the Zodiac

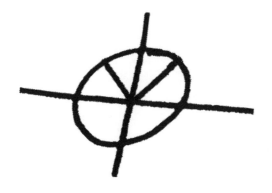

by Douglas Evander Oswell

ISBN 978-0-6151-4569-3

Typeset by the author in 11-point Monotype Plantin with chapter headings in 30-point ITC Benguiat Gothic.

Contents

Acknowledgements

To be surrounded by good women is the particular blessing of a happy man, and though he be ever so poor, a man endowed by Providence with such a boon is rich indeed. All of the women in my life are good, and while three in particular have rendered assistance in the production of this work I must acknowledge them by name. The first is my sister, Linda Dutrow, who read the first drafts of the book and offered invaluable suggestions regarding its content and its style. The second is my daughter, Michelle Oswell, whose professional abilities as a reference librarian afforded easy access to research materials that I might otherwise have not been able to obtain. The third is my wife, Diana, whose unshakable support has sustained me, not only in this endeavor, but in every single aspect of my life.

I gratefully acknowledge the indefatigable efforts of such prominent Zodiologists as Tom Voigt, webmaster of the incomparable Zodiackiller. com, Michael Butterfield (whose forthcoming book on the Zodiac affair will fill a void that has existed for the past four decades), Jake Wark, Mike Rodelli and Howard Davis. Their efforts in the realm of investigation have yielded a wealth of information that could not have been imagined even ten short years ago, when the sum total of resources available to the interested public consisted of a single yellow book.

I am indebted also to Chris McCarthy for his critique of my statistical analysis, and Ross Getman, for his long-forgotten (and now resurrected) connection of Kaczynski to *The Ring*.

This book is dedicated to MIKE RUSCONI, my talented and synoptic friend.

Preface

THE ZODIAC KILLER ("Zodiac," or "the Zodiac" as he styled himself) murdered five people between December of 1968 and October of 1969. The murders were followed by letters to the news media demanding publication of his threats and other written material, on pain of further killings. As the Unabomber, Theodore Kaczynski murdered three people and injured many more, over a period beginning in May of 1978 and continuing through April of 1995. His murders were followed by letters to the news media demanding publication of the letters themselves, and the so-called "Manifesto," on pain of further killings.

This is not a book *about* the Unabomber, nor is it a book *about* the Zodiac. To have made it either, or both, would have expanded its content to many times the present length, and needlessly complicated a subject that already is complicated enough. To accommodate the reader who may be unfamiliar with either case, or both, details of the subjects' crimes are presented wherever they are relevant, and omitted where they are not. The novice to either case will undoubtedly desire to broaden his knowledge of the criminals and their crimes. To that end he may avail himself of the numerous resources to be found in print, or on the public internet. For now, however, the following brief synopsis may suffice.

Zodiac's career of infamy began on the night of December 20, 1968, on Lake Herman Road, an isolated country thoroughfare near Vallejo, California. There, in a lonely lover's lane, he gunned down David Faraday and Betty Lou Jensen, two Vallejo teens who had come together that evening for a date. To all appearances the couple was approached by a gun-wielding man who ordered them from their car, felled young Faraday execution-style with a single bullet to the head, then fired five shots of his .22-caliber semiautomatic into the back of a fleeing Jensen. Both died at the scene.

Six months later, in the early morning hours of July 5th, the Zodiac murdered a young mother named Darlene Ferrin and wounded her companion Mike Mageau, as the pair sat talking in the parking lot of Blue Rock Springs, a golf course in Vallejo. Pulling his car up behind their parked Corvair, the killer shone a bright light into the car and fired a hail of bullets from a 9 mm semiautomatic pistol. He then quietly drove away. Darlene Ferrin expired at the scene. Mike Mageau recovered from his wounds.

Following a three-month hiatus the Zodiac struck again, this time on the shores of Lake Berryessa, a popular recreation area north of Napa, California. On October 27, dressed in a garish costume, he confronted college students Bryan Hartnell and Cecilia Shepard as they enjoyed each other's company on a blanket near the shore. Brandishing a pistol and posing as an escaped convict, Zodiac induced the couple to bind each other's hands, then proceeded to stab them with a foot-long knife. Two days later, Cecilia Shepard succumbed to injuries sustained in the attack. Bryan Hartnell survived, and related a chilling account of the assault.

On October 11, 1969, Zodiac made his final appearance in the city of San Francisco. Hailing a cab at the intersection of Mason and Geary in the downtown section of the city, Zodiac directed cab driver Paul Stine to drive him to the corner of Washington and Cherry, in posh Presidio Heights. Once the destination had been reached, his passenger held a pistol to Stine's head and pulled the trigger, murdering the cabbie with a single shot.

From a window overlooking the murder scene, three teenage partygoers watched as the killer fumbled with his victim's body, exited the cab and casually walked away. Shortly thereafter, police officers Donald Fouke and Eric Zelms passed him in their squad car as he ambled unhurriedly down nearby Jackson Street. Because the suspect had been mistakenly identified as a Negro Male Adult, the officers had no reason to stop and question the Caucasian man they saw. Proceeding onward, they allowed him to continue as he made his way from Jackson Street to West Pacific Avenue and presumably to a waiting vehicle.

He was never seen again.

Nine years later, and eighteen hundred miles away, the Unabomber kick-started his career with a package bomb addressed to Professor E.J. Smith at Rensselaer Polytechnic Institute in Troy, New York. The parcel containing the bomb was found in a parking lot of the University of Illinois at Chicago. University officials dutifully returned the parcel to its purported sender, Professor Buckley Crist of Northwestern University. It detonated when opened, inflicting minor injuries to Terry Marker, a campus security officer. The date was May 26, 1978.

On May 9th of the following year, the Unabomber struck again, this time with a bomb hand-placed in the Technical Building of Northwestern University in Evanston, Illinois. Tucked inside a "Phillies" cigar box, the device exploded when opened by John Harris, a member of the Civil Engineering Department. Harris suffered burns and lacerations.

The relatively innocuous nature of the first two bombings was belied by the potential viciousness of the third. On November 14, 1969, on a flight originating from Chicago, a bomb exploded in the baggage compartment of a United Airlines 727, filling the cabin with smoke and forcing the airplane to make an emergency landing. In the baggage compartment, authorities discovered the remnants of a bomb that had been rigged to a barometric detonating mechanism, designed to trigger the device when the aircraft reached a certain altitude. The force of the explosion had not been sufficient to damage the airplane's fuselage. Had it done so, all of the people on board would probably have been killed.

Bomb number four targeted Percy Wood, president of United Airlines, with a pipe bomb cleverly concealed in a hollowed-out copy of the novel *Ice Brothers* by Sloan Wilson, author of *Man in the Gray Flannel Suit*. Wood opened the device on June 10, 1980. It exploded, causing serious lacerations to his face and leg.

The Unabomber's fifth device consisted of a brown paper package placed in a hallway of the Business department at the University of Utah in Salt Lake City. It was discovered on October 8, 1981, by a student who immediately notified the campus police. A local bomb squad identified the package as an bomb, before safely detonating it with a small explosive charge. The device had been attached to a can of gasoline, intended to act as an incendiary. Had it worked as planned, a terrible fire would have ensued, with many people either killed or injured.

On May 5, 1982, a package addressed to Professor Patrick C. Fischer was opened by his secretary Janet Smith, and exploded in her hands. Smith suffered injuries to her face and arms. Two months later, in the faculty lounge of Cory Hall at the University of California, Berkeley, Professor Diogenes Angelakos picked up a piece of what he believed to be test equipment belonging to a student or construction crew. As he lifted its handle, the Unabomber's seventh bomb went off, causing serious injuries to Angelakos's right hand, arm and face. Like the Salt Lake City bomb, this device was also rigged to a one-gallon can of gasoline, which fortunately did not ignite.

At this juncture the Unabomber, now known as such by the authorities, had yet to score a single kill.

A three-year hush ensued before he struck anew. Once again the location was Cory Hall, at UC Berkeley. On May 15, 1985, the life of John Hauser, an Air Force Captain, engineering student, and up-and-coming astronaut, took a sudden and unexpected turn. Eyeing a notebook binder he presumed to be the project of a fellow student, Hauser raised the cover. It immediately exploded, causing instant damage to Hauser's hand and arm, including the loss of four fingers. Permanently maimed, Hauser's dream of becoming an astronaut was gone.

Around the same time as the Hauser incident, the Unabomber mailed a brown paper parcel to the Boeing Aircraft Company's Fabrication Division in Auburn, Washington. Upon partially unwrapping the device, mailroom employees at the plant became suspicious and notified the county Sheriff's office, whose bomb squad rendered it safe by detonation.

Not content with the mayhem he had already wrought, the Unabomber waited only six months before mailing his tenth device, a package bomb addressed to renowned psychologist Dr. James McConnell at his home in Ann Arbor, Michigan. Attached to the outside of the package was a letter requesting that McConnell review and critique an enclosed manuscript. When McConnell's assistant, Nicklaus Suino, opened the parcel the bomb exploded, causing serious injuries to Suino and damaging the hearing of McConnell, who had been standing nearby.

Amazingly, at this point no person had been killed by the Unabomber in his relentless crusade against society. That circumstance would change on the afternoon of December 11, 1985, in the parking lot of Rentech Computer Rental Company in Sacramento, California. Hugh Campbell Scrutton, owner of Rentech, observed in his parking lot what appeared to be a piece of wood with nails protruding from it. When Scrutton tried to move it, the "road hazard" exploded with a resounding bang. The blast ripped off his hand, while shrapnel tore a gaping hole in Scrutton's chest. Moments later he expired. Finally, after long effort, the Unabomber had succeeded in creating a lethal bomb.

Emboldened by success he struck again, this time once again in Salt Lake City. On February 20, 1987, employees of CAAMS, a computer company, watched through the blinds of an office window as an unidentified white male bent down beside a car. They saw him take from a cloth bag what appeared to be a pair of two-by-fours, studded with protruding nails, and place the object in the parking lot adjacent to the car. Sensible of the fact that he was under observation, the man walked quietly away. Shortly thereafter Gary Wright, vice-president of CAAMS, emerged from his car in the parking lot and noticed the wooden object lying on the pavement. When he attempted to move it, a hidden pipe bomb detonated, causing serious and lasting injuries to Wright.

Shocked at having been observed by witnesses, the Unabomber now went deeply underground, striving to perfect a combination of explosive and detonator that would allow small but lethal bombs to be carried through the mail.

On June 18, 1993, more than six years after the CAAMS event, he mailed a set of two identical package bombs to recipients a continent apart. Dr. Charles Epstein was a medical professor at the University of California, San Francisco. One of the packages, addressed to Epstein at his home nearby in Tiburon, exploded when he opened it, causing lasting injuries to Epstein's hand, arm, face, and hearing. Six days later, prominent computer scientist David Gelernter suffered a similar fate when he opened the second of the packages, addressed to his office at the Computer Science Department of Yale University. Following the explosion a dazed but determined Gelernter staggered to a campus clinic, where his blood pressure was recorded as zero. Miraculously, he survived.

Fortune proved not so kind to Thomas Mosser, a vice-president and general manager of the Young & Rubicam advertising agency, headquartered in New York City. On December 10, 1994, Mosser could hardly have anticipated the calamity that awaited him at his home in North Caldwell, New Jersey. Among the mail that had accumulated during a recent business trip was a small white package. A scant few seconds prior to his opening this package, Mosser's young daughter ran playfully from the room, as Mosser's wife Susan followed close behind. The blast that followed wrought terrifying damage on Mosser's body, tearing off fingers and driving nails into his flesh. He succumbed a short time later.

The career of the Unabomber was quickly drawing to a close. It did not end soon enough for Gilbert Murray, President of the California Forestry Association, headquartered in the city of Sacramento. At some point in the afternoon of April 24, 1995, a package arrived at the Association, addressed to William Dennison, Murray's predecessor at the CFA. Taking the heavy parcel from his receptionist, Murray walked into his office and closed the door behind him. Shortly thereafter a deafening explosion reverberated through the air, and Gilbert Murray, the Unabomber's final victim, was no more.

★ ★ ★

The purpose of this work is to offer the reader an analysis of the startling and thought-provoking similarities between the Unabomber and the Zodiac. In doing so, the author will demonstrate that both killers

- Possessed a common social pathology and a common criminal motive;
- Achieved emotional gratification by using murder as a vehicle for attaining nationwide publicity;
- Moved in key areas during the times of the Zodiac events;
- Possessed physical descriptions that bore a number of striking similarities, most notably the heavy structure of their facial features and the large, square jaw that was captured by forensic artists creating composite sketches rendered years apart;
- Possessed a common mathematical mindset, and shared the quality of intellectual versatility;
- Made use of literary allusion and employed a particular type of literary genre to serve up clues about their motives to the public and police;
- Offered hints pertaining to their physical locations through the use of identical allusions contained within their writings;
- Used elaborate ciphers of their own design; and
- Displayed over 40 similarities in compositional style and tone.

Additionally, within the ciphers of the Zodiac, four particular sets of *meta-codes* will be revealed, whose solutions point directly to Kaczynski. An informal comparison of handwriting specimens will demonstrate the relative ease with which the hand of Kaczynski might be disguised to form the hand of Zodiac. Finally, a logical scenario will be put forth to explain how and why the persona of the Unabomber might have evolved from the persona of the Zodiac.

There will exist an undeniable inference that by elaborating on these similarities the author is attempting to credit Kaczynski with the criminal activities of the Zodiac. The reader will not be discouraged from making such a judgement, if he is led to it naturally by the combined force of all the evidence. In order to offer a more balanced and objective analysis to any reader so inclined, the best objections to a formal linkage of the cases have been presented alongside the host of similarities. Key among these objections are the problems with Kaczynski's whereabouts during the epoch of the Zodiac, the possible disparities in physical appearance, the failure to match Kaczynski's fingerprints with the purported prints of Zodiac, the inconclusive verdict on the handwriting, and the purported evolution of Kaczynski's ability to kill. These objections have been analyzed, not necessarily with a view to rebutting them, but to convince the reader that they are by no means trump cards to a possible connection. Once again, if the reader is led to the conclusion that Theodore Kaczynski was actually the Zodiac, no attempt will be made to dissuade him from it. The good name and reputation of one cold-blooded killer can hardly be diminished by his implied association with another.

That said, the author's chief concern is not that his readers will close this book convinced or unconvinced that the case for a suspect has been made. It is, rather, that they should reach its ending imbued with a clear and unequivocal perception that something astonishingly unique has been revealed. At the very least he hopes that they will share his sense of curiosity — curiosity combined with wonderment — that the Unabomber and the Zodiac, who on the face of things appear as distant cousins, should actually be twins. He hopes that, like himself, they may store these revelations in a place where they will not be lost, against the day when further information comes to light that will either affirm the speculation, or completely strike it down. If so they will not have read this treatise, nor the author written it, in vain.

Chapter 1

Signs of the Zodiac

Thou shalt not covet thy neighbour's house, thou shalt not covet thy neighbour's wife, nor his manservant, nor his maidservant, nor his ox, nor his ass, nor any thing that is thy neighbour's.

EXODUS, 20:17

WHAT KIND of criminal was the Zodiac? What led him to kill, and how did the act of murder gratify his sensibilities?

Modern criminology divides multiple murderers into two broad categories. *Serial killers,* so named because they commit a *series* of *killings,* are defined as individuals who murder on at least three occasions, with a "cooling off" period in between each crime. *Mass murderers* are defined as those who kill four or more people, in one location, in one incident.

While these definitions are commonly accepted not only by criminologists, but by the public at large, they leave something to be desired in terms of truly delineating the nature of their subjects. Because their emphasis is purely quantitative, they tend to blur some very real distinctions between criminal classes whose psychology and motives are unique unto themselves.

Over the course of decades, the term "serial killer" has supplanted the earlier labels of "sexual sadist" and "psychopath," to describe the murderer whose gratification revolves around the control, abuse and destruction of his victims. His crimes are monstrous and their aftermath horrendous:

The two victims were a mother and her sixteen-year-old daughter. The actual intended victim was the sixteen-year-old. The mother was killed as she attempted to defend herself and her daughter. The killer had waited

13

until the victims were ready for bed. He struck the sixteen-year-old in the head with a baseball bat, which resulted in her instant death. He then confronted the mother with a knife, as she became aware of his presence in the home. The mother suffered several defense wounds to her arms and hands before succumbing to some 31 stab wounds of her body. There was evidence that she was tortured as well. Once his victims were unconscious and dead he engaged in hours of sexual deviance with their bodies. His intention was to knockout the sixteen-year-old and then torture her to death. However, he had hit her with such force that she died. He eviscerated both of his victims. He had sex with their corpses and drank their blood before posing and propping them with their body parts and inserting a baseball bat into the daughter's vagina. He removed the breasts from the mother and placed them in the bedroom on end tables on either side of the bed where the daughter's body was found. He incised the skin of the pubis from the mother and placed the tissue into her mouth. He incised the skin of the pubis from the daughter's body and placed it upon the right side of her face. He then engaged in postmortem piquerism by stabbing into the daughter's throat a total of sixteen times.[1]

Consider also this brief synopsis from criminologist J. Paul De River's classic work, *The Sexual Criminal*:

The following case illustrates the most brutal type of sadistic lust murderer. This suspect confessed to the murder and dissection of his female victims. The bodies of both women had been slashed: the first victim with a butcher knife, and the second victim with a safety razor blade. This subject had a fetish for both knives and safety razor blades. The body of the first victim had been dissected, her legs and arms disarticulated; the throats of both victims were cut, and in both cases the breasts had been slashed, and the vagina mutilated. On one of the victims he had bitten the breast, and later confessed he might have swallowed the nipple. He practiced cunnilingus on the first victim. When he was arrested his mustache showed evidence of blood.[2]

Famed killer Ted Bundy bludgeoned his victims into a state of insensibility, then followed the assaults with various acts of rape, torture, mutilation and death by strangulation. Once his victims had expired, Bundy indulged his taste for necrophilia and post-mortem mutilation. Ed Kemper committed rape, stabbing, and manual strangulation upon his living victims; decapitation and necrophilia upon the dead. Lawrence Bittaker's fancy was to torture his victims with a pair of pliers and a hammer. His partner, Roy Norris, tape-recorded their sessions of rape and torture. At the ensuing trial, a replay of those recordings sent jurors and spectators running from the courtroom in horror and disgust.

As stated above, the term "serial killer" is commonly used in reference both to a type of crime and the psychological character of the person who commits it. The classical description assumes as its premise the fact that certain killers have a tendency to continue killing until they are either caught, or some external circumstance puts an end to their murderous ways. It defines the "serial" killer as someone who commits a "series" of killings. In a very broad sense, the description serves its purpose. It fails, however, to define its subject's nature. Apart from the sheer number of times a serial killer strikes lies a bizarre, complex and frightening array of characteristics that set this type of murderer apart from all the others. The National Center for the Victims of Crime offers a chilling definition of the term that states its case with naked clarity:

> Serial murder is the supreme manifestation of violent criminality as evidenced by the horrifying acts perpetrated against innocent victims. The crime is often an interrelation and culmination of extreme sexual perversity and brutal homicide which generally leaves the victim in a condition far worse than simply the infliction of death. Many victims of serial killers endure prolonged periods of suffering until the lethal assault saves them from further torment .... Although serial murder is relatively rare in comparison to homicide or violent crime in general, the serial killer receives much more disdain from society because of the agony he inflicts upon the victim in what the public considers a senseless occurrence.[3]

By the time of its adoption in the last decades of the twentieth century, "serial killer" had supplanted the earlier terminology of "sociopath," "psychopath," and "sexual-sadist" that had been used to define the same essential kind of criminal. Although it is less fashionable nowadays to refer to killers as sociopaths, the appellation of sexual sadist is commonly employed to describe the serial killer, and to suggest that the person to whom the label applies is something more than simply a killer who takes a certain number of victims over a particular period of time.

"Sexual crimes," wrote J. Paul de River in *The Sexual Criminal*, "are probably the most demoralizing and horrifying of all crimes, and administer the greatest shock to those who come in contact with them." As illustrated in the examples above, the horror of which de River speaks is a direct result of the manner in which the sexual sadist carries out his acts. In the case of sexually-sadistic murder, death is simply the climax of a series of actions that have been scripted in the fantasies of the perpetrator long before the act itself. Those actions are calculated to gratify a warped and perverted sexual impulse that can achieve satiety only by causing and witnessing the physical suffering of another human being. They are actions planned far in advance of the actual assault, and, unless they are interrupted by some unforeseen circumstance, involve *prolonged and intimate contact* with the victim.

Let us now consider the other type of multiple killer: the *mass murderer*. The mass murderer has this in common with the serial killer: he kills. Apart from that, the two types are wholly different, not only in their motivations, but in their psychological attributes, and the manner in which they interact with their chosen victims.

In most instances, mass murder is the last act of a desperate individual. Unlike the sexually-sadistic killer, who derives a perverse sense of joy from his hidden crimes, the mass murderer acts in a single, violent paroxysm of inexplicable rage, exposing himself to identification, capture, and often death at the hands of the police. The murders are acts of desperation, serving as vehicles for bringing the perpetrator into the public eye and drawing attention to his sense of impotence, his frustration, his anger and his hostility. The mass murderer is a psychologically troubled and deeply *disaffected* individual who often seeks to preserve his ego at the expense of his existence.

The mental state of such a disaffected person is, as the dictionary defines the term, one of fathomless resentment and unending discontent. By the time he acts out his murderous intentions, the disaffected killer has reached the end of a long metaphorical rope. He looks into the mirror and despises what he sees. He compares his life's achievements with those of others whom he perceives as enjoying prominence and success. Green-eyed envy consumes his waking thoughts. Constant failure, or at least the *perception* of constant failure, imbues him with a sense of hopelessness that the future may hold brighter days in store. These feelings in their turn lead invariably to depression and despair. His ego, always precariously balanced, stands poised upon a precipice. Life becomes a prison from which there can be but one means of escape.

Ultimately, mass murder offers its participants two distinct forms of satisfaction. First, in committing violence, the disaffected killer assuages his pent-up anger and releases his hostility in a single, overwhelming act that exposes him to the risk of imprisonment or death. Second, and perhaps most significant, it affords him a stage upon which he can stand and make his statement to the world. Nothing, it would appear, is more calculated to arrest the attention of society and divert it toward a single individual than the act of murder in the mass.

Given the distinction between serial killers and mass murderers, to which class did the Zodiac belong?

The details of Zodiac's murders give evidence of motivations far removed from those of a sexual sadist or a sociopathic personality. Clearly missing is the "recreational" element so typical of sociopathic or sexually-sadistic killers. When committing murder, Zodiac's interest in the victims does not progress beyond the deed itself. (We qualify the crime at Berryessa because in that instance binding the victims served only to immobilize them for the subsequent stabbing. Likewise we qualify the Stine murder, because the events immediately following the slaying were calculated for the purpose of authenticating the attack and manipulating evidence.) He does not torture, taunt, abuse, or sexually assault them. He makes no effort to linger with the victims following their decease. With the exceptions noted above, he refrains from touching them. His immediate interest lies in dealing death, and nothing more.

In a span of only nine short months, from December 20, 1968 through September 27, 1969, Zodiac committed three crimes so alike in their nature as to suggest that it is through those three events that we are likely to achieve a true knowledge of why he killed. The horrifying incidents at Lake Herman Road, Blue Rock Springs and Lake Berryessa each involved a young couple caught alone and unawares in an isolated trysting place where they were either engaged in sexual activity or could be mistakenly thought by the killer to be engaged in sexual activity.

There is little if any doubt that the turnout on Lake Herman Road served the teenage population of Vallejo and its surrounding environs as a private place for sexual or simply affectionate liaisons. Given the loneliness and isolation of the place, one can scarcely think otherwise. The same can probably be said of the golf-course parking lot at Blue Rock Springs, as indeed it can probably be said of any parking lot, after hours, at innumerable golf courses and public parks across the nation. Lake Berryessa and its environs no doubt contain a great many informal trysting places, and it is impossible to confirm with any degree of certainty whether the site occupied by Hartnell and Shepard had been used extensively for that purpose. Regardless, based on Hartnell's account of the incident, and certain items contained in the police reports, it seems obvious that sexual activity had either been contemplated or indulged in by the couple on the day of the assault.

> The victims's [sic] personal belongings that were left at the scene of the stabbing after the ambulance had gone were turned over to the Detectives, which consisted of one army field jacket with the male victim's name on it; one car blanket, multi-colored, wool; male victim's shoes; female victim's glasses; one key; one book, party jokes; one box of partially used prophylactics.[4]

It is hardly unreasonable to conclude that in his first three Bay Area assaults, Zodiac's intention was to murder couples that he found together alone in isolated places. That is the first, and most significant principle with which we have to work. It shows a distinct pattern of victimology, suggesting a particular mindset on the killer's part. It suggests, particularly, that these initial murders were none other than acts of symbolic retribution, fostered by the killer's own sexual inadequacy. The brevity of the attacks and the abruptness of their conclusion prevent us from seeing the Zodiac as one for whom the act of murder served as a vehicle for sexual or other stimulation. Far more likely is the notion that he killed as an act of retribution against a class of persons who represented the sexual fulfillment that he himself could not attain.

In three out of four attacks, Zodiac's victims were a young male and female caught alone together in an isolated place where it could be assumed by the killer that they were engaged in sexual activity. According to the police report, Faraday and Jensen parked their Rambler at the turnoff on Lake Herman Road in order to indulge in "necking." The box of "partially used prophylactics" enumerated in the Lake Berryessa incident carries its own unavoidable interpretation. (Less titillating, though perhaps of no lesser significance, was the book of party jokes found amongst the victims' effects, signifying lightheartedness and fun.) Finally, while there exists no evidence to indicate sexual contact between the victims at Blue Rock Springs, the suggestion is unavoidable. Whatever the reason for the assignation between Darlene Ferrin and Mike Mageau, the couple placed themselves in a position where any individual who happened upon them might understandably have inferred that a tryst was taking place.

Extrapolating from these circumstances alone, we may feel confident that at the very least a provisional motive can be ascribed to the assaults. To all appearances, Zodiac's murders comprised a personal vendetta against a particular class of individuals. Fueled by envy, his primary motive was the desire to achieve revenge.

At first glance this may seem an oversimplification, based only upon the victimology alone, with no corroborating evidence to back it up. Yet the most significant aspect of the entire case — without which the name of Zodiac would never have acquired its status as a household word — lends credence to the theory. The very existence of the Zodiac correspondences serves to depict their author as a person suffering from a variety of social pathologies that manifested themselves in his inability to function both socially and sexually.

Upon the face of it, a man who murders to achieve publicity is a man who has difficulty expressing himself through the usual channels of social interaction. Apart from that, his succession of letters shows that even as late as the period from mid-1970 through 1974, when the murders had ceased and the credibility of the bomb threats had declined to nothing, Zodiac continued to take advantage of his stature as a public figure, in a series of correspondences that grew less threatening and more bizarre with each succeeding letter.

The first hint that Zodiac offers of sexual inadequacy is contained in the Three-Part Cipher, solved by the Hardins in 1969. In that correspondence, Zodiac declares that "to kill something" is "even better than getting your rocks off with a girl." Given the circumstances of the crimes, this is tantamount to saying that what Zodiac has (i.e., the ability to kill) is superior to what his victims have (i.e., sexual relations). It implies a "sour grapes" attitude toward sex, coupled with an almost snobbish inference that Zodiac's attainments are loftier and better. Freudian interpretations aside, one wonders why Zodiac would have reached for such an analogy, apart from the imputation that he was sexually inadequate himself and had never experienced the pleasure of getting his "rocks off with a girl."

The Dripping Pen Card contains yet another allusion to sexual frustration. "I get awfully lonely when I am ignored," it states, "so lonely I could do my Thing!!!!!!" This allusion to the killer's loneliness is revealing in itself. In the late sixties "doing one's thing," could be associated with a number of meanings. Chief among those meanings, however, was a thinly-veiled allusion to having sex. That the killer's "thing" ostensibly was murder, and that he identified the process as superior to sex, corroborates the notion that Zodiac, if not positively asexual, had experienced very little success in his strivings for sexual fulfillment.

Later, Zodiac's introduction of The Mikado and the character of Ko-Ko bring this notion more clearly into focus. His identification with the character of the Lord High Executioner appears extremely logical in connection with the Zodiac victimology. In his role as Lord High Executioner, Ko-Ko is tasked with executing people who have been caught in the act of flirting. Given the prudish nature of nineteenth century sensibilities, a contemporary of Zodiac might well have interpreted "flirting" more suggestively than those who had enjoyed The Mikado in its early days. Such sexual connotations would have been obvious to Zodiac, who in essence performed a role similar to Ko-Ko's by literally executing people whom he caught (or supposed he had caught) in the act of "flirting," or, more bluntly, "having sex."

The Lord High Executioner's aria offers yet another insight. In that solo piece, Ko-Ko presents "a little list" of "society offenders," comprising a select group of annoying persons with unendearing habits whose loss will be "a distinct gain to society at large." The association of this song with Zodiac is at once both cogent and transparent. We are led to assume that there is something about Zodiac's victims which he finds perturbing or annoying; something that incites his anger and exercises his sense of righteous indignation. Referring back to the role of Ko-Ko, we can perceive that this something consists of "flirting," or of sexual behavior in general. Like Ko-Ko, Zodiac's is the avenging hand that will administer justice to those found enjoying their sexuality in *flagrante delicto*.

Zodiac enlarges upon this theme in his Exorcist Letter of 1974, providing his final quote from *The Mikado*. "Titwillo" comprises yet another Ko-Ko song, concerning a little bird who dies from unrequited love. The quotation hints of suicide:

He plunged him self into
the billowy wave

and an echo arose from
the sucides grave
titwillo titwillo titwillo

The final stanza of the song (not quoted, but unavoidably implied) relates the reason for the unfortunate bird's despair:

Now I feel just as sure as I'm sure that my name
Isn't Willow, titwillow, titwillow,
That 'twas blighted affection that made him exclaim
"Oh, willow, titwillow, titwillow!"

We may interpret this as saying that, like the tom-tit in the song, an inability to achieve the object of his desires has driven Zodiac to the extreme acts of murder and perhaps (as hinted in the letter) suicide.

In offering the recurrent theme of *The Mikado*, Zodiac related, as clearly as he was able, the motivation for his crimes. Taking his victimology into account, there can remain very little doubt as to what impelled Zodiac to kill. The theme of that impulse can be stated simply as *hostile rage against a particular class of people, having its origins in sexual frustration and envy.*

Moreover, if we believe Zodiac to have been *sexually* frustrated, it almost assuredly follows that he suffered from *social* frustration as well. In fact (barring some physical problem) it is logical to assume that social ineptitude preceded any sexual dysfunction experienced by the killer. Sex is a process that is purely physical only in its culmination. The balance of the process (or rather, its precursor) is no different than that which is involved in cultivating friendships and acquaintances that are completely non-sexual in nature. People who lack the social skills necessary to form simple friendships or sustain themselves in everyday social situations are, as a matter of course, less likely to form the social relationships that will lead to sexual ones.

Zodiac became famous for his correspondences, even more so than for his murders. In many ways those correspondences support the supposition that he suffered from social ineptitude as well as sexual frustration. The very existence of the letters bears this out. In their essence they comprise a plea for attention from an individual who is mired in obscurity and seeks with desperation to be recognized. Thus it may be suggested that the murders and the letters bear something of a symbiotic relationship. Had the murders not occurred, there would have been no letters. This may seem obvious on its face, but it must be borne in mind that, without the measure of credibility fostered by the killings, Zodiac's letters would never have seen the light of day. To a lesser extent, the murders appear to have been driven at least partly by a need to achieve the credibility necessary to awaken the attention of the media. The murders and letters together comprised a complex relationship at the root of which lay a hatred of his fellow humans and a need for recognition that arose from the killer's overwhelming sense of inferiority and his inability to function in society.

Additionally, Zodiac's words and actions offer a glimpse at the depressed, despairing and suicidal impulses so often associated with the disaffected killer. In the Dripping Pen Card (mentioned above) he speaks of how "lonely" he gets when he is ignored, and associates loneliness with killing, or "doing his thing." In the Dragon Card he feels constrained to mention that the public distribution of a Zodiac button will "cheer me up considerbly," and later complains that he is "rather unhappy," when the buttons are not forthcoming. Last, the Exorcist Letter of 1974 offers several allusions to suicide, in the mention of the movie itself (wherein a central character leaps from a window); the self-destruction of the Tom-Tit in *The Mikado* (once again, by falling); and use of the word "suicide" in the song "Tit-Willow."

Finally, the Zodiac's actions associated with the Paul Stine murder offer convincing evidence of a desperation that borders on the suicidal. The slow, methodical and deliberate nature, not only of the attack itself, but of the entire process involved in going through his victim's pockets, tearing off (not cutting) a neat, rectangular piece of fabric from Paul Stine's shirt, wiping down the cab, and then, after being seen by witnesses, *walking* the entire distance from the corner of Washington and Cherry to the intersection at Jackson and Maple, suggest (if they do not absolutely prove) a desire on the part of Zodiac to tempt fate by provoking a confrontation with the police; a confrontation that very nearly came to pass. As we shall see later, flirtation with suicide by a deeply disaffected person, whose suicidal impulses do not arise to the level of actual self-destruction, is a very real phenomenon.

Given the clear distinction between the recreational (sociopathic) and the disaffected (mass) killer, we contend that Zodiac most likely belonged to the latter, rather than the former, class. His victimology suggests the treble elements of envy, hostility and rage, while his writings give evidence of a psychological need to become noteworthy in the public eye. Envy — *sexual* envy — plays a key role in his motivations. His are the essential attributes of a mass murderer, the more especially since none of the elements of sexual sadism are present and despite the fact that the requisite pattern of mass murder (four or more people in one location in one incident) is not seen. (Zodiac's published threats intimated exclusively of mass murder, e.g., the warning that he would go on a "kill rampage"; the statement that he would "wipe out" a school bus full of children; and the bombs designed to blow up passing busses.) Zodiac, in short, is a mass murderer who meets the primary requisites for that distinction in a qualitative, though not a quantitative, sense.

As some day it may hapen
that a victom must be found.
I've got a little list. I've
got a little list, of society
offenders who might well be
underground who would never
be missed who would never be
missed. There is the pest-
ulential nucences who whrite
for autographs, all people who
have flabby hands and irritat-
ing laughs. All children who
are up in dates and implore
you with im platt. All people
who are shakeing hands shake
hands like that. And all third
persons who with unspoiling
take thoes who insist. They'd
none of them be missed. They'd
none of them be missed. There's
the banjo seranader and
the others of his race and
the piano orginast I got him
on the list. All people who
eat pepermint and phomphit

Page 2 of the Zodiac's "Little List Letter," June 26, 1970.

Chapter 2

Ego Sum

I have seen the moment of my greatness flicker,
And I have seen the eternal Footman hold my coat, and snicker . . . .

T.S. ELIOT, *The Love Song of J. Alfred Prufrock*

WHAT KIND of criminal was Theodore Kaczynski? What led him to kill, and how did the act of murder gratify his sensibilities? Conventional wisdom perceives the Unabomber crimes, committed by Kaczynski, as the work of a serial killer. It is not possible to disagree with this assessment, if one takes as his model the commonly-used description of a serial killer as one who murders on at least three occasions, with a "cooling off" period between each crime. However, as we have demonstrated in the case of Zodiac, this definition is somewhat less than satisfying, because it defines the perpetrator by circumstances that may or may not be under his control, and fails to take into account such intrinsically significant features as his psychological makeup and the motivating factors behind his crimes.

Ostensibly, Kaczynski committed his bombings in order to facilitate the downfall of modern technology, which he believed to be a destructive force in human affairs. Although misgivings about the nature of technology appear in Kaczynski's early writings, it was not until the early seventies that they began to coalesce into the overriding worldview that would define him from then until the present day. Particularly, the philosophical works of the French philosopher Jacques Ellul helped form Kaczynski's personal worldview, and substantiated his own ideas on the subject of encroaching technology:

It wasn't until 1971 or '72, shortly after I moved to Montana, that I read Jacques Ellul's book, "The Technological Society." The book is a masterpiece. I was very enthusiastic when I read it. I thought, "look, this guy is saying things I have been wanting to say all along."[1]

Kaczynski's interest in the writings of Ellul led directly to what appears to have been an obsessive determination to save society from the evils of advancing technology. From approximately 1971 to the present date, he has sold himself to the public as a veritable savior of the human race, striving to halt the inevitable advance of technological progress through a personal campaign comprised half of terror and half of propaganda. "The people who are pushing all this growth and progress garbage deserve to be severely punished," the Unabomber writes, in his April 24, 1995 letter to the *New York Times*. And in his so-called Manifesto he baldly states:

> Even if these writings had had many readers, most of these readers would soon have forgotten what they had read as their minds were flooded by the mass of material to which the media expose them. In order to get our message before the public with some chance of making a lasting impression, we've had to kill people.[2]

Despite this sense of high purpose, Kaczynski's selection of victims reveals a set of motivations which, if not transparent, are at the very least translucent. Among those victims targeted (though not necessarily injured, due to various turns of fate) were a host of individuals involved primarily in mathematics and the sciences, particularly engineering. Several within this class were successful educators holding high positions in academia. Most of the targeted victims were men of prominence who had achieved great recognition and success in their chosen fields; some having published their written works to widespread public acclaim. Several others had known success as prominent figures in the business world, including Percy Wood, the President of United Airlines, and Thomas Mosser, a public relations executive for a large advertising agency.

What did these victims have in common? All were individuals who had enjoyed in life an uncommon measure of success. A considerable subset of those persons had worked in fields of endeavor similar to the one in which Kaczynski himself had sought success but failed, particularly the sciences and engineering. No matter what the field of endeavor, however, success was their common denominator, and it was as representatives of the class comprising successful people that Kaczynski assailed them with his bombs.

In the published portions of his extensive journals, Kaczynski specifies the type of people whom he despises, hates, or wishes to kill and maim. These run the gamut from "scientists, big businessmen, union leaders, and politicians," to "government officials, police, computer scientists, behavioral scientists, [and] the rowdy type of college students who left their piles of beer-cans in the Arboretum . . . ," as well as Communists. More revealing than this, however, is the manner in which he refers to such people collectively:

> There was just one thing that really made me determined to cling to life for awhile, and that was the desire for revenge. I wanted to kill some people, preferably including at least one scientist, businessman, or other *bigshot* . . . . In Montana, if I went to the city to mail a bomb to some *bigshot*, [redacted] would doubtless remember I rode [redacted] bus that day. . . . [U]sing my spare time to build a bomb or 2 or 3 or invent other means of killing or maiming *big-shots*.[3] [Author's italics]

Webster's Dictionary defines the word "bigshot" as "a person of consequence or prominence." Here, Kaczynski uses the term in a sneering sense, as if the bigshots in question carry a loftier estimation of their importance than the circumstances (in Kaczynski's eyes) might warrant. It is the eternal cry of the little man, condemning the big man for his prominence, though in Kaczynski's case it is something more. For Kaczynski himself, at least in the beginning, possessed the attributes of the big man class, and would, but for his social pathologies, have eventually found himself in the "bigshot" category as well. He was a first-rate mathematician who, even as a student, had published high-quality, original research in the most prestigious mathematical journals in the world. Had it not been for his social pathologies, which were extreme to the point of actual dysfunction, there is little reason to doubt that he would inevitably have attained prominence and world-renown in his chosen field. His creative inclination, for which there is evidence, might well have led to prominence in other fields, such as engineering and invention; fields in which the rare combination of creativity and analytical reasoning is much in demand. He had everything to gain — and everything to lose as well. His use of the word "bigshot," is incredibly revealing, for it shows quite plainly the true nature of his resentment towards the people he targeted as victims. These were people enjoying a stature that Kaczynski desperately wanted to attain, and because he could not attain it, he hated them with all the passion at his command.

Contrary to what he might like the public to believe, the Unabomber was no altruist. He was a highly intelligent man with an ugly disposition and a proclivity to seek revenge against anyone possessing attributes which he himself desired. A man of Kaczynski's intelligence and pride would hardly have been inclined to admit that to himself, even though, deep inside, he may have known it to be true. Imagine looking at yourself in the mirror every day and admitting that you're a loser in every regard; that you live a sexless life because you can't relate to women; you can't hold down a job; you're a disgrace to the parents who worked so hard and sacrificed so much to raise and educate you. What kind of person could expose his ego to such condemnation and refrain from suicide? But if one is a Kaczynski, one is intelligent enough and creative enough to construct a *weltanschauung* — a personal perspective on the cosmos — that not only excuses him for his shortcomings and places the blame on society, but affords a justification for lashing out at the people one envies as well. Though degraded, such a person may hold his head aloft, believing that not only is *he* in the right, but that *everyone else* is clearly in the wrong. In doing so, he salvages his ego, assuages his hostilities, and effectively saves his life.

Kaczynski achieved satisfaction by killing, not because he thought it would save the world (an impossible goal by any standard) but because it assuaged his hostility against the people he envied. This is a classic characteristic of disaffected killers, whether they be bombers, shooters, or Muslim terrorists flying airplanes into buildings.

Writing about Kaczynski, famed criminologist and profiler John Douglas sums it up both bluntly and succinctly:

> Anyone this clearly intelligent who makes such ridiculous demands and has such ridiculous goals isn't interested in reforming society. He's got a personal ax to grind based on his own deep problems and inadequacies.[4]

Kaczynski's Luddite philosophy, with which he blamed technology for the ills of the world generally, and his own personal ills particularly, served as a smokescreen for the hostility he felt against those who had succeeded in areas where he had failed, and the inward self-loathing his ego must have felt as a consequence of those failures.

Based on what we know of his true motivational profile, we can safely and positively assert that in his guise as the Unabomber, Theodore Kaczynski committed murder as an act of retribution against a class of persons who represented the material successes which he himself could not attain.

Comparing Kaczynski's motivations as the Unabomber with those we have inferred in reference to Zodiac, we can clearly see a least-common-denominator of *"symbolic revenge against a class of individuals whose possessions or attainments were envied by the killer."* At a bare minimum, both killers shared that quality. The difference is that, in the case of Kaczynski, the coveted attainment was success in the realm of technology, while Zodiac's source of envy appears to have been nothing more than a lack of sexual fulfillment.

Is the difference significant? Perhaps. But bear in mind that the analysis of Kaczynski's motivations as the Unabomber involves a period of time that is more than a decade removed from the crimes of Zodiac. People change with time, and for a true comparison between the motivations of the Unabomber and those of Zodiac we must go back farther in time and have a look at Kaczynski during the heyday of the Zodiac. The results may prove enlightening, to say the very least.

A veritable epigraph to the Unabomber's life may be written from the following quotation, taken from the Stephen Dubner interview of Kaczynski in 1999:

> At Harvard, Ted felt socially isolated by other students. He recalls that "their speech, manners, and dress were so much more 'cultured' than mine." There was an even greater unease in Ted's life; he suffered from what he calls "acute sexual starvation." Sexual references run throughout his book, and although he never ties them into a knot, one cannot help wondering if sexual frustration was his main despair.[5]

Acute sexual starvation. The words are Kaczynski's own, and they conjure images of a psychological syndrome no less unpleasant for the fact that this is a coined term, and neither a theoretical nor a clinical diagnosis. It is, in fact, Kaczynski's personal assessment of a condition that profoundly affected not only his own life, but sadly, the lives of others whom he never knew or associated with.

Kaczynski was born in 1942 to parents who have been described as "working-class intellectuals." Of modest social and academic attainments, Ted Sr. and his wife Wanda attuned themselves to the world of books and learning — virtues they imparted to their two sons, Ted and David, who quickly learned that the surest way to please their parents was by success in anything involving the application of their mental powers.

Prodded by the indefatigable efforts of a doting mother (herself a person of considerable intelligence), Kaczynski's youth was marked by a rapid intellectual advancement that progressed at the expense of his adjustment to social life and situations. Kaczynski entered his senior year of high school two full years in advance of his peers and two full years behind his regular classmates, both in age and social adaptation. A classmate observed:

> While the math club would sit around talking about the big issues of the day, Ted would be waiting for someone to fart. He had a fascination with body sounds more akin to a 5-year-old than a 15-year-old.[6]

His intellectual precocity, coupled perhaps with the natural desire of his parents to bask vicariously in the light of his achievements, had devastating effects on Kaczynski's ability to mature both socially and sexually. All available evidence indicates that by the age of sixteen, when he was bundled off to Harvard, Ted's experience with the opposite sex had been limited to at most a couple of minor dates. In the summer between high school and Harvard, he apparently attempted to cultivate a relationship with a young woman of the Catholic faith, but did not pursue the relationship because he feared that her beliefs would be unacceptable to his mother, an atheist by some accounts, and an agnostic at best. His younger brother David has opined that this was nothing more than a rationalization on the part of Ted — an excuse for avoiding a relationship that sorely tried his deficient social skills.

During his entire four-year stay at Harvard, Kaczynski appears to have attempted no more than a single relationship, a short-lived affair about which nothing is publicly known, apart from its existence. He admits to a "relationship" with a "Ms. Z" during his five-year stay at the University of Michigan, which apparently went nowhere. At Berkeley, where he lived for two years amid the most frenetic excesses of the sexual revolution, he did not have so much as a single date.

In 1974, while working at a truck stop in Montana, Kaczynski tried to woo the affections of a waitress by the name of Sandra Hill. Ted's ministrations to Hill came in the form of three letters. In the first letter, Kaczynski asked the woman to go to Canada and become his "squaw." In the second missive, he presented his credentials, including his academic degrees and a bibliography of his published works. The last of the correspondences was an admission of defeat, and a formal surrender by Kaczynski in the pursuit of her affections.

In the spring of 1978 Kaczynski moved back to the Chicago area and took a job at Foam Cutting Engineers, where he worked briefly as a machine operator. While there he initiated a short-lived relationship with 29-year-old Ellen Tarmichael, his immediate supervisor at the plant. The extant quotes from Kaczynski's journals contain a single reference to this relationship:

> But this affair with [redacted] has done strange things to me. In the first place it aroused in me hope — a hope for something worthwhile. Perhaps foolishly I did hope that I might win, if not her love, then at least a reasonable amount of affection — physical sex too, of course, but it would have been more important to me to have her care for me than to have physical sex with her. I could get by with just holding her hand if necessary, if I thought she really cared for me. Of course, kissing her was immensely pleasurable . . . .[7]

Six weeks after their first meeting, Tarmichael and Kaczynski went apple picking and returned to Ted's parents' house where they baked an apple pie. At that point, the woman informed Ted that she no longer wished to see him "on a social basis," since they had little in common other than their employment at Foam Cutting Engineers. Humiliated, Ted responded by placing copies of "crude" and "insulting" limericks in various locations around the foam-cutting plant. When he refused to leave off, David (a supervisor) instructed his older brother to "go home," effectively dismissing him from his job.

Tarmichael was fortunate that Kaczynski's resentment did not play out to the extent he planned. As related by Dr. Sally Johnson in her court-ordered psychiatric evaluation of Kaczynski (hereafter styled the *Psych Report*) his journals disclosed a far worse scenario for revenge:

He indicated that he had started a relationship with a female manager at the foam cutting plant where he was working with his brother and father. After three dates that relationship had failed. . . . He remembers contemplating suicide by hanging at that time, and then describes that he became full of rage and instead decided to take a knife and mutilate the woman. He proceeded to the parking lot at the work site and got into her car. At that time he changed his mind and again felt very sad.[8]

In a 1991 letter to his brother, Ted complained:

Women are gentle, nice, pleasant to be with, they represent warmth, joy, family life, love and, of course, sex. Naturally, women have their faults too and moreover not all women have the good qualities I've just mentioned. But for 37 years I've desired women. I've wanted desperately to find a girlfriend or a wife but have never been able to make any progress toward doing so because I lack the necessary social self-confidence and social skills.... I am tormented by bitter regret at never having had the opportunity to experience the love of a woman.[9]

In February of 1996, David Kaczynski gave an interview to the FBI. Among other statements he observed:

Ted's inability to make friends or establish any ongoing relationships is also a lifelong characteristic of his. Since he had not thought Ted was much interested in relationships with women, Dave was surprised when Ted told him he had advertised in the paper for female companionship during TED's time at the University of California at Berkeley (UCB) in 1968–69. DAVE believes TED continued to be unsuccessful in his quest.[10]

The inability to form sexual relationships became a source of immense frustration for Kaczynski who, as the years progressed, grew increasingly resentful of the role his mother had played in steering him toward exclusively intellectual pursuits. By 1991 these feelings had grown venomous; so much so that he informed Wanda by letter that he would forever hate her for the "harm" she had done. It is a moot point for this discussion whether his accusations were correct, but at least it underscores the fact that unrequited sexual frustration formed a large part of the phenomenon that was Ted Kaczynski.

In an autobiography written ca. 1979, Kaczynski claimed that during his high school years he developed a personal philosophy of hatred and amorality. This is important to bear in mind when delving into the possibility of his implication in later crimes.

> By the time I was, say, 12 years old, my system of morality had evolved into an abstract, artificial construction that could not possibly be applied in practice. I never told anyone about this system, since I knew they would never take it seriously.

> By and by I got bored with this game. One day when I was 13 years old, I was walking down the street and saw a girl. Something about her appearance antagonized me, and, from habit, I began looking for a way to justify hating her, within my logical system. But then I stopped and said to myself, "This is getting ridiculous. I'll just chuck all this silly morality business and hate anybody I please." Since then I have never had any interest in or respect for morality, ethics, or anything of the sort.[11]

In his sixteenth year, when Kaczynski entered Harvard University, he began leading an obscure existence marked only by extreme solitude and study. Obscurity and isolation continued during his graduate years at Michigan, from 1962 through 1967. The psychological profile taken of Kaczynski during the course of the Unabomber trial lists only one female relationship during five years of study, involving a woman identified by Kaczynski only as "Ms. Z."[12]

Constant study, part-time work, and a frustrating series of setbacks involving a doctoral dissertation may have diverted Kaczynski's attention from the lack of social interaction and sexual gratification that marked his first four years at Michigan. By the beginning of his fifth year, however, something was ready to give. The nature of this crisis, taken from Kaczynski's 1978 autobiography, is related by Dr. Sally Johnson in the Psych Report:

> While at the University of Michigan he sought psychiatric contact on one occasion at the start of his fifth year of study. As referenced above, he had been experiencing several weeks of intense and persistent sexual excitement involving fantasies of being a female. During that time period he became convinced that he should undergo sex change surgery. He recounts that he was aware that this would require a psychiatric referral, and he set up an appointment at the Health Center at the University to

discuss this issue. He describes that while waiting in the waiting room, he became anxious and humiliated over the prospect of talking about this to the doctor. When he was actually seen, he did not discuss these concerns, but rather claimed he was feeling some depression and anxiety over the possibility that the deferment status would be dropped for students and teachers, and that he would face the possibility of being drafted into the military. He indicates that the psychiatrist viewed his anxiety and depression as not atypical. Mr. Kaczynski describes leaving the office and feeling rage, shame, and humiliation over this attempt to seek evaluation. *He references this as a significant turning point in his life.*[13] [Author's italics]

In a later section this incident is given further elaboration, including Kaczynski's own account, written ca. 1979:

In the summer after his fourth year, he describes experiencing a period of several weeks where he was sexually excited nearly all the time and was fantasizing himself as a woman and being unable to obtain any sexual relief. He decided to make an effort to have a sex change operation. When he returned to the University of Michigan he made an appointment to see a psychiatrist to be examined to determine if the sex change would be good for him. He claimed that by putting on an act he could con the psychiatrist into thinking him suitable for a feminine role even though his motive was exclusively erotic. As he was sitting in the waiting room, he turned completely against the idea of the operation and thus, when he saw the doctor, instead claimed he was depressed about the possibility of being drafted. He describes the following, "As I walked away from the building afterwards, I felt disgusted about what my uncontrolled sexual cravings had almost led me to do and I felt humiliated, and I violently hated the psychiatrist. Just then there came a major turning point in my life. Like a Phoenix, I burst from the ashes of my despair to a glorious new hope. I thought I wanted to kill that psychiatrist because the future looked utterly empty to me. I felt I wouldn't care if I died. And so I said to myself why not really kill the psychiatrist and anyone else whom I hate. What is important is not the words that ran through my mind but the way I felt about them. What was entirely new was the fact that I really felt I could kill someone. My very hopelessness had liberated me because I no longer cared about death. I no longer cared about consequences and I said to myself that I really could break out of my rut in life and do things that were daring, irresponsible or criminal."[14]

This, then, was the precipitating factor in Kaczynski's determination to embark upon a career of murder, beginning in September of 1966:

> He describes his first thought was to kill someone he hated and then kill himself, but decided he could not relinquish his rights so easily. At that point he decided "I will kill but I will make at least some effort to avoid detection so that I can kill again." He decided that he would do what he always wanted to do, to go to Canada to take off in the woods with a rifle and try to live off the country. "If it doesn't work and if I can get back to civilization before I starve then I will come back here and kill someone I hate." In his writings he emphasized what he knew was the fact that he now felt he had the courage to behave irresponsibly.[15]

At approximately the same time, other events were transpiring that may have affected Kaczynski's ever-increasing sense of sexual frustration and resentment. As described by Kaczynski in his autobiography:

> I often had fantasies of killing the kind of people whom I hated (e.g. government officials, police, computer scientists, behavioral scientists, the rowdy types of college students who left their piles of beer-cans in the Arboretum, etc., etc., etc.) and I had high hopes of eventually committing such crimes. . . . The back half of the house where I roomed during my fifth year at Michigan consisted of an apartment occupied by a bunch of rowdy jocks who belonged to the hockey team. My room was adjacent to their apartment, and, as the wall was thin, I heard a great deal of what went on there. These jocks were respectable bourgeois: They were clean-shaven, short-haired, neatly dressed, and went to church on Sunday like typical clean-cut college boys. They also smoked pot, held wild parties at which they would get drunk and continually shout words like "fuck" and "cunt" at the tops of their voices, and they would go to bed promiscuously with various girls — no great sin perhaps, but one of them [redacted], had a girl named [redacted], whom he was engaged to marry. When [redacted] was at Michigan for . . . .[16]

Disappointingly, the continuation of these recollections has not been made publicly available. Years later, in an unpublished manuscript, Kaczynski described a promiscuous woman he once knew as a "damned animal." It is tempting to suppose that the "damned animal" of Kaczynski's recollections is none other than the girlfriend of the "jock" next door to Kaczynski's apartment at Michigan, whose name was redacted by the FBI.

The *Psych Report* offers elaborated details of Kaczynski's experiences at Michigan:

> It was during that period of time that he was staying at a rooming house, managed by a graduate student, (REDACTED). He began to experience difficulty with the noise from the other rooms, particularly the sounds resulting from sexual activity of other renters. He reported the noises he heard in the house to the University System, with the hope that action would be taken against Mr. (REDACTED). He describes three experiences where he perceived he overheard the landlord providing negative information about him which subsequently resulted in a negative outcome. The first involved an Engineering student by the name of (REDACTED), who was coming over to get help with math problems. Although Mr. Kaczynski couldn't clearly hear a conversation, he eventually heard a statement by (REDACTED) indicating that he had "only come to get help with math." He perceived that Mr. (REDACTED) must have said something negative to (REDACTED) about him. On the second occasion, he had given an individual information about rooms to rent at the house where he was residing. Again, he heard a voice which he thought belonged to the individual he had spoken with, but he never came up to see him, and the next time he saw him, he was snubbed by him. On the third occasion, he had received a letter from his mother referencing that the daughter of some of their friends was interested in the woods and might like to look him up; they had given her his address. Subsequently, several weeks later he thought he overheard a woman's voice in the foyer area of the house and Mr. (REDACTED) say "Oh hi (REDACTED)" and then he said something negative about him, and the woman left without ever visiting him.[17]

Also reported was a series of journal entries that offer a surprising contradiction to the idea that Kaczynski was driven by hatred of technology alone:

> He wrote in his journal about him *not fitting into organized society* and *not wanting to fit into it,* and seeking avenues of escape from it. In his words *in the early 1970s,* he wrote "[t]rue I would not fit into the present society in any case but that is not an intolerable situation . . . . It's not merely the fact that I cannot fit into society that has induced me to rebel, as violently as I have, it is the fact that I can see society made possible by science inexorably imposing on me."

> Near the end of his autobiography in 1979, Mr. Kaczynski describes his motives for writing, to include that he intended to start killing people and

that when caught, he was concerned people would perceive him to be a "sickie." His writings were an effort to prevent the facts of his psychology from being misrepresented. He also describes some type of relief, sexual or otherwise, he obtains by writing. *He describes his sources of hatred as his perceived social rejection* and the "fact that organized society frustrates my very powerful urge for physical freedom and personal autonomy." *He also describes experiencing anger from other sources and then turning his hatred towards organized society.*[18] [Author's italics]

The foregoing incidents sketch a portrait of a disturbed individual who is almost completely alienated from normal human society. They depict the young Kaczynski as both sexually and socially dysfunctional, sexually immature, and sexually frustrated to the point where he began to question his sexual identity. They show faint but distinct signs of a growing resentment toward a specific class of individuals (the "rowdy jocks" and "rowdy types of college students") and their social and sexual habits (i.e., beer drinking and promiscuous sex).

They also show, quite clearly, a well-defined correlation between those resentments and a growing desire to kill, expressed in a series of plainly stated resolutions beginning late in 1966 with the psychiatrist whose only fault was to have unknowingly presided over the humiliation and shame surrounding Kaczynski's pondered sex-change operation.

There is a heated immediacy to his stated desire to lash out against society, even considering that the autobiography from which the quotes were taken was not composed until 1979. Whether Kaczynski, in the midst of a white-hot anger driven by his sexual frustrations, would have waited a full twelve years to requite that burning rage, is a point to be deferred for now. What is significant here is the fact that if Kaczynski *had* killed in the years between 1966 and 1969, his motivations would have been similar, if not identical, to those we have set forth in reference to the Zodiac. Sexually desperate, and frustrated to the point where (1) he had seriously considered sexual mutilation as an antidote to his woes; (2) he felt constrained (unsuccessfully) to advertise in the newspapers for a woman; and (3) his mounting sexual frustration led directly to a dark and desperate resolution to practice murder, there can be no question whatsoever that if *any* individual were inclined to assail young couples alone in lovers' lanes, such a person would certainly have been Theodore Kaczynski.

★   ★   ★

Like Zodiac, Kaczynski's writings give evidence of a suicidal ideation involving some kind of violent confrontation with the police:

> My very hopelessness had liberated me. Because I no longer cared about death, I no longer cared about consequences . . . . My first thought was to kill somebody I hated and then kill myself before the cops could get me. . . . But, since I now had new hope, I was not ready to relinquish life so easily. . . . Then I thought, "Well, as long as I am going to throw everything up anyway, instead of having to shoot it out with the cops or something . . . ."[19]

As referenced above, Kaczynski first entered this state of mind following his aborted sex-change consultation in 1966. It was a theme repeated more than a decade later, following his failed attempt at romance with Ellen Tarmichael in 1978:

> For these reasons, I want to get my revenge in one big blast. By accepting death as the price, I won't have to fret and worry about how to plan things so I won't get caught.[20]

> Following that I had a vague intention of taking to the woods . . . and, from ambush, murdering snowmobilists, motorcyclists, outboard motor users, or the like; in the end shooting it out with the authorities and not permitting myself to be taken alive.[21]

These entries, especially those relating to Kaczynski's later years at Michigan, circa 1967, are especially relevant in light of the Stine murder, in which, as argued above, Zodiac appears to tempt fate by deliberately inviting a confrontation with the police. Note the three separate references to the possibility of such a confrontation in the Kaczynski quotes: "before the cops could get me", "shoot it out with the cops", and "shooting it out with the authorities."

"Suicide by cop" is a classic phenomenon employed by mass murderers and other disaffected types, who have resolved to end their own lives while lashing out at the society which they feel has done them wrong. It offers a means of throwing off all restraint and maximizing the carnage that can be wrought in a single outburst of violence. Zodiac appears to have contemplated the notion, while Kaczynski most

certainly mulled the idea; perhaps even obsessed over it. Yet in the actual event, neither killer succumbed to the impulse. Despite what might
have been his actual proclivity in that regard, Kaczynski took great care
to plan his crimes in such a way as to minimize personal risk. Among
his writings are the following entries:

> But, since I now had new hope, I was not ready to relinquish life so easily.
> So I thought, "I will kill, but I will make at least some effort to avoid de-
> tection, so that I can kill again."[22]

> For these reasons, I want to get my revenge in one big blast. By accepting
> death as the price, I won't have to fret and worry about how to plan
> things so I won't get caught. Moreover, I want to release all my hatred
> and just go out and kill. When I see a motorcyclist tearing up the moun-
> tain meadows, instead of fretting about how I can get revenge on him
> safely, I just want to watch the bullet rip through his flesh and I want to
> kick him in the face while he is dying.

> However, it would have been very tempting to just hang onto my job at
> Prince Castle indefinitely, even though I have nothing to look forward to.
> The truth is, I don't want to die![23]

As killers, both Kaczynski and Zodiac transcended the usual tendency
of mass murderers, which is to spend their rage in a single incident of
overwhelming violence that exposes them to death or capture. (The
one possible exception to this pattern was the Stine incident, where
Zodiac appears to have invited a confrontation by deliberately lingering
at the scene. It should be borne in mind, however, that the Stine slaying
concluded the Zodiac's violent career.) These were deeply disaffected
killers, possessing the mentality of mass murderers, who were not
"ready to relinquish life" as stated by Kaczynski, but carefully planned
their murders so that they might live to kill again. So successful were
they in that regard that they conferred upon themselves the appellation
of serial killer, despite the fact that their personalities were completely
at odds with the term. Moreover, each killer asserted himself patiently
through a series of small (though sensational) incidents, as opposed to
the more usual method of "going out" in a short-yet-spectacular explosion.

said to myself, "Why not *really* kill that psychiatrist... and anyone else whom I hate." What is important is not the words that ran through my mind, but the way I felt about them. What was entirely new was the fact that I *really felt* I *could kill someone*. My very hopelessness had liberated me. Because I no longer cared about death, I no longer cared about consequences, and I suddenly felt that I really could break out of my rut in life and do things that were "doing, "irresponsible", or criminal.

My first thought was to kill somebody I hated and then kill myself before the cops could get me. (I've always considered death preferable to long imprisonment.) But, since I now had new hope, I was not ready to relinquish life so easily. So I thought, "I will kill, but I will make it at least some effort to avoid detection, so that I can kill again." Then I thought, "Well, as long as I am going to throw everything up anyway, instead of having to shoot it out with the cops or something, I will do what I've always wanted to do, namely, I will go up to Canada, take off into the woods with a rifle, and try to live off the country. If that doesn't work out, and if I can get back to civilization before I starve, then I will come back here and kill someone I hate." What was new here was the fact that I *really* had the *courage to behave* "irresponsibly".

All these thoughts passed through my head in the length of time it took me to walk a quarter of a mile. By the end of that time it had acquired bright new hope, an angry, vicious kind of determination, and high morale.

I didn't feel I wanted to take off into the wilderness in autumn, with the cold northern winter coming on, and frankly

Kaczynski's first-stated desire to kill, from a journal entry composed ca. 1978–1979, and referencing events that transpired during the start of his final year at the University of Michigan, 1966.

Chapter 3

Public Address

"The press is a mighty engine, sir," said Pott.

CHARLES DICKENS, *The Pickwick Papers*

DESPITE THE VIOLENCE of their murders, neither the Unabomber nor the Zodiac owes his place in the annals of crime to the act of dealing death *per se*. Their fame arose directly from multiple correspondences with the media and (by proxy) the police, which took the form of daring taunts, in-your-face derision of the authorities and the demand for continued publicity on pain of further killings, particularly involving mass murder. For these two famous killers, the desire for prominence in the public eye comprised a secondary motive, which both drew upon and complemented the mayhem of their deeds.

In each, the media preferred was a large-circulation daily newspaper serving a major metropolitan area. Zodiac chose the *San Francisco Examiner, San Francisco Chronicle* and finally the *Los Angeles Times* as vehicles for his correspondences, all sent in the form of letters to the editor, and in two cases addressed personally to staff columnist Paul Avery. Similarly, Kaczynski chose the *San Francisco Examiner, San Francisco Chronicle*, the *New York Times*, and the *Washington Post*, with a handful of letters addressed personally to Warren Hoge of the *New York Times*. Both killers directed letters to specific individuals in response to provocations by those persons — in Zodiac's case to Vallejo Police Chief Jack Stiltz (the Examiner II Letter); in Kaczynski's case to Professor Tom Tyler, head of the psychology department at the University of California, Berkeley (the Tom Tyler Letter). Stiltz had requested more information from Zodiac to corroborate his confession to the crimes at Lake Herman Road and Blue Rock Springs, while Tyler had authored a newspaper article commenting on the Unabomber from a psychological perspective.

One of the first elements of these letters that stands out and strikes the observer as particularly unique is the need of the writer to establish his *bona fides*, ensure that the public is convinced they are authentic, and freely acknowledge that their author has committed certain crimes for which he alone must receive the credit. It is interesting to note that in both cases the first correspondence did not appear until after the writer had established his credibility as a killer. For Zodiac, that event occurred almost four weeks after the Blue Rock Springs attack, while Kaczynski mailed no correspondences for more than seven years, until a series of frustrating setbacks and general failures culminated finally in the successful murder of Hugh Scrutton at his computer store in Sacramento. He immediately sent a lengthy letter to the editor of the *San Francisco Examiner*, the contents of which are not fully known, though portions of the missive were made available by the prosecution at Kaczynski's trial in 1998. (We will examine the excerpts later, but for now it must suffice to point out that the first correspondences of both Kaczynski and the Zodiac were sent to the *San Francisco Examiner*.)

There exists a clear sense that in each of these criminal enterprises the desire for publicity at least equals the psychological need represented by the killings themselves. Each killer is keenly sensible of the way in which he "packages" himself for public consumption, and he gravitates toward large media outlets that will afford the broadest scope for publicity. Each invents for himself a moniker and a trademark symbol by which he will be known — in Zodiac's case the name of Zodiac and the crosshair circle device; in Kaczynski's case the initials FC and the corresponding letters formed in punched-out pieces of metal on the bombs he made. In neither enterprise is a murder successfully effected without some subsequent attempt at communication with the media and/or the authorities.

Even more significantly, the communications of both killers afford their author a safe means of committing public terror by drawing on the credibility fostered by the murders. This is well illustrated by Zodiac's school-bus threat of 1969, with its subsequent retraction, and the 1995 threat by the Unabomber to blow up an airliner out of the Los Angeles Airport, also with its subsequent retraction. (Interestingly, while Kaczynski's retraction letter was sent to the *New York Times*, the threat letters of both the Zodiac and Kaczynski were mailed to the *San Fran-*

cisco Chronicle.) Credibility, of course, was a key element in fostering terror on the scale attempted by the murderers. Once that credibility had been attained, the authorities could not be certain that murder on a massive scale would not have been beyond the will, or the ability, of the killer. Thus, each killer could enjoy the psychological satisfaction of terrorizing a large regional population (something he could not have done through murder on a small scale alone) with no attendant risk.

With Zodiac, there is a clear sense that his letter-writing campaign provided a source of emotional gratification very nearly equal to that achieved by his murders. He craved publicity, and demanded it from the media on pain of further killings. "If you do not print this cipher," he writes in his first letter to the *Examiner*, "I will go on a kill rampage . . . ." In the Seven-Page Letter of 1969 he warns, "Be shure to print the part I marked out on page 3 or I shall do my thing." In April of 1970 he continues by insisting on publication, not only of his bus bomb diagram, but the "Zodiac buttons" as well, to be worn by "a lot of people." And, in the Exorcist Letter of 1974, he closes with the dire threat to "do something nasty, which you know I'm capable of doing" if he does not see his letter in the *Chronicle*. Despite the varied nature of the Zodiac's threats (shootings, bombings and something not clearly defined) they can easily be distilled into a common formula which roughly equates to "publish this material or else I will commit mass murder."

Zodiac's correspondences grew increasingly bizarre as time progressed, with each threat taken less seriously as no new murders transpired. It would have been highly instructive to see just what course the Unabomber's writings would have taken had they been allowed to progress beyond the point where he had ceased to kill and continued his activities through the surrogate means of the idle threat — something he had already begun to do in 1995. Unfortunately (for the purpose of our assessment) Kaczynski's career came to a sudden halt before this could come to pass. Even so, the brunt of Kaczynski's threats, as stated to the media, comprised the same essential message as that of Zodiac more than a quarter-century earlier: "publish this material or else I will commit mass murder."

Please see to it that the answer to our offer is well publicized in the media so that we won't miss it. Be sure to tell us where and how our material will be published and how long it will take to appear in print once we have sent in the manuscript. If the answer is satisfactory, we will finish typing the manuscript and send it to you. If the answer is unsatisfactory, we will start building our next bomb. . . . We encourage you to print this letter.[*] [Times Letter II]

If the enclosed manuscript is published reasonably soon and receives wide public exposure, we will permanently desist from terrorism in accord with the agreement that we proposed in our last letter to you . . . . [Times Letter III]

So desperate was Kaczynski for the publicity afforded by the letters and his Manifesto that he willingly accepted the high degree of risk attendant upon their publication worldwide in the most accessible media markets, particularly the Internet. Whatever his criminal predilections, or psychological peculiarities, Kaczynski was, and is, no fool. He knew full well that the tenor of his writings, all reflective of his life's philosophy, could easily be traced back to him by the people with whom he had shared those ideas over the course of many years. This was particularly so in reference to his brother, who not only was aware of those ideas, but at one point shared them with his elder sibling. Yet so strong was his need for national publicity that Kaczynski insisted on publication of the Manifesto, using all the credibility fostered by his killings to blackmail the *New York Times* into making it, and its corresponding links to him, accessible to the entire world.

As with the Zodiac, there is something peculiar about the mindset of Theodore Kaczynski that in criminal terms reaches out beyond the bounds of simple murder. Why this should be in regards to the latter remains something of a mystery, though perhaps it pertains to a particular type of upbringing in which public recognition was accorded Kaczynski by virtue of his superior, even freakish, intellect.

As a youth, Kaczynski's mental abilities appear to have afforded him an avenue to public recognition and parental approbation. Kaczynski's high school years saw him win high praise for an intellect that made him stand out, as nothing else, amongst people his own age at Evergreen Park High School in Evergreen Park, Illinois. Observed classmate Loren De Young, "Everybody fussed over his brilliance to

---

[*] See Appendix A for a listing of correspondences attributable to the Unabomber and the Zodiac. Quotations from the letters will be cited with their common nomenclatures, as given in the appendix.

a great degree, he was a focal point at our school."[1] Tom Quinlan, an assistant district attorney in Modesto, California, whose brother had been a classmate of Kaczynski, recalled:

> The only thing I can remember is my mother being very impressed when it appeared in the newspaper in Chicago that he was graduating from high school at 15 years old and going on to Harvard ....[2]

Such recognition — a fifteen-year-old working-class boy from Evergreen Park getting a writeup about his intelligence in a big Chicago newspaper — must have been especially gratifying to a youth who by all accounts (including his own) spent the majority of his teenage years aloof from social activities and other areas from which acceptance, self-esteem and recognition might have come. In fact, it appears to have formed Kaczynski's primary source of parental approval. In his autobiography he observed:

> ... my parents' main task in life was to bring me up properly. Thus, I tended to feel that I was a particularly important person and superior to most of the human race. Generally speaking, there was nothing arrogant or egotistical in this feeling, nor did I ever express any such feeling outside the immediate family. It just came to me as naturally as breathing to feel that I was someone special.[3]

During his teenage years, Kaczynski appears to have sustained his ego and forged an identity for himself by way of his scholastic accomplishments. In his senior year those accomplishments were crowned by the receipt of a National Merit scholarship that would allow him to attend virtually any college of his choice. Eschewing others, he settled on Harvard.

But while the notion of going off to Harvard at sixteen years of age might have proven initially gratifying to Kaczynski's ego, the gratification appears to have been short-lived. From being a child prodigy and a "focal point" at Evergreen Park, Kaczynski matriculated at Harvard to find himself cast into obscurity as simply one intelligent student among thousands. Based upon her perusal of Kaczynski's journals, Dr. Sally Johnson wrote, "Upon entering Harvard, he was struck with the realization that he was no longer smarter than all the other students."[4]

By the time he began his graduate studies at Michigan, Kaczynski apparently had reconciled himself to a career in academia. There, Kaczynski appears to have enjoyed the recognition of his mathematical peers, and distinguished himself by publishing a number of scholarly papers in prestigious mathematical journals. Nevertheless, those papers were of such a nature as to preclude Kaczynski's winning any kind of admiration or recognition outside the limited sphere of individuals (a mere handful in the entire country, according to one advisor) who could assimilate their meaning. It can hardly be doubted that his parents were impressed by their son's accomplishment, although there is no evidence at hand to indicate the nature of their reaction. Yet there is no doubt that, intelligent though they were, the elder Kaczynskis would have been unable to appreciate the scope and import of the papers Kaczynski published while at Michigan.

In 1967 Kaczynski applied for and won a tenure-track position as assistant professor of mathematics at the University of California, Berkeley. Although being hired to such a prestigious position was an accomplishment in itself, it did not automatically ensure a successful, long-term position in the academic realm. He continued to publish mathematical papers in scholarly journals, and one may be tempted to think that scholarly research comprised the only outlet for Kaczynski's desire to achieve recognition. In fact, Kaczynski fancied himself an author. His early attempts at the craft included such pieces as "Three Worthy Artisans," which he solicited his mother to send to *Harper's Weekly*, "How I Blew Up Harold Snilly," written under the pseudonym of Apias Tuberosa, and "The Wave of the Future," a wry, dry, thousand-word satirical essay actually published in the "Phoenix Nest" column of the *Saturday Review* in June of 1970. Sardonically predicting the future advent of an imaginary process called "cloud control," Kaczynski offers his own take on the phenomenon:

> Now, I can predict in advance that there are going to be some senti-mental old ladies who will object to this. For instance, they will say there are some people who like to look at clouds, and they will point out that children like to imagine faces and animals and such in the funny shapes of clouds. They will claim that controlled clouds would be too boring to look at. However, this difficulty can not only be remedied, but turned to advantage. The scientists of the future will be able to make clouds move and change in definite patterns, so that they will make pictures and act

out stories, just like television. Thus the clouds of the future actually will be far more interesting and entertaining to look at than those of today. In fact, there will be regular, planned, educational programming in the sky, which will help teach children all the scientific facts they will need to know to get along in the world of tomorrow. And cloud-vision will be even better than educational television, because people won't be able to switch to a channel with violence on it.[5]

Despite being published in the well-known *Saturday Review,* and even considering the later encomium offered to Kaczynski by Martin Levin, editor of "The Phoenix' Nest,"[6] Kaczynski apparently failed to duplicate his success in future attempts at publication. In fact, the "Phoenix Nest" article appears to have been his only publishing success from 1970 until the time the Manifesto appeared in a special segment of the *New York Times* for all the world to see. Even there, Kaczynski as much as admits that his attempts at publication, *sans* murder, have been less than satisfactory:

> *If we had never done anything violent* and had submitted the present writings to a publisher, they *probably would not have been accepted.* If they had been accepted and published, they probably would not have attracted many readers, because it's *more fun to watch the entertainment put out by the media than to read a sober essay . . . .* In order to get our message before the public with some chance of making a lasting impression, *we've had to kill people.*[7] [Author's italics]

Like Zodiac, Kaczynski used murder in the service of a secondary goal — the desire to attain publicity and personal notoriety on a national scale. In both cases this tendency went above and beyond whatever particular demons drove their subjects to kill. It very much served as an end unto itself. Both Kaczynski and the Zodiac possessed it.

★ ★ ★

Distinct from, but undoubtedly related to the drive for publicity, were the telephone calls placed by the Zodiac to police agencies immediately following the Blue Rock Springs and Lake Berryessa events:

> I want to report a double murder. If you will go (1) one mile east on Columbus Parkway to the public park you will find the kids in a brown

car. They were shot with a 9 MM luger. I also killed those kids last year. Goodbye.[8]

I want to report a murder, no, a double murder. They are two miles North of Park Headquarters. They were in a white Volkswagen Karmen-Ghia .... I'm the one that did it.[9]

Like the written correspondences, these clandestine calls did nothing to further the actual crimes to which they were related. They appear, however, to be signature elements of the crimes — peculiar aspects of the criminal enterprise that appear to afford their perpetrator a form of emotional gratification indispensable to achieving satisfaction from the crime. FBI profiler John Douglas explains this phenomenon in layman's terms:

But as we studied more and more serial offenders and developed our profiling methods, we came to realize that while M.O. was important, in certain types of crimes it wasn't nearly as important as what I call "signature" — the unique aspect that was critical not so much to accomplish the crime as to *satisfy the perpetrator emotionally* ....[10] [Author's italics]

Though it may be difficult to discern precisely what kind of emotional gratification Zodiac received from his calls to the police, we may with some degree of confidence offer a speculative opinion based on the evidence at hand. The most significant piece of evidence resides in the Zodiac missives themselves. In that forum (a public forum), Zodiac carries out a continuous taunting of the police who have failed to catch him, and under whose noses he has carried out the most audacious crimes. Open jibes, such as "Hey pig, doesnt it rile you up to have you[r] noze rubed in your booboos?" vie with understated or indirect taunts like "[t]he S.F. Police could have caught me last night if they had searched the park properly instead of holding road races with their motorcicles seeing who could make the most noise." At the very least, the running "score" presented at the end of each missive (i.e., Me – 37, SFPD – 0) clearly evinces a desire to taunt the police and deride them for their ineptitude. Moreover, it seems logical to assume that the telephone calls served a similar, if not identical, purpose. Both were made to police agencies relevant to the jurisdiction in which the crimes had been committed, from pay phones in close proximity to police headquarters, and at a time very shortly removed from the murders them-selves. Like the Stine slaying, committed in a wealthy residential neigh-borhood almost literally under the noses of the police, the calls were the killer's own unique way of "rubbing their noses" in the boo-boos of the authorities.

It would prove both tempting and instructive to find a similar ten-dency associated with the Unabomber's crimes; and indeed, there is a single instance at hand. *Time* magazine's 1996 treatise on the Una-bomber cites an incident that occurred in Sacramento, California on April 23, 1995, one day prior to the explosion at the California Forestry Association headquarters that killed Gilbert Murray:

> The next day, a Thursday, a shoebox-size package and four letters were posted from Oakland, California. The following Sunday [April 23], as these items wended their way through the mails, an anonymous man with a gravelly voice called the Association of California Insurance Companies in Sacramento at 10:52 a.m. and breathed into the answering machine, "Hi. I'm the Unabomber, and I just called to say 'Hi.'" . . . The Una-bomber had never preyed upon insurance targets. Perhaps he — or who-ever — had misdialed. *The insurance association's phone number was 440-1111. The sheriff's office number was 440-5111, just one digit off.*[11] [Author's italics]

The likelihood of this phone call having been placed by anyone other than Kaczynski is small. Not only was he in the Bay Area at the time, a relatively short distance from Sacramento, but he had just mailed the package containing the bomb directed to the California Forestry Association, which exploded in Sacramento only a day after the call. Assuming that he had indeed misdialed – and this is not an outrageous assumption – it would appear that, like Zodiac, he possessed a pen-chant for taunting the police by telephone.

This circumstance becomes more cogent yet when seen in light of Kaczynski's longstanding attitude about the authorities. It is per-haps easy to perceive why Kaczynski might have disliked the police, grouping them together with all of the elements of official authority that limited his sphere of freedom. "I often had fantasies of killing the kind of people whom I hated (e.g., government officials, police . . . .)" wrote Kaczynski in his autobiography. Additionally, the Unabomber correspondences contain instances of taunting similar to the sarcastic jabs taken by Zodiac at the San Francisco police:

> Clearly we are in a position to do a great deal of damage. And it doesn't appear as if the FBI is going to catch us any time soon. The FBI is a joke. [Times Letter II]

> For an agency that pretends to be the world's greatest law enforcement agency, the FBI seems surprisingly incompetent. They can't even keep elementary facts straight. [Times Letter III]

> The FBI's theory that we have some kind of a fascination with wood is about as silly as it gets. [Times Letter III]

> The FBI must really be getting desperate if they resort to theories as ridiculous as this one about the supposed fascination with wood. [Times Letter III]

Taken in this context, Kaczynski's anonymous telephone call — apparently intended for the Sheriff's office but mistakenly directed to the wrong party — satisfied a personal need to taunt the authorities who had thus far failed to capture him. It is a trait he shares with the Zodiac, as is the call itself.

Finally, the Zodiac's Lake Berryessa attack is associated with the peculiar phenomenon of the handwritten graffiti left on the door of Brian Hartnell's car. This does not appear to have been a spontaneous action on the part of Zodiac, since he came equipped with a felt-tipped marker in addition to the other paraphernalia that he used to commit the crime.

Likewise, Kaczynski's career as the Unabomber is marked by one instance of the planned and calculated use of a graffiti. In the spring of 1993, James Hill, a chemistry professor at California State University in Sacramento, observed a number of instances of a strange graffiti, spray-painted on the walls of buildings near the office where he worked. Hill described these graffiti as "a peace symbol-like circle with the letters FC inside."[12] Questioned by Mike Rusconi in 1996,[13] Hill described the "peace symbols" as having been rendered upside-down. Outside some of the circles, the word ANARCHY had been seen.

If an attempt is made to visualize this device, one can readily perceive that very little difference exists between the graffiti seen by Professor Hill and the Zodiac's crosshair circle, which he drew on Brian Hartnell's car. One can easily be converted into the other by the simple expedient of moving the lateral arms a mere 45 degrees either up or down. Note the following examples, in which the appearance of the Unabomber symbols is extrapolated from the descriptions tendered by Professor Hill:[14]

Zodiac device   **Kaczynski device,**   **Kaczynski device,**
                     lines outside   **lines within**
                        circle   **circle**

Since "FC" stood for "Freedom Club," the name of Kaczynski's supposed terrorist group, and since Freedom Club was defined by Kaczynski as an anarchist "organization" it seems apparent that the graffiti were deliberately produced at Sacramento State as part of the 1993 bombing that severely injured geneticist Charles Epstein. The return address on the package containing that bomb was that of Professor Hill, who had seen the graffiti on the campus buildings at Sacramento State and reported to the same to the FBI, though by that time the writings had been removed.

Like Zodiac, nearly 25 years before, the Unabomber felt the need to mark his presence by the use of a line-in-circle graffiti which he went out of his way to produce and for which he deliberately brought materials — in Zodiac's case a felt-tipped pen; in Kaczynski's case a can of paint. The difference is not significant.

groops of parking about 10 min
apart then the motor cicles
went by about 150 ft away
going from south to north west.
ps. 2 cops pulled a goof abot 3
min after I left the cab. I was
walking down the hill to the
park when this cop car pulled up
+ one of them called me over
+ asked if I saw any one
acting sapicisous or strange
in the last 5 to 10 min + I said
yes there was this man who
was running by waveing a gun
+ the cops peeled rubber +
went around the corner es
I directed them + I dissop —
eared into the park abbout +
a half away never to be seen
again.
    "Hey pig doesn't it rile you up
to have you noze rubed in your
booboos ?
If you cops think Im going to take
on a bus the way I stated I was,
you deserve to have holes in your
heads .

Above: Page 3 of Zodiac's Seven-Page Letter, with its wryly-worded retraction of the earlier school bus threat. Below: the Unabomber's wryly-worded retraction of his airline bombing threat. Both missives were mailed to the San Francisco Chronicle.

Note. Since the public has a short memory we decided to play one last
prank to remind them who we are. But no, we haven't tried to plant a
bomb on an airliner (recently).

Chapter 4

Loco Motions

One of the wild suggestions referred to, as at last coming to be linked with the White Whale in the minds of the superstitiously inclined, was the unearthly conceit that Moby Dick was ubiquitous; that he had actually been encountered in opposite latitudes at one and the same instant of time.

HERMAN MELVILLE, *Moby Dick*

PROXIMITY to the murder scenes or locations of the letter-mailings forms what is perhaps the most tenuous link connecting Theodore Kaczynski to the Zodiac events — tenuous, only because the facts are not complete. For while Kaczynski has never offered an alibi for any of the Zodiac events, his general movements at the times of their occurrence, far from eliminating him as a suspect, actually serve to draw suspicion toward him as a possible author of those events.

Following his graduation from the University of Michigan in the spring of 1967, Kaczynski relocated to Berkeley, California, where he maintained an official residence until his resignation from the University of California, effective June 30, 1969. According to the Turchie Affidavit [the warrant related to Kaczynski's arrest], David Kaczynski recalled that

> [I]n June, 1969, Theodore Kaczynski quit his job at UCB. Shortly thereafter, David met his brother in Wyoming and they travelled in Theodore Kaczynski's car to British Columbia, Canada to find some land. Theodore Kaczynski found some land near Prince George and filed homesteading-type applications for the land. Theodore Kaczynski returned to his family's home in Lombard, Illinois, in the summer of 1969, where he lived while awaiting word from the Canadian government on his land application.[1]

The distance in time covered by the words "shortly thereafter," cannot be determined, and might range from a few days, to a few weeks, or even more. Even assuming its sufficiency (at least four days) to cover the time leading to the Blue Rock Springs incident, the implication clearly exists that Kaczynski's official residency at Berkeley was long enough to cover only the December 20, 1968 (Lake Herman Road) and July 4, 1969 (Blue Rock Springs) events.

Additionally, a *New York Times* article of 1996 suggests that the actual duration of the Canada trip taken by Kaczynski and his brother might have covered two months, or portions of two months. If that is so, then it appears that the trip's itinerary might have overlapped with Zodiac's July 31 and August 3 mailings to the *Vallejo Times-Herald, San Francisco Chronicle* and *San Francisco Examiner*.

Clearly the implications are (1) that Kaczynski could not or would not have composed those correspondences in the presence of a second party, and (2) he was not in the Bay Area on the dates they were put into the mail. Given the facts as they are known, neither of those implications is wholly credible. Though it might (or might not) be true that Kaczynski would not have composed the missives in the presence of his brother, there is simply no evidence to suggest that the two were in continual contact during the period in question. Moreover, whether the Canada trip included a visit to the Bay Area remains an open question that has yet to be answered by either party. Nevertheless, it is interesting to note that no account has been given as to the manner in which Kaczynski moved his personal belongings from Berkeley to Illinois. According to David, the brothers spent the duration of their trip in Kaczynski's 1967 Chevelle, camping in the woods and essentially living off the land. It is difficult to believe that all of Kaczynski's personal effects could have been carried about in that vehicle, along with two grown men and the equipment necessary for such an extended trip. At some point in time, Kaczynski must have returned to Berkeley in order to settle the arrangements for moving his possessions. Such an event has never been mentioned, nor has the time that would have been involved in it been accounted for.

Moreover, the author is in possession of a series of correspondences by a resident of Idaho who claims to have seen Kaczynski at the University of Idaho in the *late spring* of 1969. The first of these very interesting communications[2] begins:

I was reading the Zodiac site and your posts regarding Kaczynski. In several places it is mentioned that he officially ended his term in June . . . . The idea that he stayed until June is confusing to me because I met him in N. Idaho in the spring of 69.

If you would like to discuss this let me know.

The succeeding correspondence proved to be more interesting still:

Let me tell you why my memory is that it was the spring of 69. I graduated from high school in 68 and went to the University of Idaho that next fall. I spent my freshman year living in a dorm.

That spring there was a dance at one of the men's dorms and a group of girls from mine decided to go there. Some how I got dragged along.

I don't remember the exact time but it was not cold outside so it had to be in the later spring. I even remember what I wore that night which I don't usually. White slacks and a bright lemon green Nehru jacket . . . . The jacket was just a light cotton with no lining so it couldn't have been very cold.

I only spent my freshman year living at the dorm so it had to be that spring. Also I normally wore my hair long but had cut it that year in the early spring. That is one of the few times in my life I wore it short. I guess you would have to be a woman to remember that stuff.

Anyway that was where I met him.

We had a very long conversation that night and in retrospect it is amazing what things we discussed.

Solicited for further details, she graciously provided the following account:

I already told you about the timing so I wont go into that.

I went to the dance and this guy who looked a little older than I was came over and asked me to dance. He had longish hair at that time and for the U of Idaho that was pretty much unusual. We danced a few dances and he was pretty interesting so we ditched the dance and walked down to the student union building to the cafeteria. We got some pop and found an out of the way (still in the cafeteria) place to talk. I am a pretty curious person and I love to talk politics so we talked till late.

I keep hearing how he doesn't know how to be sociable but he seemed very nice and we talked about a lot of things including his stay at Berkeley. He said he had been a math assistant and I was pretty impressed. I told him he must be pretty smart and he just laughed about that . . . . Anyway I asked about how it was down there in Berkeley. Now you should know I was a republican at that time. So I thought Berkeley was pretty much like a zoo.

He did not like Berkeley. He said he had joined a young republican group once but said they were just there for the partying and were not serious. In fact he admired the SDS more even though their politics were diametrically opposite his. At least they were committed to their cause.

I told him well maybe but bombing places isn't a great idea. He asked why I thought that and I told him that no matter how careful you are to just destroy a place you are eventually going to kill innocent people. He said that people always die in war and that was what it was.

While I agreed that a cause can be war I still insisted that there has to be other ways to get your point across. I don't know if he thought I had made a good point or not. We also talked about his opinion of technology so that was not something that developed later. He was pretty adamant about it too.

I am trying to remember what else we discussed. I know we talked about his dislike of leftwing causes. Which was pretty funny when they were saying when he was first caught that he was a leftwing person.

When he introduced himself he said his name was Theodore Kaczynski and I couldn't say his last name. He laughed. He told me he preferred being called Theodore but most called him Ted. You could tell he really hated it and I sympathized cause I hate being called [redacted]. It was easy to remember his first name cause that's my grandfather's name. I got the impression that he used the name as a gauge to tell if people were going to listen to what he was saying or just go off on their own lines of thought. I think I picked up on that cause I do that myself.

There were other things we talked about but that's all I can think of at the moment.

I asked him why he was at the University of Idaho cause it was a bit out of his way. He said he and his brother David were up there looking at property to buy. Somewhere quiet and out of the way. He said they had looked at a bunch of places but didn't like any of them so far.

He said his brother was off talking to the people showing the property. Now this is something that puzzles me a lot. I definitely had the impression that David made the decisions and Theodore went along with them. I asked why he was at the dance and he said David told him he had no social life and to go find a dance and socialize. He said David was worried that he didn't socialize enough. I keep hearing how David looked up to his brother but I have to wonder if it really wasn't the other way around. David got along easy with people and he didn't that easily.

On this same issue I did not notice that he could not handle being around a woman. He was certainly nice and considerate to me. In fact the sweetest thing happened when he took me to my dorm.

He opened the door and let me through then he shook my hand. Then he said that it was one of the nicest nights he had spent because I not only listened to him but actually understood what he was talking about and formed my own opinions on them and discussed them. Then he said the other thing he enjoyed so much was that I didn't try to jump his bones or expect him to jump mine. (My wording not his.) He said there was so much pressure to do that normally that it was one reason he didn't like to socialize much. I never once got the impression he didn't feel attracted to women but he didn't like the pushiness he had seen. I admit that I was very flattered and remembered him positively for it.

Years later I was in SLC [Salt Lake City] when there was a bombing. A sketch came out in the paper and I kept looking at that sketch. It really bothered me. I told [redacted] that I would swear I had seen that person and it was at the U of I. Then I realized it reminded me of the Theodore I had met at that dance. I told [redacted] (my husband) that was who it looked like and reminded him of what I had told him of Theodore. Later when he was captured I was shocked to find it really was him. And disappointed that he hadn't agreed with me in the end about bombing.

Sorry this is so long and rambling. I am sure I haven't included everything but I, at least, have always thought it was interesting that the Theodore isn't quite the man normally portrayed. I am not a groupie of his and in fact after SLC when ever I thought of him it was with a dark feeling of foreboding.

An obvious contradiction exists between this unsolicited account and the testimony of David Kaczynski as given to agents of the FBI. If the account is true, it sets the beginning of the Canada trip back a month or more and places the Kaczynski brothers in the state of Idaho, doing in the spring what they purportedly had done in the summer of 1969, and doing it in a place not mentioned in the younger brother's story. And while his correspondent has expressed a desire to remain anonymous, the author is aware of her identity and, by his own reckoning, has found her to be credible.

Whatever the case, there is no doubt that at some point in the latter third of 1969, Kaczynski moved his place of domicile from Berkeley, California, to his parents' small residence in Lombard, Illinois. While it may seem obvious to some that his relocation effectively removed Kaczynski from the scenes of any further Zodiac events, it is precisely this circumstance that attaches the greatest suspicion to Kaczynski in terms of proximity. For, though he lived in Lombard, Kaczynski quite simply did not stay put.

In the *New York Times* article of May 26, 1996, David Kaczynski stated:

> David returned to school, and Ted moved in with his parents, who by then had moved back to the Chicago area .... Living at home, [Ted] kept mostly to his bedroom. Awaiting word on his land application, he did nothing for more than a year. His parents urged him to get a job .... But the effort failed.[3]

In reality, David Kaczynski was in no position to account for his brother's day-to-day activities during the period covering Ted's residence in Lombard. During that time, David, by his own account, was finishing his final year at Columbia University. In the summer of 1970, after taking his degree, David moved from Columbia to Great Falls, Montana, where he found employment working for the Anaconda Copper company. The recollections of Ted's mother, Wanda, should be viewed as more reliable than those of David, considering that Ted lived directly with her during his stay in Lombard. Her knowledge of that period, as conveyed to the *Washington Post*, paints a somewhat different picture of Kaczynski's movements during those two years:

> There was another shutdown when Canada rejected his land application. And then, *as there had been several times before*, an abrupt leave-taking .... Wanda, an early riser, remembers lying in bed one morning and hearing him puttering around. "The thing that gave me a disturbed feeling was *the way Ted would leave*," she recalled. "He didn't tell us he was leaving. We had nothing."[4] [Author's italics]

The context of these remarks indicates not only that the reference was to the two-year period of Ted's residence in Lombard, but also that Kaczynski's leave-taking had occurred on more than one occasion. Kaczynski's mother did not simply say "the way Ted left," as she would had she been referring to only one occasion. "The way Ted would leave," assumes that this particular way of leaving was habitual, and had occurred more than once over the period of years in question.

Such peregrinations on the part of Ted Kaczynski have been documented for at least two occasions coinciding with periods of Zodiac activity. The first is found within the pages of the *Psych Report*:

> Throughout the summer of 1970, Mr. Kaczynski continued to look for wilderness land in Alaska and subsequently learned that his application for land in Canada was denied.[5]

"Looking for land" is a theme with Kaczynski that recurs on three occasions between 1969 and 1980. The first instance is the 1969 trip to Canada. The second, as seen above, is documented in Kaczynski's records as reviewed by Dr. Johnson for the Psych Report. The third occurred in 1980, following Kaczynski's unsuccessful attempt to make a life for himself in Chicago, away from his wilderness home.

> After quitting his job at Prince Castle, he lived with his parents in Lombard, Illinois and in the early summer of 1979 returned to his cabin in Montana. He remained there until mid 1980, when he traveled to Canada, again in search of wilderness land.[6]

Referring to the same time period, David Kaczynski gave similar information to the FBI:

> DAVE advised that after TED quit his job at Prince Castle in Addison, he borrowed DAVE's 1975 Datsun for a trip to Saskatchewan, Canada . . . .[7]

There is some confusion between the two accounts as to exactly in what year — 1979 or 1980 — Ted began his third "search for land" in Canada. What is not in doubt, however, is the fact that Ted spent the interval between "summer" of 1979 and November of that same year, not searching for land, but acquiring materials and building the bomb that nearly brought down an American Airlines flight from Chicago to Washington, D.C.

> I mentioned a plan for revenge on society. Plan was to blow up airliner in flight. Late summer and early autumn I constructed device. Much expense because had to go to Gr. Falls to buy materials ....[8]

If David's recollections are correct, the implication clearly is that the "search for land" was nothing more than a pretext, probably for Ted to induce Dave to lend him his car, which he would have needed not only for the return trip to Montana and back to the Chicago area in November, but for trips to Great Falls and perhaps elsewhere in search of materials. And if that is so, it also implies that "searching for land" is really nothing more than a pretext generally; an excuse for Kaczynski to get away for an extended period of time with no explanation as to his specific whereabouts, or specific activities.

"Summer of 1970," during which time Kaczynski allegedly began his second "search for land" in Canada, coincides with the June 26, July 24, and July 26 Zodiac mailings that included the Mt. Diablo map and code, the Kathleen Johns reference and the Mikado paraphrase. There is, of course, no evidence to prove Kaczynski's actual presence in the Bay Area during the period in question. However, the fact of his being in the western United States, thousands of miles from his domicile in Illinois, with his actual whereabouts completely unaccounted for, cannot be seen as other than suspicious.

At some point either late in 1970 or early in 1971 (the actual date remains unclear) the Canadian government informed Kaczynski that his land application had been denied. This precipitated a period of psychological withdrawal, at the end of which Kaczynski decided to leave his parents' home and seek a new place of residence in Montana, near his brother's new apartment in Great Falls. In a *People* magazine article dated August 10, 1998, David Kaczynski said:

> I had gone to Montana in [1970] and taken a job as a steelworker. I got a letter from my parents saying Ted had left, and they didn't know where he had gone. They were worried. He had left a note that sounded suicidal. *Several weeks later*, he showed up at my apartment. He had a plan for us to buy land in Montana, and we bought 1.4 acres near Lincoln, where he built his cabin.[9] [Author's italics]

Based on interviews with David, the *New York Times* article "Prisoner of Rage" enhances this:

> In the spring of 1970, David graduated from Columbia. Unsure what to do with his life, he remembered the beauty of Montana and decided to return. "I got a job in a smelter, in Great Falls," he said. Meantime, Ted continued to live in Lombard. Then *in the spring of 1971*, David recalled, Ted "showed up one day" in Montana, and soon he found the piece of land he wanted.[10] [Author's italics]

Extrapolating from these recollections, it is completely reasonable to conclude that at some point during or near the spring of 1971, Ted Kaczynski left his parents' home in Lombard and traveled to his brother's apartment in Great Falls, Montana, arriving there after an absence of several weeks. The period of time concerned is tantalizingly close to the period of Zodiac activity marked by the L.A. Times letter and the Pines postcard; those missives dated March 13, 1971 and March 22, 1971 respectively. Once again, though Kaczynski cannot positively be placed in the Bay Area during that period, it is highly suspicious that at that particular juncture he had left his place of domicile in Lombard, Illinois and traveled to the western United States, during which time his whereabouts for a period comprising several weeks remained completely unaccounted for.

Following the March 22, 1971 Pines Card, the next authenticated Zodiac correspondence, the Exorcist Letter, was mailed to the San Francisco Chronicle on January 29, 1974. At that point, Kaczynski's place of residence was the small cabin he had built on the jointly-purchased land in Montana. Once, again, however, his whereabouts for the entire winter of 1974 remain a mystery:

> In the winter of 1974, Theodore Kaczynski wrote the family a letter to say that he would be away camping for a while and that they should not worry if they did not hear from him.[11]

Though Kaczynski's actual whereabouts during this period of "camping" remain unknown, a passage from the Psych Report may offer a clue:

> During the period of late 1972 until December 1973, Mr. Kaczynski worked at a variety of jobs in Chicago and Salt Lake City, Utah. He re-

turned to his cabin in Montana in June 1973. In September 1974, for two to three weeks, he worked at a gas station in Montana, earning a few hundred dollars. *In January 1975 he traveled to Oakland, California, and returned to his cabin in March.*[12] [Author's italics]

Based on the documentation, it appears that in the early 1970s Kaczynski spent the winters away from his cabin in Montana, working odd jobs in various metropolitan areas. Having spent the entire winter of 1975 in the San Francisco Bay area (Oakland), it is not illogical to assume that he might have spent the previous winter (that of 1974; a period not accounted for) in the same location. If that is so, it places him once again at a considerable distance from his official domicile, near the scene of a Zodiac event. (Perhaps not surprising is the revelation that Kaczynski spent nearly the entire winter of 1975 in Oakland, a period of time only slightly removed from the suspicious December, 1974 greeting card — the Donna Card — sent to the sister of Donna Lass and connected to two earlier correspondences in the hands of the San Francisco police, the Pines and Monticello Cards. The postal code on both the Exorcist Letter and the Donna Card is 940, indicating that they were mailed in Alameda County, which encompasses the city of Oakland.)

The fact remains that, all hearsay aside, Kaczynski cannot be eliminated as a Zodiac suspect on the basis of his known whereabouts during the periods of Zodiac activity from 1968 through 1971 and even beyond, to 1974. Further, the act of traveling a considerable distance toward the areas of Zodiac activity, at the times of their occurrence, makes him far more suspect than an individual whose primary place of domicile was near those areas during the times in question.*

---

* See the author's website at http://unazod.com/eureka.html for a discussion of Kaczynski's whereabouts as they pertain to the discovery of the Eureka Card, a suspected Zodiac correspondence mailed in December, 1990 from Eureka, California.

Chapter 5

Eyewitness News

William Bird, tailor, deposes that he was one of the party who entered the house. Is an Englishman. Has lived in Paris two years. Was one of the first to ascend the stairs. Heard the voices in contention. The gruff voice was that of a Frenchman. Could make out several words, but cannot now remember all. Heard distinctly "sacre" and "mon Dieu." There was a sound at the moment as if of several persons struggling — a scraping and scuffling sound. The shrill voice was very loud — louder than the gruff one. Is sure that it was not the voice of an Englishman. Appeared to be that of a German. Might have been a woman's voice. Does not understand German.

EDGAR ALLAN POE, *The Murders in the Rue Morgue*

IT SEEMS CURIOUS that, despite his having been seen by at least five eyewitnesses on four separate occasions, no definite consensus exists regarding the Zodiac's appearance. This is not surprising. Mike Mageau, the Blue Rock Springs survivor had been badly wounded by the time he caught a glimpse of Darlene Ferrin's killer, as he writhed in pain from 9 mm gunshot wounds to his elbow, shoulder, knee and jaw. Survivor Bryan Hartnell, who viewed his assailant at Lake Berryessa from the ground up, saw nothing more than the form of a man towering over him with a handgun and a knife, clad sloppily in loose-fitting apparel topped off with a square black hood. The teenaged eyewitnesses at Presidio Heights got an unobstructed look at Zodiac as he left the cab scant minutes after murdering Paul Stine, though their view was by street lighting and at a distance of approximately 50 feet. Finally, Officer Fouke of the San Francisco Police caught a passing glance at a solitary man who almost certainly was the killer of Paul Stine, in bad light, from a moving car, and at a time when the appearance of a white man walking casually down an adjacent street, nearly two blocks away from the crime scene, did not draw his attention.

Following the Blue Rock Springs attack, officer Hoffman of the Vallejo Police Department recorded the first eyewitness account given by the badly-wounded Mageau:

> Subject appeared to be short, possibly 5'8", was real heavy set, beefy build. States subject was not blubbery fat, but real beefy, possibly 195 to 200 or maybe even larger. Stated he had short curly hair, light brown, almost blond. He was wearing a short-sleeved shirt, blue in color. Cannot remember if it was light or dark blue. States he just saw subject's face from the profile, side view, and does not recall seeing a front view. States there was nothing unusual about his face, other than that it appeared to be large. Michael stated the subject did not have a mustache, nor was he wearing glasses or anything. He could not recall anything unusual except that he had a large face. Michael reemphasized that he really did not get a good look at subject other than his profile. Also, it was dark out and it was hard to see the subject. . . . Stated subject was a white male, approximately 26-30 years. Was unable to judge real well what his age was.[1]

Three to four weeks later, Mageau offered a revised description to the *Vallejo News-Chronicle*:

> He got his first look at the slayer when he was walking away and was partly illuminated by his own headlights. . . . He was of stocky build and short, about 5 feet 8 or 9 inches, weighing about 160 pounds, Mageau said. His face was full, he was bareheaded and had "wavy or curly light brown hair," and looked about 25 to 30 years old. He wore a blue shirt or sweater.[2]

In other interviews, Mageau described the killer's hair as short, curly and light-brown, worn in a "military-style" crew cut and remarked that the hair had been "combed up and back in a kind of pompadour." His pants had pleats, according to Mageau, and he wore a Navy-type windbreaker.[3]

Likewise Bryan Hartnell, who survived the attack at Lake Berryessa despite being stabbed six times in the back with a foot-long knife, gave varying accounts of Zodiac's appearance. One day after the attack, on September 28, 1969, Detective John Robertson of the Napa

County Sheriff's Department, interviewed a sedated Hartnell in his hospital room:

B.H. . . . I was really trying to see what he looked like, you know. He had on pleated pants, these old type of suit pants, you know, and they were either black or dark blue, I can't remember now. And I can't remember what he was wearing for shoes. But he had on this cotton coat. You've seen the kind, that you just turn the collar up once, there's a zipper down the front, you know. They're real light, super-thin, you know . . .

J.R. Kind of a windbreaker . . .

B.H. Yeah, like a windbreaker. And it's got this blue, this little collar, sometimes the guys wear them standing up, you know.

J.R. What color was that?

B.H. That was dark blue, And I don't know. Maybe he had something in his pouch. I just took it as being a . . . as being a . . . you know, he was stout because he looked kind of heavy. I think he was weighing two and a quarter, two fifty, somewhere in there. And I got kind of a look at his hair . . . I looked through his hair. I[t] kind of looked like it was combed, you know, like this . . . it was a brownish, you know, dark brown hair.

. . .

And I don't know how tall he was. Maybe 5-8 or maybe 5-10, 6 feet, somewhere in there. I've a very poor judge of height because of my height.

. . .

J.R. Okay. You said his hair looked dark brown. How could you see his hair?

B.H. 'Cause I saw it from where those goggles fit. I looked so closely to find out. And when he turned you know they kind of flittered . . . I could see his hair. It looked kind of greasy.

J.R.   Now was he as heavy as I am?

B.H.   Well I can't say 'cause he wasn't wearing those type of clothes. They were sloppy clothes, you know. And he just had on this old pair of pleated pants. I don't know . . . how tall are you?

J.R.   I'm about five eleven.

B.H.   Well, like I say, he was dressed kind of sloppily, you know. His pants real tight up here and his stomach kind of pouched a bit, you know. I don't know . . . it's hard to say 'cause I can't judge you with being in a suit and all, you know, and him not being professional-looking at all. He could be about the same. It's hard to say. He was so sloppily dressed.[4]

In a later interview, reported by author Robert Graysmith in an obscure appendix to his *Zodiac*, Hartnell offered a somewhat different account:

He had to be fairly lightweight (without puffed-up jacket). All the guys the police had me look at were really fairly husky guys. This guy I think was in his thirties and fairly unremarkable.[5]

Hartnell also gave information to the producers of the television series "Crimes of the Century" in or around the year 1989. Among other things he declared that he had "grossly misjudged" his assailant's height and weight; that the perpetrator's jacket "was loose" and that he could have been "big or small."[6]

Just over two weeks after the attack at Berryessa, a newspaper account of the Paul Stine murder, that ran on the morning after the slaying, offered the following description:

The suspect was described as white, about 40, 170 pounds, a blond crewcut, wearing glasses. He was wearing dark shoes, and dark grey trousers and jacket.[7]

The police report offered additional detail, taken from the eyewitnesses who had seen Zodiac walk out of the cab and disappear down Cherry Street toward the Presidio:

Description was obtained from reportees, whose observation point was directly across the street (50ft.) and unobstructed . . . . WMA, in his early forties, 5'8", heavy build, reddish-blond "crew-cut" hair, wearing eyeglasses, dark brown trousers, dark (navy blue or black) "Parka" jacket, dark shoes.[8]

In succeeding days, SFPD issued two bulletins, each containing a composite drawing and description of the suspect. The initial bulletin, No. 87-69 showed a youngish-looking man and described the suspect as "WMA, 25–30 Years, 5'8" to 5'9"[,] Reddish Brown Hair – Crew Cut, Heavy Rim Glasses, Navy Blue or Black Jacket." On October 18 SFPD issued a revised bulletin, showing the earlier composite alongside a second drawing depicting an older-looking man with a large, square chin and a receding hairline. The description was modified to read "WMA, 35–45 Years, approximately 5'8", Heavy Build, Short Brown Hair, possibly with Red Tint, Wears Glasses."

Among contemporary Zodiac researchers, confusion still exists over the origin of the second, revised composite. With no real corroborating documentation, some opine that this composite was the result of an interview with officers Donald Fouke and Eric Zelms, who apparently saw the suspect as he casually made his way east on Jackson Street before turning north onto Maple. Others assert that the composite was made on the basis of a second interview of the teenaged eyewitnesses to the event. By some accounts, Fouke has denied involvement in making the revised composite sketch, though one is led to wonder why his input would have been ignored. Fouke's formal description of the suspect was tendered one month after the event, in a memo addressed to the Department:

> . . . The suspect that was observed by officer Fouke was a WMA 35-45 Yrs about five-foot, ten inches, 180–200 pounds. Medium heavy build — Barrel chested — Medium complexion — Light-colored hair possibly greying in rear (May have been lighting that caused this effect.) Crew cut — wearing glasses — Dressed in dark blue waist length zipper type jacket (Navy or royal blue) Elastic cuffs and waist band zipped part way up. Brown wool pants pleeted [sic] type baggy in rear (Rust brown) May have been wearing low cut shoes. Subject at no time appeared to be in a hurry walking with a shuffling lope, Slightly bent forward . . . .[9]

In later interviews Fouke offered essentially the same information with slight variations in terms of height and weight:

> The individual I saw that night was a white male adult approximately 35 to 45 years of age, 5 feet 10 inches, 180 to 210 lbs.[10]

> 35-40, 5'11" tall, 190 lbs., with a cloth bomber jacket and boots.[11]

When asked his impression about the wanted poster sketches, he said that he felt that Zodiac had a more receding hairline (i.e., was at the older end of the "35–45" age range) and had more of a traditional, "flat-top" crew cut. He also stated that there was "something about the chin" but could not put his finger on precisely what about it was not right.[12]

To the foregoing physical descriptions must be added the accounts of Vallejo P.D. switchboard operator Nancy Slover, Bryan Hartnell, and Napa P.D. switchboard operator David Slaight. Slover variously described Zodiac's voice as "a youthful male voice,"[13] and "young sounding."[14] In the official police report she stated "[w]riter could distinguish no trace of accent in voice . . . . Subject spoke in an even, consistant voice (rather soft but forceful) . . . . Subject's voice was mature."[15]

In the September 28, 1969 interview by Detective Robertson, Bryan Hartnell described his assailant as having an unidentifiable drawl, which he later qualified as "not a Southern drawl." To the media, Officer

Slaight described the killer's voice as "sounding like a young man,"[16] and "[a] male voice, young sounding, possibly early twenties."[17]

Obviously these descriptions, relating to the killer's height, weight, age, hair color and general body type, cannot all be correct. It is especially curious to see the range of descriptions that fall within the scope of a single eyewitness's accounts, quite apart from the noticeable divergence that occurs from one eyewitness to the next. Zodiac's weight varies from a low of 160 to a high of 250 pounds, while his height is given variously as ranging anywhere between 5'8" and 5'11". Body type goes from "stocky" to "stout" to "fairly lightweight," while hair color shifts between light brown, dark brown, reddish-blonde, brown with a red tint, and graying in the rear. Age estimates vary from a low of "early 20s" to a high of 45 years.

It is well-known in the criminological profession that eyewitness accounts are notorious both for their inaccuracy and unreliability. This is especially so when the witness has been traumatized, when events transpire suddenly, and when external conditions are less than perfect for facilitating vision. All three of these factors played, to one extent or another, into the descriptions given by Mike Mageau and Bryan Hartnell. While not physically traumatized, the teenagers who saw the Zodiac at Presidio Heights had the disadvantage of being approximately 50 feet away, and no doubt excited by what was happening in the cab across the street. Street lighting would have provided the only source of illumination, and between that, and the distance, conditions could not have been optimal for a precise description. Similar qualifications would probably have held true for the Fouke sighting on Jackson Street, although in that instance it would have been indifference, and not excitability, that made the resulting description less perfect than it would have been had Fouke's attention been directed toward the appearance of a white male adult, and not the negro male adult that was being sought on account of the dispatcher's mistaken directive. Once again, lighting conditions were not good, the eyewitness was in a moving vehicle, and there was no intimation of anything noteworthy about the suspect until several minutes after the sighting.

What all this signifies is that very few people can actually be excluded as Zodiac suspects on the grounds of physical appearance alone. Favored suspects run the entire gamut, from the relatively thin to the almost morbidly obese, while even within the categories of height and age there is considerable disparity. To this must be added the distinct possibility that Zodiac employed some element or elements of disguise, as he boastfully asserted in his seven-page letter of November 9, 1969.

★ ★ ★

Ted Kaczynski is by no account a "stocky" man. Neither, however, is he a particularly small man. When arrested at his cabin in Montana, following an extremely harsh winter of living off the land, his weight was listed as 150 pounds, on a 5-foot nine-inch frame. No doubt during better times, especially during the years at Berkeley, his weight might have gone as high as 160 to 165 pounds. While this does not make him "stocky" by any matter or means, it creates a solid foundation for a disguise that can leave an eyewitness with the distinct impression of bulk or stockiness, by the simple expedient of wearing extra clothing.

Consider the descriptions of Bryan Hartnell, who estimated Zodiac's weight as high as 250 pounds, then gradually proceeded to back off that estimate until at one point he actually described his assailant as "fairly lightweight," while allowing that he had misjudged the killer's height and weight. Reading the Robertson interview, one is immediately struck by the fact that from the beginning Hartnell attempted to qualify his weight estimates by pointing out the sloppiness of his assailant's garb. Pressed by Detective Robertson, Hartnell failed to say whether the killer was as large as the detective, continually referring back to the "sloppy" manner in which Zodiac had been dressed. This tendency toward sloppiness is buttressed by Officer Fouke's description of his subject as wearing pleated pants that were "baggy in the rear." In all the eyewitness sightings, Zodiac is said to have worn some kind of jacket, descriptions ranging from a "windbreaker" to a "parka-type" to a "cloth bomber jacket."

This type of clothing severely complicates any attempt to define Zodiac's actual weight and build. Was this really a stocky man the witnesses were beholding, or simply a man of modest proportions, hiding behind layers of loose-fitting apparel?

The question, of course, has no definite answer. Either alternative is possible. But at 5'9" tall and an estimated weight of around 160 pounds, Ted Kaczynski might certainly have added 20 to 30 pounds to his appearance simply by donning an extra layer or two of clothing. This would have changed the appearance of his body type from middling to heavy, especially amongst witnesses laboring under the combined effects of such factors as pain, stress, anxiety, visual distance and poor lighting.

In fact, as the Unabomber, Kaczynski was no stranger to the use of such an artifice. One of his journal entries, made publicly available by the prosecution at his trial, describes the means by which he disguised himself when purchasing a piece of pipe:

> When I bought this pipe, I was wearing a bulky cloak, with a jacket inside, so I would appear heavier than I am ....[18]

Clearly he was aware of the value extra clothing played in giving witnesses a false impression of his body type.

Kaczynski's abilities in the realm of disguise included such tricks as glasses, chewing gum or facial tissue stuffed under the lips and into the nostrils, dyes for the beard, and an ingeniously devised pair of shoes with a normal-sized sole fitted atop a smaller sole, designed for the express purpose of leaving footprints smaller than his own.

In various photos, the color of Kaczynski's hair ranges from medium to dark brown, with what appears as a reddish tint both to the hair and beard. There is, of course, great variance in the descriptions of the Zodiac's hair color, though in the final analysis some shade of brown is likely to be the closest we can come to the actual truth. Lighting was bound to have played some role in the eyewitness accounts of his hair color, because hair can appear lighter than it actually is when reflecting light. Mageau caught only a glimpse of Zodiac by the headlights of Zodiac's own car, while the teens at Presidio Heights would have seen their subject by the light of street-lamps, shining from above. Hartnell claimed to have seen dark brown hair while looking up through the eye slits in Zodiac's hooded mask. Because there was still adequate daylight during the event, and because of his close proximity, Hartnell's description is undoubtedly the most accurate of all, assuming that the killer neither wore a wig, nor dyed his hair. (The use of either artifice under an elaborate hood, however, would probably have been seen by the killer as superfluous.) In explaining the disparity between what was witnessed two weeks later at Presidio Heights, it is probably safe to say that in the latter assault Zodiac lightened his hair in some manner; perhaps by bleaching, or perhaps simply by cropping it closer than it apparently was at Lake Herman Road or Berryessa.

Mike Mageau described his assailant's hairstyle in ways that appear to be conflicting. Though his first description was "short" and "curly," he later added that Zodiac's hair had been worn in a "military-style" crew cut, "combed up and back in a kind of pompadour." The contradiction here is somewhat puzzling. For many people "crew cut" refers to a hairstyle in which the hair is close-cropped to the same length all around, usually one-quarter inch or less. This, however, is not a universal appraisal. For some, the term applies to hair that is generally short with a small allowance for additional length on top. Mageau, obviously, was of this class, which is why he could describe the killer's hair in the same context as short, curly and combed up in a pompadour-like arrangement. Had Zodiac sported a traditional "buzz cut" style, he would not have used those terms.

Consensus was much more consistent among the witnesses to the Presidio Heights event, and the accounts given there are supported by two police composites, each depicting an individual with evenly cropped hair, cut short, though not "buzzed" as the term is understood. There is no suggestion of a "kind of pompadour," which implies that the killer changed his hairstyle somewhat between the July 4th and October 11th attacks.

Kaczynski's hair is thick, moderately wavy, and fairly stiff; so much so that it will stand up of its own accord. His favorite hairstyle over the years, as seen in numerous photos ranging from youth to middle age, is one in which the hair is cropped closely (but not "buzzed") at the top and sides, with a greater allowance of growth in the front, combined up and back in what can well be described as a "semi-pompadour." Extant photos taken at various other times have shown him sporting a modest-length "Beatle-style" cut, parted at the side with a large growth of extraneous hair combed over the forehead, and a close-cropped cut without the extra growth in front.

Despite the use of the "crew cut" terminology, the composites made of the Presidio Heights accounts show short, dense hair that is combed completely back above the forehead. The second composite shows what appears to be a receding hairline, an element evidently derived from the accounts. Whether Zodiac's hairline actually was receding is a question not easily resolved. The first accounts failed to mention this feature, nor was it noticed by Mike Mageau at Blue Rock Springs. A logical explanation for the discrepancy is that Zodiac possessed a more-or-less prominent widow's peak, defined as "a V-shaped point formed by the hair near the top of the human forehead." This, combined with short, even hair combed directly up and over the forehead might well give the appearance of a receding hairline, since a true receding hairline will often mimic the appearance of a widow's peak. Kaczynski's hair has never receded, though he possesses a noticeable and prominent widow's peak, which is all that can, or need be said upon the subject.

Looking at the composites, one can readily discern that the most noteworthy change between the first and the second rendition is that of the subject's lower jaw, or chin. While the facial structure of both appears to be somewhat large, the chin of the second comprises a prominent feature, something the artist deliberately applied, and not explainable by the vagaries of composite production. While Officer Fouke has been cited as denying that he or Officer Zelms (now deceased) had anything to do with this composite, it is interesting to note the remark in his 2004 Rodelli interview that there was "something about the chin." If indeed he had nothing to do with the second composite, one must assume that the teenaged eyewitnesses also noticed a peculiarity — in their case a prominence — of that feature in the subject.

Kaczynski's facial structure is quite heavy, and stands in rather stark contrast to the rest of his body form. His head is large in comparison with the rest of his body, and his most prominent feature, by far, is the large, square chin, which appears to jut out noticeably from his face.

It seems remarkable, but the progression of police composites in the Unabomber case appears to parallel the succession of composites made from the Presidio Heights accounts of Zodiac. Immediately after the event at the CAAMS Computer Store in Salt Lake City, in which an eyewitness had actually seen Kaczynski planting the bomb that injured Gary Wright, a composite was made showing a youngish-looking individual with nondescript features and a modest facial structure. At some point after the event a second artist was called in, who from the eyewitness's elaborate description produced a drawing that showed the subject with a markedly heavy facial structure, and a prominent chin that is for all intents and purposes an identical copy of that seen in the second Zodiac composite. [See Figure 1, next page]

Obviously this is the kind of feature that fixes itself upon the impressions of a witness, and it is curious that the same feature should be expressed in the cases of both the Unabomber and the Zodiac composites. Bear in mind also that Mike Mageau was unable to give any description of his assailant's face other than "large" or "full."

A visual comparison of Kaczynski's Berkeley photograph with the two San Francisco composites, as well as a side-by-side comparison of the first San Francisco composite and a photograph of Kaczynski from his college days, may offer the reader some foundation for a subjective analysis of the similarities and dissimilarities between the three. [See Figures 2 and 3, next page]

In his memo of November 12, 1969, Officer Fouke described his subject as "walking with a shuffling lope." This is a rather vague description, and no one can say precisely what it means, even after numerous interviews of Fouke in the succeeding years. To "lope" implies a springing step, while "shuffling" implies the opposite. Fouke has said only that the term "lumbering," which Robert Graysmith ascribed to his account, is not an accurate description of what he meant by "a shuffling lope." The only inference that can be made with any confidence is that the subject observed by Fouke walked with a peculiar gait that somehow impressed itself on his observer's mind.

This is of interest to us because of a description of Theodore Kaczynski that was tendered by his brother to the FBI in 1996:

Ted's left foot is noticeably pigeon toed which affects the way he walks.[19]

Zodiac's use of glasses might or might not have constituted an element of disguise. Glasses are commonly used to mask the features, though a criminal might wear them for the legitimate purpose than visual correction. Kaczynski certainly wore glasses as part of a disguise, though these were dark, aviator-style sunglasses, and not the clear, prescription-type glasses used by Zodiac at Presidio Heights. Nonetheless, there is extant an account by Chris Waites, Kaczynski's neighbor in Montana, that elaborates on something unusually relevant to our discussion here:

Figure 1.

Figure 2.

Figure 3.

Ted had several pairs of glasses; all protective in nature, needed to keep wind, rain, dust, sleet or snow — depending on the season — out of his eyes. Sometimes when riding his bike he wore a full, dark, rimmed pair that looked like reading glasses, or corrective lenses, but he didn't need glasses to see.[20]

In summation it can be said that while nothing in the physical descriptions of the Zodiac can be used to effectively exclude Kaczynski as a suspect, a number of elements contained in those descriptions point directly to him in a completely inclusive sense. In and of itself, this fact does not identify him as the Zodiac, and indeed, it is safe to say that no one will be prosecuted in the Zodiac affair on the basis of his physical appearance alone. On the other hand, it adds to the more salient aspects of the comparison, which will grow even stronger as we progress.

Chapter 6

Figuratively Speaking

I'm very well acquainted, too, with matters mathematical,
I understand equations, both the simple and quadratical.

GILBERT AND SULLIVAN, *The Pirates of Penzance*

THE FACT THAT Ted Kaczynski was a brilliant mathematician is hardly news to anyone today. In September of 1995, however, few people had any intimation of that fact, apart from a particularly astute subscriber to the internet newsgroup sci.math, who anticipated the revelation by six full months. In a September 30, 1995 posting to the group, he bluntly stated, without qualification, that the Unabomber was a mathematician, arguing for his position on the basis of certain phrasings within the newly-published Manifesto. These phrasings included terms such as "rational calculation," "the pursuit of goal x," "the sum of two components," and "new, ordered community."[1]

Certain occupations tend to be filled by people having particular qualities of mind and mental ability. The nature of mathematics is such that no person is likely to succeed in its pursuit unless he has been endowed both with the intellectual capacity and the organizational mindset necessary for dealing with the concepts of numbers and abstractions. Those qualities, being ingrained in their possessor, will manifest themselves in virtually every aspect of his relations with the world in which he lives.

That Ted Kaczynski possessed the intellectual capacity to succeed in mathematics is not in question, because he did indeed succeed, at least until his social pathologies drove him from the field. In other respects, however, his mathematical mindset — the mindset that led to his success — is equally apparent. His Manifesto, for example, though frequently described by ill-schooled journalists as "rambling," turns out to be nothing of the sort. For while it can certainly be described as dry, its dryness is actually a manifestation of the extreme orderliness of the way in which it is composed, with grammatically-precise sentences laying out the premise of Kaczynski's worldview in a clear and logical progression that moves toward a natural conclusion in harmony with the document's stated theme. This is not an aberration. It is simply a habit with Kaczynski, and a trait that indelibly marks everything he writes. Rambling is not an option for Kaczynski, whose writing is imbued with an inflexible precision that is never florid, never excessive, and never deviates or strays off tangentially from the subject at hand. He practices the habit of enumeration, as clearly displayed in the carefully numbered paragraphs of his Manifesto, and the numbering of specific points in his letters to the media, particularly the *New York Times* letter of 1995 and the various documents written by Kaczynski over the span of his entire life. The following examples are indicative of the whole:

> Our offer to desist from terrorism is subject to three qualifications . . . *First:* Our promise to desist will not take effect until all parts of our article or book have appeared in print. *Second:* If the authorities should succeed in tracking us down . . . we reserve the right to use violence. *Third,* we distinguish between terrorism and sabotage. [Times Letter II] [Author's italics]

> Practically all of my property held by the government falls into one of three categories:
>
>> 1. Property other than firearms and ammunition . . . .
>> 2. Property that . . . may have been the instrumentality . . . .
>> 3. Firearms and ammunition.[2]

> Since thick, heavy envelopes cannot be left on the bars, I suggest four possible alternative solutions: (1) All outgoing mail can be left on the inmates desk . . . (2) When going out to rec . . . inmates can ask the officers . . . (3) Mail collection could be scheduled so that . . . (4) Thick envelopes . . . can be bent around the bars . . . .[3]

I don't have the technical expertise to judge whether such a machine is plausible, nevertheless I suspect that your "Hyperflux System" is a hoax. Here's why:

1. You are apparently a student of the arts, and . . . .
2. Your mention of the science fiction story by Phillip K. Dick . . . .
3. Your picture of the "Hyperflux System" is just too cute . . . .
4. The name "Hyperflux System" too is just too cute . . . .
5. There would seem to be some degree of inconsistency . . . .
6. You have scheduled your press conference for April 1 . . . .[4]

Like a mathematician, or someone possessing the mindset of a mathematician, Zodiac mirrors Kaczynski's habit of enumerating things. In this context, enumeration signifies the habit of numbering things that do not require numbering because they are placed in a direct order, one item immediately following the other:

Christmas
1 brand name of ammo — Super X
2 10 shots fired
3 Boy was on his back with feet to car
4 Girl was lyeing on right side feet to west
4th of July
1 girl was wearing patterned pants
2 boy was also shot in knee
3 ammo was made by Western [Examiner Letter]

1 I look like the description passed out . . . .
2 As of yet I have left no fingerprints behind . . . .
3 my killing tools have been boughten . . . . [Seven-Page Letter]

If you dont want me to have this blast you must do two things. 1 Tell every one about the bus bomb with all the details. 2 I would like to see some nice Zodiac butons wandering about town. [Dragon Card]

Zodiac's missives are riddled with spelling errors, considered by many to have been deliberately contrived. Allowing for the possibility that those errors were nothing more than red herrings meant to confuse the authorities as to Zodiac's true intelligence, his writing style can be described as clear, rational and imbued with many, if not all, of the qualities displayed in Kaczynski's written word. Far from rambling, he proceeds directly to the point he wishes to make with no unnecessary detours or distractions along the way. His statements show clear indications of logical thought with none of the mental meandering that would typify the thought processes of an individual not in absolute control of his faculties. If we remove the distraction occasioned by his misspellings we can easily discern, and perhaps even admire, the clean and unembellished style of Zodiac. The following paragraphs of the Stine Letter have been edited to remove the obvious errors in spelling and punctuation:

> This is the Zodiac speaking. I am the murderer of the taxi driver over by Washington Street and Maple Street last night; to prove this here is a bloodstained piece of his shirt. I am the same man who did in the people in the North Bay area.
>
> The S.F. Police could have caught me last night if they had searched the park properly, instead of holding road races with their motorcycles, seeing who could make the most noise. The car drivers should have just parked their cars and sat there quietly waiting for me to come out of cover. [Stine Letter]

As one would expect of a person trained in mathematics, Zodiac displays a penchant for precision in the details he relates. Where he cannot describe an object with exactitude he invariably qualifies that object with the word "about" or "approx." Hence in the Seven-Page Letter of 1969 the dogs are "to the west", there are "2 groups of barking," and the motorcycles go "from south to north west," while in the same missive the groups of barking are *"about* 10 min apart," the motorcycles go by *"about* 150 feet away," and the two cops pull a goof *"about* 3 min" after Zodiac leaves the cab. In the same letter, the battery-powered clock required for the bus bomb will run for *"aprox* 1 year." In the mass mailings of July 31, 1969, all the details given are precise, while in the Examiner Letter of two days later, the shabbily-dressed negro is described as *"about* 40–45," and the circle of light is *"approx* 3 to 6 in. across."

Zodiac offers further proof of his penchant for precision in sentences from the Seven-Page Letter and the Belli Letter respectively. In the first of these usages he writes, "I think you do not have the man power to stop this one . . . ." Notice the placement of the word "think," which appears *before* the negation signified by "not." The usual phrasing for such a sentence would be "I do not think . . . ." Yet clearly there is a difference between *thinking* something and *not thinking* something: the first is active, while the other is completely passive.

The second usage occurs within the Belli Letter, where the Zodiac declares, "[b]ut if I told back too long from no nine I will loose ~~complet~~ all controol of my self & set the bomb up." Notice, in this instance, how he has stricken out the word "complet[e]" and replaced it with the simpler "all." This is no caprice, but rather, an effort on the writer's part to render his meaning more precise. For should he lose *complete* control, there remains an inference that he will retain some level of *incomplete* control — in other words, he will not have lost the totality of his control. By catching himself and substituting "all" in place of the less-precise "complete," he satisfies himself that his meaning will be interpreted exactly as intended, though no one but a pedant, perhaps, might appreciate the difference.

These usages give evidence of the type of mindset — precise to an extreme degree — that is compatible with that required by, and typical of, a mathematician. Moreover, they evince an intelligence higher than the average.

The essence of mathematics is providing proof of various propositions. In his communications with the media, Zodiac displayed a near-obsession with providing proof to the authorities that he alone had committed the crimes for which he took the credit:

I am the killer . . . to prove this I shall state some facts which only I & the police know. [Times-Herald Letter]

This is the murderer . . . .To prove I killed them I shall state some facts which only I & the police know. [Chronicle Letter]

I am the killer . . . .To prove this I shall state some facts which only I & the police know. [Examiner Letter]

In answer to your asking for more details about the good times I have had in Vallejo, I shall be very happy to supply even more material. [Examiner II Letter]

I am the murderer of the taxi driver . . . to prove this here is a blood stained piece of his shirt. [Stine Letter]

To prove that I am the Zodiac, Ask the Vallejo cop about my electric gun sight which I used to start my collecting of slaves. [Seven-Page Letter]

Additionally, Zodiac left the graffiti on Bryan Hartnell's Karmen Ghia in order to take credit for the crime at Berryessa, and used pieces of Paul Stine's bloody shirt to fully authenticate two of his next three correspondences.

Though the Unabomber never used a physical object to authenticate his letters, the desire he displays to offer proof appears to have been equally as strong. In lieu of a bloody shirt, Kaczynski supplied the authorities with a nine-digit authenticating number, and used it to "prove" his authorship of the Unabomber correspondence. His statements are eerily similar to those of Zodiac:

> To prove that we are the ones who planted the bomb at U. Of Cal. last May we will mention a few details that could be known only to us and the FBI who investigated the incident. [Examiner Letter]

> This is a message from the terrorist group FC. To prove its authenticity we give our identifying number. [Times Letter II]

> To prove that the writer of this letter knows something about FC, the first two digits of their identifying number are 55. [Chronicle Threat Letter]

> Warren Hoge of the New York Times can confirm that this note does come from FC. [Sharp Letter]

During his student years at the University of Michigan, one of Kaczynski's advisors remarked that Kaczynski would typically offer more proof than necessary when working with mathematical issues.

A mathematical statement is defined as the statement of a mathematical relation. Such statements are to mathematical proofs as hypotheses are to scientific theories; the statement providing a declaration or assumption that will be put to the test. It is interesting to mark the occasions upon which Zodiac employs the words "state" or "stated" in lieu of the verb "to say." In each of the three letters of July 31, 1969, he writes that "to prove" he is the killer, he will "*state* some facts." In the August 2, 1969 letter he observes, "They did not openly *state* this, but implied this . . . ." And the Seven-Page Letter of November 9, 1969, contains the sentence "If you cops think Im going to take on a bus the way I *stated* I was, you deserve to have holes in your heads."

Not surprisingly, Ted Kaczynski makes frequent use of the same expression. His Manifesto contains nine separate instances of the words "state" or "statement" in reference to something that is declared. As the Unabomber, his correspondences show a similar tendency:

> We decided that before attempting to make a public statement we ought to go back to experimenting . . . . By the way, contrary to statements made by the FBI, the[s]e are not pipe bombs (except in the case of the Mosser bombing). [Penthouse Letter]

> Some news reports have made the misleading statement that we have been attacking universities or scholars . . . . It may be just as well that failure of our early bombs discouraged us from making any public statements at that time . . . . [Times Letter II]

> In that letter we stated . . . . Statements we made in our letters to associate us with anarchism and radical environmentalism . . . . [Times Letter III]

In his correspondences, and particularly in his ciphers, Zodiac used a variety of abstract symbols typically employed by mathematicians to represent arithmetical functions, unknown quantities and abstruse concepts peculiar to the discipline:

+	Addition
−	Subtraction
×	Multiplication
/	Division
=	Equality
<	Less than
>	Greater than
Δ	Triangle
■	Q.E.D.
⊙	Binary operator
□	Square
⊥	Perpendicular
∧	Logical conjunction
∨	Logical disjunction

Perhaps Zodiac's most significant use of abstract symbolism was the crosshair circle by which he identified himself from the very beginning of his career. While the most obvious interpretation of the device is that it represents a gun sight, Zodiac's use of the symbol in conjunction with numbers suggests a meaning less readily apparent. In mathematics, the unit circle is defined as a circle having a radius of one unit, centered at the origin 0,0 in the Cartesian coordinate system in the Euclidean plane. Graphically, it is depicted as a circle intersected at its center by two perpendicular lines — in other words, an exact facsimile of the Zodiac crosshair circle.

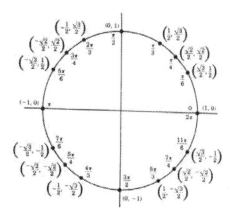

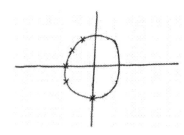

In two separate instances Zodiac employed the crossed circle in a context clearly apart from its presumed significance as a gun sight. Page six of the Seven-Page Letter shows such a circle, subdivided by small dots into twelve equal segments, with Xs placed at the six, eight, nine, ten and eleven positions.

The Mt. Diablo map shows a similar circle, not subdivided, with the numerals 0, 3, 6 and 9 at the ends of the perpendicular axes.

Even more significant is Zodiac's remark that the map, coupled with the code, will lead the reader to a location where a bomb has been placed. It is tempting, and not wholly implausible, to speculate that the ostensible purpose of the device is to solve a cipher by the use of some kind of mathematical procedure. This speculation is reinforced by the hint given one month later at the tail end of the Little List Letter:

> PS. The Mt. Diablo Code concerns Radians & # inches along the radians[.] [Little List Letter]

As a first-rate mathematician, Kaczynski was more than familiar with the concepts represented by the radian and the unit circle. At least two of his published works, in identical wording, make pointed mention of the unit circle:

> Let D be the open unit disk in the complex plane and let C be its boundary, the unit circle.[5,6]

Somewhat curious is Zodiac's use of the term "*along* the radians," since radian measures typically apply to the measurement of angles, as opposed to arcs. Zodiac's reference to "inches *along* the radians" almost certainly refers to a measurement of arc, since one does not measure anything *along* an angle, though one may measure along the length of an arc which is subtended by an angle. The same two works by Kaczynski cited above, each published in the year prior to the Mt. Diablo Letter, refer to measurements *along* an arc:

> Let γ' be an <u>arc</u> with one endpoint at $(0, 0, b)$ such that $\gamma' - \{(0, 0, b)\}$ $\subseteq K°$ and f approaches a limit <u>along</u> γ'.[7] [Author's emphasis]

> ...$f_n(z)$ approaches 0 as $z = re^{i\theta}$ approaches any point of C <u>along</u> any <u>arc</u> that does not meet Ω_n.[8] [Author's emphasis]

Finally, it is instructive to note the way in which Zodiac uses the symbol for equivalence ($=$) to mark a relationship between two dissimilar yet connected objects. Hence in the Dripping Pen Card, the "score" is tallied as "Des July Aug Sept Oct = 7." Similarly, the 1970 Cid Letter contains the tally "[Zodiac] = 10 SFPD = 0" and the Mikado Letter gives it as "[Zodiac] = 13 SFPD = 0." The Pines Card contains the

Chapter 7

General Eclectic

In a letter say that, "scientists consider themselves very intelligent because they have advanced diplomas (advanced degrees) but they are not as intelligent as they think because they opened those packages." This will make it seem as though I have no advanced degree.

THEODORE KACZYNSKI, *Journal Entry*

IT GOES WITHOUT SAYING that Theodore Kaczynski is a person of great intellectual prowess, not only within the field of mathematics, but in many other areas as well. Intellectual versatility moved his abilities far beyond the pursuit of purely mathematical goals, and manifested itself in a wide variety of scholarly interests and pursuits, including literature, languages, history, anthropology, chemistry and ecology. Kaczynski's unusual intelligence afforded him the ability to excel in many areas beyond the scope of his formal education.

Given the relative dearth of information left us by the Zodiac it is impossible to determine, with any degree of certainty, the extent of his formal education. Those who casually approach the case are apt to mistake the misspellings in his letters as indicative of someone poorly-educated and of little more than middling intelligence. Yet there is little doubt amongst those who have delved more deeply into the case that the misspellings were deliberately contrived in an effort to confuse the authorities as to Zodiac's true level of intelligence. More compelling than the misspellings themselves are the instances where Zodiac renders his grammar and orthography correct. In his authenticated missives, Zodiac

- Correctly uses the semicolon;
- Spells "patterned" correctly;

- Misspells "cipher" then spells it correctly one sentence later;
- Hyphenates "Exam-iner" correctly;
- Hyphenates "end-ed" correctly;
- Uses the semicolon three times in the Examiner Letter of August, 1969;
- Hyphenates "cover-age" correctly;
- Hyphenates "trans-parent" correctly;
- Drops the silent "e" from the end of "needle" in "needling" and from "irritate" in "irritating" but pretends that he doesn't know the rule in reference to simple words like "have" and "wipe";
- Hyphenates "disap-pear" correctly;
- Spells "ammonium nitrate" correctly, but can't manage "fertilizer";
- Spells "photoelectric" correctly;
- Spells "continually" correctly;
- Spells "billiard" correctly;
- Spells "inflicting" correctly;
- Hyphenates "irritat-ing" correctly;
- Spells "judicial" correctly;
- Hyphenates "comedy" correctly;
- Spells "capable" correctly;
- Understands the distinction between "to" and "too" and doesn't confuse them;
- Never confuses possessive pronouns with contractions;
- Never confuses plurals with possessives;
- Uses contractions correctly and correctly places the apostrophe; and
- Does not use the apostrophe to form a plural — a common mistake even among educated people.

Moreover, as we have previously noted, Zodiac's syntactical abilities appear quite good when considered apart from the misspellings. In the following example, Zodiac's misspellings are corrected, removing them as a source of distraction from the grammar and syntax displayed:

This is the Zodiac speaking. In answer to your asking for more details about the good times I have had in Vallejo, I shall be very happy to supply even more material. By the way, are the police having a good time with the code? If not, tell them to cheer up; when they do crack it they will have me.

On the 4th of July:

I did not open the car door. The window was rolled down already. The boy was originally sitting in the front seat when I began firing. When I fired the first shot at his head, he leaped backwards at the same time, thus spoiling my aim. He ended up on the back seat, then the floor in back, thrashing out very violently with his legs; that's how I shot him in the knee. I did not leave the scene of the killing with squealing tires and racing engine as described in the Vallejo papers. I drove away quite slowly so as not to draw attention to my car.

The man who told the police that my car was brown was a negro about 40—45, rather shabbily dressed. I was at this phone booth having some fun with the Vallejo cop when he was walking by. When I hung the phone up the damn X @ thing began to ring and that drew his attention to me and my car.

Last Christmas:

In that episode the police were wondering as to how I could shoot and hit my victims in the dark. They did not openly state this, but implied this by saying it was a well-lit night and I could see the silhouettes on the ho-rizon. Bullshit, that area is surrounded by high hills and trees. What I did was tape a small pencil flash light to the barrel of my gun. If you notice, in the center of the beam of light if you aim it at a wall or ceiling, you will see a black or dark spot in the center of the circle of light approximately 3 to 6 in. across. When taped to a gun barrel, the bullet will strike exactly in the center of the black dot in the light. All I had to do was spray them, as if it was a water hose; there was no need to use the gun sights. I was not happy to see that I did not get front page coverage. [Examiner II Letter]

Even a cursory reading of this production should suffice to dem-onstrate that its author, far from being an unschooled semi-literate, has acquired excellent grammatical and composition skills, through formal education, or a longstanding exposure to the written word, or both. The syntax displayed is quite good, while the sentences are al-most exclusively complex. The writer uses the semicolon to separate clauses and uses the proper adjectival forms of the adverbs "slow" and "violent." He correctly spells numerous words of moderate difficulty, such as "material," "leaped," "violently," "described," "attention," "ho-rizon," "ceiling," "barrel," "exactly," and "coverage." Curiously, he mis-spells "squealing" by doubling the "l," ("squealling") which suggests that he understands the doubling rule involved but has misapplied it in this case.

Readability statistics on the body of the letter show passive voice in only nine percent of the sentences, with a readability index of 79.7, and a grade-level index of 6.1 on the Flesch-Kincaid scale of readability.[1]

Curiously, this fails to jibe with the same analysis performed on a selection of Theodore Kaczynski's composition, as taken from the following passage of the Unabomber Manifesto:

> 1. The Industrial Revolution and its consequences have been a disaster for the human race. They have greatly increased the life expectancy of those of us who live in "advanced" countries, but they have destabilized society, have made life unfulfilling, have subjected human beings to indignities, have led to widespread psychological suffering (in the Third World to physical suffering as well) and have inflicted severe damage on the natural world. The continued development of technology will worsen the situation. It will certainly subject human beings to greater indignities and inflict greater damage on the natural world, it will probably lead to greater social disruption and psychological suffering, and it may lead to increased physical suffering even in "advanced" countries.

> 2. The industrial technological system may survive or it may break down. If it survives, it MAY eventually achieve a low level of physical and psychological suffering, but only after passing through a long and very painful period of adjustment and only at the cost of permanently reducing human beings and many other living organisms to engineered products and mere cogs in the social machine. Furthermore, if the system survives, the consequences will be inevitable: There is no way of reforming or modifying the system so as to prevent it from depriving people of dignity and autonomy.[2]

Flesch-Kincaid statistics for this portion of the Manifesto assign a readability score of 21.9 and a grade level of 12, with no use of passive voice in the text. Clearly this is a far cry from the Zodiac. But since the Manifesto was presented as a scholarly document, with no effort made to hide the intelligence of its author, a better approach might be to analyze specimens of Kaczynski's writing more in harmony with the context presented in the correspondences of the Zodiac. Contrary to popular belief, Kaczynski's general writing style, while syntactically excellent and grammatically precise, is by no means as high-blown and scholarly as the prose contained in the Manifesto. A very good example of Kaczynski's unbuttoned style can be seen in his sarcastic letter to Joe Visocan, a former employer with whom Kaczynski had disagreed:

> Dear, sweet Joe:
> You fat con-man. You probably think I treated you badly by quitting without notice, but it's your own fault. You gave me this big cock-and bull story about how much money I could make selling tires and all that crap. "The sky's the limit" and so forth. If you had been honest with me I would not have taken the job in the first place, but if I had taken it, I wouldn't have quit without giving you a couple of week's notice. Anyhow, I have a check coming. I am enclosing a stamped, self-addressed envelope in which you can send it. I had better get the check, because I know what authorities to complain to if I don't get it. If I have to complain about the check, then, while I'm at it, I might as well complain about the fact that you don't have a proper cage for putting air in split-rim tires, which, if I am not mistaken, is illegal.
> Love and Kisses,
Ted Kaczynski[3]

Many years later, in a "cop-out" (complaint) to prison authorities, Kaczynski registered his dissatisfaction with the activities of a fellow inmate:

> October 12, 8:30 PM. The guy in the cell above mine has been hitting his shower button constantly for the last seven hours or more. The water runs down into my cell, and I have to keep sopping it up with a towel. Why not shut off his water?
>
> P.S. He kept hitting his shower button all night without stopping until after 4:30 AM. That shower makes a fairly loud clunk when it shuts off, so he kept me awake most of the night. This is unreasonable. I shouldn't have to put up with this.[4]

A third example, less formal still, is the "Wild Carrot Letter," written *circa* 1994, in which Kaczynski gives a Montana neighbor explicit instructions for planting a gift of carrot seeds:

> Plant these just as you would regular carrots. Some will probably put up seed stalks the first year. Pull these out, since the roots get tough as soon as they put up seed stalks. The white roots have only so-so flavor. The

tasty roots are the pale-yellow ones. If you like them and want to grow the seeds, dig around the plants in the fall to see which ones have large, pale-yellow roots. Leave these in the ground over the winter, with soil mounded up over them to prevent mice from getting at them, and the second year they will put up seed stalks.[5]

Readability statistics for the foregoing examples fall more in line with those attributable to Zodiac in the Examiner Letter, as shown in the following chart:

Function	Zodiac Examiner II Letter	Manifesto	Visocan Letter	Cop-out	Wild Carrot Letter
Passive voice	9%	0%	0%	0%	0%
Readability	80.0	21.9	74.7	72.7	81.9
Grade Level	6.0	12.0	7.3	6.0	5.5

While the chart clearly shows a vast difference between the statistics for the Examiner II Letter and the Manifesto, it shows the same divergence between the Manifesto and the informal written productions of Kaczynski. Additionally, there is a marked similarity in all parameters between Kaczynski's "unbuttoned" style and the style shown in the Examiner Letter.

Given the disparities between these productions and the Manifesto, and the proximity between them and the Examiner II Letter, it is not possible to exclude Kaczynski as the author of the latter on the basis of complexity alone. One may logically conclude that the author of the Examiner II Letter was at least as grammatically proficient as Kaczynski when writing in a non-formal mode.

★ ★ ★

Zodiac demonstrates a certain degree of mechanical ingenuity with his "electric gun sight" and the design of the bombs with which he threatened to destroy a school bus. In the Examiner II Letter one is struck by the meticulous, even loving manner in which Zodiac describes the invention he claims to have used in the Lake Herman Road assault. Later, in his Seven-Page Letter, he refers to the device again, and bestows the name of "electric gun sight" upon it.

In the same correspondence, Zodiac presents in detail the bomb intended to destroy a school bus full of children. He begins with a general description of the explosive that will be used:

> Take one bag of ammonium nitrate fertlizer & 1 gal of stove oil & dump a few bags of gravel on top & then set the shit off & will positivily ventalate any thing that should be in the way of the blast. [Seven-Page Letter]

Then, following a brief digression, he elaborates upon the mechanical details of the device:

> 1 bat. pow clock — will run for aprox 1 year
> 1 photoelectric switch
> 2 copper leaf springs
> 2 6V car bat
> 1 flash light bulb & reflecter
> 1 mirror
> 2 18" cardboard tubes black with shoe polish inside & out.

The list of components is then followed by a hand-sketched diagram showing the actual manner in which the device is to be armed and actuated. While not professionally rendered, this diagram is actually very good in illustrating how the bomb is expected to work, especially in point of the elaborate mechanism that will supposedly set it off. It clearly shows the manner in which light from the flashlight bulb will shine through one of the cardboard tubes, strike the mirror on the other side of the street, and be reflected back through the second cardboard tube to the photoelectric switch that will detonate the bomb when the beam of light is broken by a passing bus. The arming mechanism, a clock, is represented by a large circle with a single hand arising from the center. A curved arrow indicates the direction which the hand, carrying its copper leaf-spring contact points, will travel to complete the circuit between the photoelectric assembly and the string of bombs itself. Two separate side-views of the clock mechanism are provided, in addition to a separate drawing showing a car and a school bus traveling side-by-side on what is clearly meant to depict a crowned road, with arrows showing light from the trigger mechanism being broken by the larger vehicle.

In theory, this device could have worked exactly as it was shown. In actual practice, however, it would have been difficult, if not impossible, to align the cardboard tubes in such a manner as to allow the feeble beam of light from a single flashlight bulb to be directed across the street to a small mirror and reflected back to the switch on the second tube. Zodiac himself lamented this fact in the Belli Letter of December, 1969, saying that "the trigger mech requires much work to get it adjusted just right." This is no doubt why in April of the following year he submitted a second diagram, showing improvements in the bomb's design. This second bomb design proposed the use of sunlight rather than a flashlight bulb to arm the triggering device, and added a second photoelectric switch as "cloudy day discon[n]ect" to prevent the bomb going off "by accid[ent]." The number of batteries was reduced from two to one.

Zodiac's descriptions of these devices provide us with nothing definite that we can use in forming an opinion as to the extent of his educational attainments. Nevertheless, he gives us sufficient information to postulate that he had *at least* a cursory knowledge of chemistry and electronics, coupled with *at least* an understanding of mechanical things and how they work.

Despite the common perception of Theodore Kaczynski as a man consumed by intellectual activities, the years of his youth and adolescence were not completely wiled away in the pursuit of academics. Dale Eickelman, who went to junior high school with Kaczynski, recalled that Ted was "good at chemistry and making explosives."

> We would go out to an open field, and I remember Ted had the know-how of putting together things like batteries, wire leads, potassium nitrate and whatever, and creating explosions . . . . We would go to the hardware store, use household products and make things you might call bombs.[6]

His proficiency in fashioning mechanical devices enabled Kaczynski to construct a working .22 caliber pistol using nothing more than hand tools and bits of scrap material found near his cabin in Montana:

> A few days ago I finished making a twenty two caliber pistol. This took me a long time, for a year and a half, thereby preventing me from working on some other projects I would have liked to carry out. Gun works well and I get as much accuracy out of it as I'd expect for an inexperienced

pistol shot like me. It is equipped with improvised silencer which does not work as well as I hoped. At a guess it cuts noise down to maybe one third. It is said that it is easy for machinist to make a gun, but of course I did not have machine tools, but only a few files, hacksaw blades, small vice, a rickety hand drill, etc. I took the barrel from an old pneumatic pistol. I made the other parts out of several metal pieces. Most of them come from the old abandoned cars near here. I needed to make the parts with enough precision but I made them well and I'm very satisfied. I want to use the gun as a homicide weapon.[7]

A photo of this device appears in the 2003 book *Harvard and the Unabomber* by Alston Chase. Apart from its functionality, the weapon appears amazingly well-fashioned in its resemblance to a factory-made device, and, along with its description, demonstrates quite plainly Kaczynski's skill in producing practical and ingenious mechanical contraptions.

The Turchie Affidavit lists a letter from Kaczynski's mother, dated July 16, 1958, and found by the authorities in his Harvard file:

Much of his time is spent at home reading and contriving numerous gadgets made up of wood, string, wire, tape, lenses, gears, wheels, etc.; that test out various principals in physics. His table and desk are always a mess of test tubes, chemicals, batteries, ground coal, etc. He will miss greatly, I think, this browsing and puttering in his messy makeshift lab.[8]

While in his unpublished manuscript titled "How I Blew Up Harold Snilly," Kaczynski wrote:

When I was in high school I took a course in chemistry. There was only one aspect of the subject which interested me, as any chemist could have seen from a brief inspection of my rather specialized home collection of reagents; (sic) powdered aluminum, powdered magnesium, powdered zinc, sulfur, potassium nitrate, potassium permanganate . . . in suitable combinations these things are capable of exploding. One day in the laboratory, having finished my assigned experiment early, I though I might as well spend the extra time pursuing my favorite line of research. On theoretical grounds, a mixture of red phosphorus and potassium chlorate seemed promising. (I did not know at the time that it is the red phosphorus in the scratching surface of a match-book, together with the potassium chlorate in the match-head, that makes a match light so readily.

I later found that the mixture is extremely sensitive to friction and practically impossible to work with. The reader is advised not to play with it.[9]

The evolution of Kaczynski's bomb-making skills shows great creativity and sophistication in the development of explosives and triggering devices. Typical of his early efforts were the first two bombs, as detailed in the Turchie Affidavit:

> 16. An analysis of the components of the [first] explosive device by the ATF Laboratory revealed that it was constructed of a one inch diameter galvanized pipe approximately nine inches in length sealed on one end with a wooden plug. The explosive charge consisted of two types of smokeless powders and match heads. The pipe containing the main charge, together with an improvised mechanical firing mechanism consisting of a nail held under tension by multiple rubber bands, was encased in a homemade wooden box. The cover of the box was designed to release tension on the firing pin causing the nail to strike the match heads, thus igniting the smokeless powder.

> 19. An analysis of the components of the [second] explosive device by the ATF laboratory revealed that the main charge explosives consisted of match heads and a fusing system, consisting of two independent circuits each of which could detonate the device. Each circuit consisted of two C-cell batteries wired to two improvised wooden dowel initiators. Each initiator contained a pair of wires routed through a wooden dowel. The wires were joined at their termination point by a thin bridge wire. The termination point was inside the explosive main charge. When the box was opened, the electrical circuit was completed, and the thin bridge wire was heated, thereby igniting the mixture of smokeless powder and match heads. The above materials were contained in a "Phillies" brand cigar box which incorporated an anti-open switch designed to trigger the device upon opening the box lid.[10]

Of all Kaczynski's triggering devices, the one that showed the most creativity and sophistication was the barometric switch that detonated the bomb in the mail hold of a Boeing 727 in 1979:

> The fuzing system consisted of four C-cell batteries wired to a modified barometer switch and a loop switch to two improvised wooden dowel initiators. The device was contained in a homemade wooden box with a lid hinged at the rear. The barometer switch was designed to initiate the device as the aircraft gained altitude.[11]

Kaczynski himself described the bomb in his encrypted journal:

> LATE SUMMER AND EARLY AUTUMN I CONSTRUCTED DE-
> VICE. MUCH EXPENSE, BECAUSE HAD TO GO TO GR. FALLS
> TO BUY MATERIALS, INCLUDING BAROMETER AND MANY
> BOXES CARTRIDGES FOR THE POWDER. I PUT MORE THAN
> A QUART OF SMOKELESS POWDER IN A CAN, RIGGED
> BAROMETER SO DEVICE WOULD EXPLODE AT 2000FT. OR
> CONCEIVABLY AS HIG[H] AS 3500FT. DUE TO VARIATION OF
> ATMOSPHERIC PRESSURE.[12]

Equally ingenious was his tiny "detonating cap," the invention of which enabled Kaczynski to avoid the use of a bulky pipe in the construction of his bombs. He described this device in his April 20, 1995 letter to the *New York Times*:

> [A]fter a long period of experimentation we developed a type of bomb that does not require a pipe, but is set off by a detonating cap that consists of a chlorate explosive packed into a piece of small diameter copper tubing. (The detonating cap is a miniature pipe bomb.)[13]

Government agents published Kaczynski's hand-sketched drawing of this "detonating cap," which in its rendering comes across as amazingly similar to the bus bomb diagrams of Zodiac.

The point to be made here, however, is not the similarity of the devices, but the undeniable fact that in both cases the conception of bombs and detonating mechanisms shows great creativity and intellectual versatility on the part of both Kaczynski and the Zodiac. Each contrives his devices from common, easily-obtainable components, difficult, if not impossible, to trace. Each shows originality in the creation of specific components, as seen in Zodiac's photoelectric detonator and Kaczynski's miniature blasting cap and barometric switch, while each, at a minimum, demonstrates a knowledge of chemistry sufficient to understand the nature of explosives. Extrapolating from what is understood of each criminal's contemporary knowledge, one might reasonably conclude that in 1969 Kaczynski possessed bomb-making skills that were approximately at the same level as those displayed by the Zodiac.

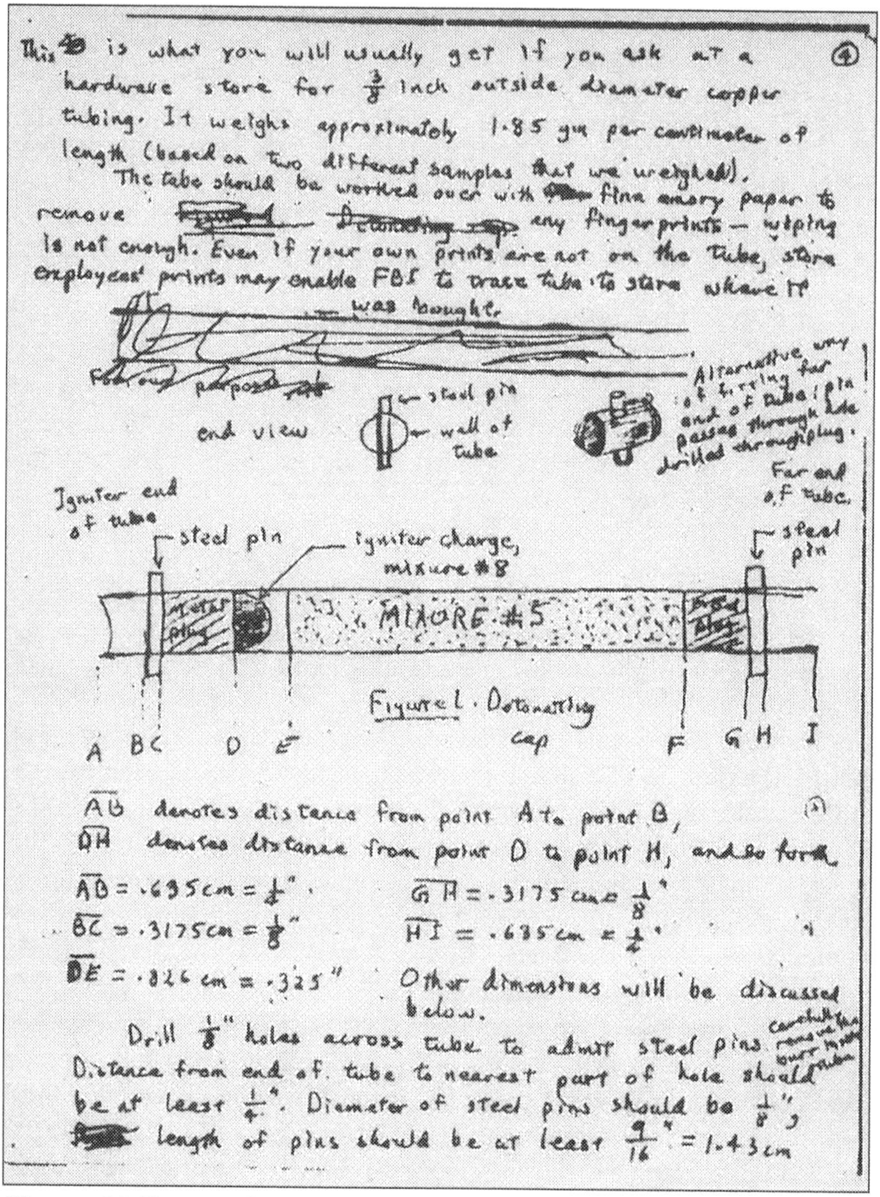

(4)

This is what you will usually get if you ask at a hardware store for $\frac{3}{8}$ inch outside diameter copper tubing. It weighs approximately 1.85 gm per centimeter of length (based on two different samples that we weighed).

The tube should be worked over with fine emery paper to remove any fingerprints — wiping is not enough. Even if your own prints are not on the tube, store employees' prints may enable FBI to trace tube to store where it was bought.

For our purposes

end view

steel pin

wall of tube

Alternative way of fixing far end of tube: pin passes through hole drilled through plug.

Far end of tube.

Igniter end of tube

steel pin

igniter charge, mixture #8

steel pin

metal plug

MIXTURE #5

metal plug

Figure 1. Detonating cap

A B C D E F G H I

$\overline{AB}$ denotes distance from point A to point B, $\overline{DH}$ denotes distance from point D to point H, and so forth.

$\overline{AB}$ = .635 cm = $\frac{1}{4}$" $\overline{GH}$ = .3175 cm = $\frac{1}{8}$"

$\overline{BC}$ = .3175 cm = $\frac{1}{8}$" $\overline{HI}$ = .635 cm = $\frac{1}{4}$"

$\overline{DE}$ = .826 cm = .325" Other dimensions will be discussed below.

Drill $\frac{1}{8}$" holes across tube to admit steel pins (carefully remove the burr from hole). Distance from end of tube to nearest part of hole should be at least $\frac{1}{4}$". Diameter of steel pins should be $\frac{1}{8}$", length of pins should be at least $\frac{9}{16}$" = 1.43 cm

Kaczynski diagram showing the miniature blasting cap with which he detonated powerful explosives in his later bombings.

Chapter 8

Light Motif

Are you chaste?

RICHARD WAGNER, *Parsifal*

ONE CURIOUS aspect of Zodiac's behavior is his use of literary allusion, both in defining himself and in offering clues as to his pathology and motives.

"I want you to print this cipher," he writes to the *San Francisco Chronicle*, in 1969. "In this cipher is my iden[t]ity."

Those who believed that the word "identity" was synonymous with "name" were disappointed when, the cipher having been solved by Donald Harden and his wife, nothing remotely resembling a name appeared. What *did* appear was something far closer to the dictionary definition of the word.

"I like killing people because it is so much fun," began the decrypted message. "It is more fun than killing wild game in the forrest because man is the most dangerou[s] anamal of all."

With this statement, Zodiac uses a literary allusion for the purpose of defining himself and presenting the "identity" of which he spoke in the earlier correspondence. It is a pointed allusion to the famous short story *Most Dangerous Game* by author Richard Connell, in which a bored aristocrat, Count Zaroff, relieves his *ennui* by hunting human prey:

> For a moment the general did not reply; he was smiling his curious red-lipped smile. Then he said slowly, "No. You are wrong, sir. The Cape buffalo is not the most dangerous big game." He sipped his wine. "Here in my preserve on this island," he said in the same slow tone, "I hunt more dangerous game."

Later, in his twin missives of July, 1970, Zodiac introduces *The Mikado*, a comic opera produced by the creative duo of William S. Gilbert and Sir Arthur Sullivan in 1885. The first allusion follows naturally from a recitation of the various "tortures" that Zodiac claims he will inflict upon his "slaves":

> Some I shall tie over ant hills and watch them scream & twich and squirm. Others shall have pine splinters driven under their nails & then burned. Others shall be placed in cages & fed salt beef untill they are gorged then I shall listen to their pleass for water and I shall laugh at them. Others will hang by their thumbs & burn in the sun then I will rub them down with deep heat to warm them up. Others I shall skin them alive & let them run around screaming. *And all billiard players I shall have them play in a darkened dunge[o]n cell with crooked cues & Twisted Shoes.* [Mikado Letter] [Author's italics]

Those familiar with *The Mikado* will recognize this allusion as a more-or-less direct paraphrase of the Mikado's lines in "The Punishment Fit the Crime":

> The billiard sharp whom any one catches,
> His doom's extremely hard,
> He's made to dwell,
> In a dungeon cell
> On a spot that's always barred.
> And there he plays extravagant matches
> In fitless finger-stalls
> On a cloth untrue
> With a twisted cue
> And elliptical billiard balls!

Two days after mailing what by consensus is known as the Mikado Letter, the *San Francisco Chronicle* received a second correspondence alluding to the opera; this time at greater length and with similar deviations from the libretto. Claiming that he now has a "little list," Zodiac proceeds with his paraphrase of the Lord High Executioner's aria, better known as "I've Got a Little List." In this production, for the first time, Zodiac appears to be identifying with the role of Ko-Ko, the Lord High Executioner of the town of Titipu, whose function is to execute all those caught in the act of flirting.

That notion is supported by Zodiac's last signed missive, the Exorcist Letter of January, 1974:

> I saw & think "The Exorcist"
> was the best saterical comidy
> that I have ever seen.
> Signed, yours truley:
> He plunged him self into
> the billowy wave
> and an echo arose from
> the sucides grave
> titwillo titwillo
> titwillo [Exorcist Letter]

This correspondence contains two distinct literary allusions and one possible literary allusion that, for the sake of organization, we will refrain from presenting now. The first reference is to the renowned cinematic production of *The Exorcist*, based on the best-selling novel by William Peter Blatty. The second allusion is once again to *The Mikado*; in particular, to the song "Tit-willow," sung by the Lord High Executioner in his wooing of that bloodthirsty and decidedly un-lovely character, Katisha.

These instances provide us with five distinct examples of literary allusion referencing three different literary sources, used by Zodiac in his correspondences from July of 1969 through January of 1974. Of these three sources, two (*Most Dangerous Game* and *The Mikado*) offer revelations pertaining to Zodiac's motivations as a killer. Moreover, a sixth possible literary allusion is contained in the sarcastic note accompanying the Dragon Card of April 28, 1970, with its reference to a novelty lapel button reading "Melvin eats blub[b]er." Intended as a jibe at attorney Melvin Belli (whom Zodiac had contacted with the Belli Letter of 1969), the jest appears to have been based upon an actual button reading "Herman Melville Eats Blubber," purportedly worn by college professors and other intellectuals in the late 1960s.

Apart from the fact that these allusions belie the view of Zodiac as an uneducated semi-literate, they point toward an individual keenly aware of the value that such allusions have in conveying complex meaning beyond the realm of simple narrative.

Ted Kaczynski's exposure to literature began at an early age, under the example of his mother, who was said to have been "steeped" in the subject. A *New York Times* article from 1996 illustrated the extent of her influence over Ted in that regard:

> Wanda Kaczynski was especially well-read and articulate, familiar with science and the works of Shakespeare, Austen, Dickens, Thackeray and other authors whose books crowded her shelves . . . . Wanda kept a diary about her boy and read to him daily from children's books, then from classic boys' literature and later from surprisingly advanced materials. A neighbor said Teddy was in grade school when Wanda began reading him articles from Scientific American that a college student might find challenging.[1]

"Kaczynski," wrote Alston Chase, "was an omnivorous reader and prolific, albeit mostly unpublished, writer and correspondent with synoptic interests . . . . His cabin shelves contained hundreds of books and scholarly papers . . . . as well as a wide range of classics by Conrad, Dostoevsky, Steinbeck, Dickens, Shakespeare, George Eliot, and many Spanish and German writers."[2] Chase also cites Kaczynski's father's love of books, and his general respect for the intellectual life, though he himself was a blue-collar worker with only modest formal education.[3]

According to his brother David, Ted "loved word games" and "punned incessantly."[4] The younger brother recalled a disagreement he had once had with Ted concerning the Freudian interpretation of an unspecified piece of literature. By David's account, he was "argued down" by Ted.[5]

Kaczynski's interest in languages and linguistics is borne out by the titles of books and papers discovered in his cabin. Such works as *201 Russian Verbs, A Finnish Grammar, Basic Conversational Russian, Beginning Latin Book, Egyptian Language, German Grammar, Lost Languages, Prose Edda* and *Early History of Indo-European Languages* mark their owner as someone whose interest in languages and word origins goes well beyond a merely practical desire to learn a second language.

As the Unabomber, Kaczynski employed both language and literature as elements of *leitmotif,* or constantly-recurring themes that defined both his identity and his *raison d'être*. His communications are riddled with word play and allusion; some of it transparent, some semi-transparent, and some so arcane that its actual significance remains obscure. In *Harvard and the Unabomber,* Alston Chase observed:

Kaczynski's actions imitated not just any art but the literary classics. History and literature enhanced his capacity for cold-blooded murder because he thought they provided justification for it. He apparently imagined himself as a character in this great historic, literary, and continuing drama . . . . [6]

Among the less transparent of Kaczynski's allusive devices are those that pertain to the operatic productions *Der Ring des Nibelungen* (*The Ring Cycle* or simply *The Ring*) and *Parsifal*, both by the famous nineteenth-century composer Richard Wagner. Foremost among these are the particular names and addresses (some real and some contrived) used by Kaczynski in his mailings.

Kaczynski addressed his first bomb to Professor E.J. Smith of Rensselaer Polytechnic Institute in Troy, N.Y. The return address bore the name of Buckley Crist of Northwestern University. *Per se*, there is nothing of significance in either of the names, nor has any evidence been uncovered to suggest that Kaczynski harbored any ill-feeling against the men who bore them.

"I picked the name of an electrical engineering professor out of the catalogue of the Rensselaer Polytechnic Institute," read an entry in his journal, "and addressed the bomb-package to him."[7]

The engineering profession employs thousands of practitioners, and it is difficult to understand exactly why Kaczynski chose Buckley Crist and E.J. Smith, among all others, to be the putative sender and potential recipient of a bomb — difficult, that is, unless one takes a closer look at the names and what meanings they imply. "Smith," is the name of a specific occupation — particularly, one who forges metals — while "Crist" is immediately recognizable as a possible reference to Christ. In Wagnerian terms, the names are highly significant, especially as they relate to *The Ring* and *Parsifal*.

Smithing or smithery comprises a key element in the construction of the theme upon which *The Ring* is founded. In *Das Rheingold*, the Nibelung dwarf Alberich, after stealing the Rhine gold, fashions the gold into a ring, which will grant all power to its owner. Later, he forces his brother Mime, a *smith*, to *forge* the helmet Tarnhelm, which will confer upon him the power of invisibility. In the third part of the cycle, *Siegfried*, Mime attempts in vain to re-forge the shattered pieces of the sword Nothung. Exasperated by his lack of progress, the young Siegfried reduces the parts to slivers, melts them down, and taking to the anvil forges the sword anew. Having done so, his first act is to strike the anvil with the sword, cleaving it asunder.

For Kaczynski, the concept of smithing, especially as practiced by the Nibelung dwarves, would have represented human industry and the rise of the technological society which he hated with such fervor. Ultimately Nothung, forged at the anvil by human hands, breaks the divine spear of the great god Wotan and ushers in the gods' demise. Smithery becomes a metaphor for human progress which, unaltered, will lead to disaster, not only for the human race, but the gods as well. Siegfried the hero breaks the anvil that symbolizes human endeavor in the material world; using the sword to destroy the means of its own creation. This is Kaczynski's entire worldview, encapsulated in a single act. Technology will produce the means of its own destruction, at the hands of a superman — a Siegfried or a Kaczynski — who wields the power to forge and heft the implement.

Such a view would not have been simple fancy on Kaczynski's part. Caught up in the political fervor of his times, Wagner lent his rhetoric and support both to revolutionists and anarchists, not least of whom was the renowned anarchist Bakunin. In light of this association, The Ring and its themes have been interpreted as allegories pertaining to the industrial revolution and the dislocations within Western society that it occasioned. It depicts a world in which virtue has been over-shadowed by avarice, deceit, and a mindless materialism that enervates the cosmos. Within that world, the smith and his anvil comprise the most poignant symbols of technological progress through the exploitation of the human race.

Further hints pertaining to The Ring can be found in the return addresses associated with the third, fifth and ninth bombs, mailed on June 10, 1980, May 5, 1982 and May 8, 1985, respectively. The ficti-tious sender of the 1980 bomb was given the address of "Ravenswood Street," while the 1982 device was return-addressed from Leroy Wood Bearnson, a professor at Brigham Young University. The 1985 device, bearing the name of "Weiburg Tool and Supply," listed its sender's spur-ious address as "10 Hagenberger Ct."

In Norse mythology, the figure of Wotan, or Odin, is accompanied by a pair of *ravens*, Huginn and Munnin by name, who sit perched on the shoulders of the god and represent the qualities of thought and memory. In the final opera of the cycle, *Götterdämmerung*, Wotan sends the ravens forth into the world to spy and bring back news. Later they appear as the harbingers of Siegfried's death. "Ravenswood," as the word is employed by Kaczynski, evokes both the *ravens* and the haunts (the *woods*) in which they (and Kaczynski) live.

For those familiar with *The Ring*, the name Leroy *Wood Bearnson* evokes images of Scene One of the first act of *Siegfried*, in which young Siegfried makes his entrance from the *wood* leading a huge *bear* by a rope. Up until this point, Siegfried has been raised and nurtured by the smith Mime in the false belief that he is the latter's *son*; a deception to which Mime is later forced to admit. In the context of *The Ring*, "Bearnson" would imply both the *bear* and the *son* (bear-and-son). It is clearly a reference to the hero Siegfried.

Obvious as this may be, Kaczynski's most transparent allusion to *The Ring* is contained in the return address of "10 Hagenberger Ct." The "Hagen" of *Hagen*berger can be no other than *Hagen*, the son of Alberich the dwarf, who murders Siegfried in *Götterdämmerung*. It is a pointed and unequivocal reference to a particular character in *The Ring*.

So patent is this last allusion that it must settle any doubts concerning Kaczynski's references to *The Ring*. Nevertheless, there are further allusions to the Wagnerian classic that we must not refrain from presenting here.

Paragraph 26 of the Turchie Affidavit lists the components of the 1980 bomb package sent to Percy Wood. Curiously, among the components listed was one item marked as "[c]ardboard from 'Bugles Cereal' box."[8] The disinterested observer may find himself bemused as to why Kaczynski would have included such an article within the relatively small confines of the book-sized parcel containing the device — unless, that is, he is aware of Wagner and *The Ring*. For in *The Ring* the hero Siegfried is accompanied by a musical instrument, a hunting *horn*, which heralds his presence and symbolizes his character in the same artistic sense as St. Jerome and the lion, St. Andrew and his cross, or Moses and his staff. Siegfried's horn hangs continually at his side, and plays a seminal role in the *leitmotif* of its character while signaling his appearance wherever it occurs. Siegfried's horn is essentially a *bugle*, defined as a small horn with no valves or other mechanical devices for controlling pitch. Visually, it is depicted in the classical shape of an animal horn, curved and tapering from end-to-end — precisely the shape of the snack food contained within the "Bugles cereal" box.

Kaczynski's 1980 bomb was mailed inside a hollowed-out copy of the 1974 novel *Ice Brothers* by Sloan Wilson, author of the well-known *Man in the Gray Flannel Suit*. *Ice Brothers* is a World War II novel detailing the exploits of a Coast Guard trawler engaged in the Greenland patrol. Its protagonist owns a yacht named the *Valkyrie*, synonymous with the legendary female warriors who in Norse mythology carry the bodies of slain warriors to Valhalla, and also the title of the second opera in the *Ring* cycle, *Die Walküre* (*The Valkyries*). The novel's action takes place around the frigid coasts of Greenland, itself a key location in Nordic history and mythology.

Kaczynski's knowledge of Wagnerian opera and *The Ring* seems apparent in light of his words to a correspondent in 1998:

> Have you ever seen a performance of the Ring Cycle? I haven't. But I've read the text. I was listening to a radio program on CBC — one of those programs to which people call in with requests. Some woman called in and the host, after chatting with her for a few minutes, asked, "Now what song would you like to request?" The woman answered, "The Ring Cycle." The host didn't catch the joke; she was just confused. Probably had never heard of Richard Wagner or the Ring Cycle.[9]

The fact that Kaczynski had read *The Ring*, as opposed to having seen it in performance, might indicate that his first exposure to Wagner came in consequence of his studies in German. Kaczynski is apparently fluent in the language, as attested by his high school membership in the German Club, and, more recently, a letter in his own hand, written in German, and pertaining to the production of a film, *Das Netz*. Moreover, Kaczynski appears to have cultivated a lifelong interest in Nordic things, particularly as they pertain to language. At Harvard he took a course in Scandinavian studies,[10] while, among the list of books found in his cabin were such titles as *A Finnish Grammar, Cartas Finlandesas — Hombres Del Norte, German Grammar, German-English Dictionary, History of the German Language, Norse Discovery of America*, and a copy of the *Prose Edda*.[11] Of these, the last is undoubtedly the most interesting of all, since the *Prose Edda*, written by Snorri Sturluson around the year 1220 A.D., is a compendium of Norse tales comprising the most significant source of material for our contemporary understanding of Norse mythology.

Moreover, Kaczynski's use of what appeared as an "upside-down peace symbol" in the graffiti he left on the campus at Sacramento State forms yet another connection to Nordic symbolism. The device is actually a stylized representation of one of the fundamental aspects of Norse mythology, called Yggdrasil, or the World Ash. Yggdrasil itself was a legendary tree, whose roots, trunk and branches comprised the nine worlds of Norse cosmology. Stylized as a union of lines, similar to the letter "Y" or the Greek letter Psi (Ψ) within a circle, the symbol has been appropriated in modern times by anarchist, neo-fascist and other revolutionary groups that draw their inspiration from the Nordic myths. It also forms one of the characters in the Runic alphabet, or *Futhark*, the old Norse alphabet dating from approximately the first century A.D.; its equivalent in the Latin alphabet is the letter "Z." Interesting, too, in this connection is the February 14, 1974 SLA Letter, attributable by many to the Zodiac:

> Dear Mister Editor:
> Did you know that the
> initials SLAY (Symbionese
> Liberation Army) spell "sla,"
> an Old Norse word
> meaning "kill."
> a friend

All of these elements and more are present in *The Ring*, with which Kaczynski, by his own admission, was familiar. Further, among the list of books discovered in Kaczynski's cabin[12] was a copy of *Tristan and Iseult*, the medieval tale of ill-fated lovers upon which Wagner based the opera *Tristan und Isolde* — yet another link between Kaczynski and the great composer.

★   ★   ★

Christian themes are missing from *The Ring*, unless one perceives in the panoply of Nordic gods a symbolic reference to the role of the Christian faith in fostering the political stability and learning that led to the inevitable rise of civilization in the West. With Wagner, however, one need not look to *The Ring* in order to discover Christian symbolism of the deepest meaning.

In choosing Buckley Crist as the purported sender of the bomb parcel addressed to E.J. Smith, Kaczynski commenced a series of references that pointed directly to images of Christ, Christianity, and the Wagnerian opera *Parsifal*.

In and of itself, the name Crist is insufficient to lead us back to *Parsifal* and Wagner. Bomb number three, however, mailed by Kaczynski in June of 1980 and addressed to Percy (*Percival*, a variant of *Parsifal*) Wood, president of United Airlines, bore a fictitious return address with the name of Enoch W. *Fischer*. Likewise, bomb number six was addressed by Kaczynski to Patrick C. *Fischer*, a professor at Vanderbilt University.

Wagner based his *Parsifal* on two Christian legends: the Holy Grail and the Fisher King. The legend of the Grail concerns a sacred vessel, a cup or chalice associated with Christ, possessing magical powers and sought by a fraternity of knights. Linked to this sacred vessel is the so-called Spear of Longinus, revered as the implement used to pierce the side of Christ, following his death upon the cross.

The legend of the Fisher King is a strange one, probably rooted in pagan mythology, wherein the ruler of a mysterious land has suffered a grievous wound that will not heal, leaving his kingdom both barren and infertile. The name of "fisher" derives from several sources. The fish itself is a well-known symbol of Christianity, pertaining to the occupation of the apostles prior to joining Jesus in his mission. In various versions of the legend, the impotent king wiles away the time by fishing in the river near his castle. Finally, the French words for "fisher" (*pêcheur*) and "sinner" (*pécheur*) are practically identical, differing only in the pronunciation of a single vowel.

In *Parsifal*, the eponymous Christian hero must overcome temptation in order to gain possession of the Sacred Spear (the Spear of Longinus), with which he will heal the injury to the Fisher King (Amfortas) and restore the Kingdom of the Grail to its original vitality. Like Siegfried in *The Ring*, Parsifal is a "superman"; a transcendent individual whose powers rise above those of ordinary mortals. Unlike *The Ring*, with its purely pagan symbolism, *Parsifal* draws on Christian themes alone, and it is in this context that we must view Kaczynski's allusions to it, in the form of the names Crist (Christ), Percy (Percival or

Parsifal) and those of the two Fischers, one of them a real person and the other created by Kaczynski.

It may seem surprising that an avowed atheist like Kaczynski should have reached for Christian symbolism in making a reference to a literary work that comes across as Christian in its import. This is less surprising in light of the fact that his allusions reflected, not only his worldview, but himself, personally, as well. For his worldview, how-ever eccentric, is no mystery: he makes no effort to conceal it from the public. His *personal identity* — the qualities that define *him* — is another matter altogether. Like Zodiac, who uses *The Mikado* to merely hint at what he dares not openly admit; namely, that he has taken it upon himself to "clean up" society by executing those caught in the act of flirting, Kaczynski uses Wagner to relay his opinion of himself as a tran-scendent being, superior to the masses. He is both the hero Siegfried and the hero Parsifal. In his autobiography he writes:

> Thus, I tended to feel that I was a *particularly important person* and *superior to most of the rest of the human race.* Generally speaking, there was nothing arrogant or egotistical in this feeling, nor did I ever express any such feeling outside the immediate family. It just came to me as naturally as breathing to feel that I was someone special.[13] [Author's italics]

In the same document, however, he asserts:

> I have always had a strong tendency to admit an unpleasant truth to my-self, rather than trying to push it away with self-deception or rationaliza-tion. I am certainly not claiming that I've never indulged in self-decep-tion — I only claim that I have much less tendency to self-deception than most people.[14]

Through his implied references to Siegfried and Parsifal, Kaczyn-ski's egotism is well expressed. Yet *Parsifal* affords him an opportunity to hint at the darker side of his identity and leave his audience a clue that, while accurate, will prove both highly personal and unflattering in the extreme. The subject of *chastity* comprises an overarching theme in *Parsifal*; one that runs the entire gamut of the work. Chastity is repre-sented as synonymous with piety, while sexual incontinence is made to stand for sin in general. By succumbing to sexual temptation through the wiles of the magician Klingsor, King Amfortas (the Fisher King) becomes wounded by the sacred Spear, sustaining the injury that cannot be healed. Prior to this event, Klingsor has sought admission to the Brotherhood of the Grail, but cannot be admitted because he lacks the necessary quality of chastity. In an effort to force virtue upon himself, and thus take possession of the Grail, Klingsor commits the criminal act of self-emasculation, which leads Amfortas to drive him from the Kingdom. Becoming a master of the magic arts, Klingsor creates a magic garden, a garden of sensual delights, where Knights of the Grail are diverted from their vows of virtue and led to acts of unchastity by beautiful, yet hellish women. Seeking redress, Amfortas himself is led astray, only to suffer the injury that lays his kingdom low. It is given to Parsifal alone, the "pure fool" of the prophecy, to fight Klingsor, overcome temptation, recover the Spear, and restore the Kingdom to its original vitality.

"*Bist du keusch*? — Are you chaste?" the temptress Kundry inquires of the magician Klingsor, and her question is loaded with bitter irony. Equally bitter is the reply:

> Frightful necessity! Untamed strife of longing; terrible longing born of hell, which I quieted by force!

Klingsor, naturally unchaste, has tried to *force* chastity upon himself by the act of self-castration. Despite this self-inflicted violence, Klingsor cannot be chaste, because the quality of chastity is itself an act of transcendence against temptation, and one cannot be transcendent against a temptation that does not exist.

This is patently Kaczynski. Kaczynski, the ever-chaste, for whom chastity is a necessity and not a virtue. Kaczynski, who, overcome by insatiable desire, sought relief from that desire through a contemplated act of self-emasculation — the sex change operation that he pondered in 1966. Like Klingsor, Kaczynski's chastity is not transcendent, but imposed by the force of circumstance. He is chaste because he cannot be otherwise.

Seen in this light, the name of Enoch Fischer, putative sender of the Percy Wood bomb in 1980, becomes less mysterious than it appeared to the authorities at the time. Because it was a contrived name, and not that of a genuine individual, we may safely assume that its two components, Enoch and Fischer, each bore some significance for Kaczynski.

The novel *Ice Brothers*, in the hollowed-out leaves of which the Wood bomb had been placed, presents a character named Seth Farmer, a boatswain aboard the trawler *Arluk*. In this context, "Enoch Fischer" points rather obviously toward "Seth Farmer." Biblically, Enoch was the son of Cain, a *farmer*, while the biblical Seth was a son of Adam, brother to Cain. In *Ice Brothers*, Seth Farmer, before joining the Coast Guard, earns his living as a *fisherman*. Not surprisingly, the word "Enoch" sounds suspiciously like a play on "eunuch," which is, of course, an emasculated male.

Moreover, this theme of sexual renunciation, so manifest in *Parsifal*, has its parallel in *The Ring*. In *Das Rheingold*, the dwarf Alberich is obliged to forswear love in order to take possession of the golden treasure and master the magic by which he may forge it into the Ring. Mocked and humiliated by the Rhine Maidens, whom he tries in vain to woo, the ugly Alberich immediately makes the deal, renouncing love in favor of the power that the Ring will confer. For Alberich, the bargain is an easy one to make, not only because he is both inwardly and outwardly unlovely, but because his amorous advances have been thoroughly scorned by the beautiful objects of his desire. Like Klingsor, his supposed virtue is nothing more than a necessity.

Amazingly, both *The Mikado* and *The Exorcist* contain overt themes relating to chastity and sexual continence. *The Mikado* is fairly straightforward in that regard: by order of the Mikado, any man caught "flirting" must lose his head. As sung by the character Pish-Tush:

> Our great Mikado, virtuous man,
> When he to rule our land began,
> Resolved to try, a plan whereby
> Young men might best be steadied.
> So he decreed, in words succinct,
> That all who flirted, leered or winked,
> Unless connubially linked,
> Should forthwith be beheaded.

Key here are the words "unless connubially linked." Marriage confers sexual prerogatives not allowable to bachelors, who are to be "steadied" by rigid adherence to the laws of chastity. "Flirting" in the context of this meaning becomes a proper nineteenth-century euphemism for any kind of sexual activity occurring outside marriage. Clearly, Zodiac al-

luded to *The Mikado* not only for its theme of enforced sexual continence, but also for his identification with the character of Ko-Ko, the
arbiter of premarital chastity and a victim of the ordinance himself.
Also present in the Exorcist Letter is the image of the lovelorn bird
whose "blighted affections" lead him to despair and suicide. Like Alberich the dwarf, and Klingsor the magician, Ko-Ko abandons love in
favor of a more practical end — in his case, life itself. "Oh, Yum-Yum,
Yum-Yum! Bother Yum-Yum!" he cries, upon coming to the realization
that unless he gives her up to Nanki-Poo his scheme to save his own
head will be of no avail. "Take Yum-Yum and marry Yum-Yum, only go
away and never come back again."

Because Zodiac sought to link *The Exorcist* with *The Mikado*, to
which he had already alluded by the time the Exorcist Letter was composed, it seems likely that both contain common elements which he
perceived as pertaining to himself. At first glance, the two have very
little in common, the one a dark tale of demonic possession and the
other a lighthearted frolic meant simply to amuse. In *The Exorcist*, however, there exists an underlying theme of chastity in the strong contrast
between the gross excesses of the possessing entity — nearly all of them
sexual in nature — and the transcendent virtue of the priests who perform the rites to exorcise the demon. Christian love, which triumphs
in the end, is presented as a pure love that exists beyond the realm of
the merely sexual. In *The Exorcist*, the latter form of love is typified by
those sophisticated laypersons — nearly all of them Hollywood types
— who require the services of the exorcist. As in *Parsifal*, only chaste
love bears the power to destroy evil and defeat the power of demons
and magicians.

The Exorcist Letter offers a final clue in the form of the strange
symbol appearing at the bottom of the note. This inscrutable device
has baffled all attempts at decipherment. Some have seen it as a stylized example of Chinese writing, while others have tried, with great
manipulation, to extract a name from the main body of the symbol, by
rearranging its elements to form certain letters of the alphabet. Over
the years, such machinations have yielded nothing in the way of a satisfactory result. Most of the "solutions" are simply too strained to be
taken seriously.

In looking at the device, however, one is struck by the fact that it
appears to consist of two distinct components, one upon the left and
one upon the right.

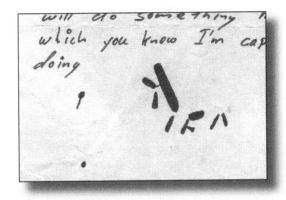

The leftmost of these components consists of a small circular dot, above which can be seen a second dot with a line emerging from its lower end, about twice the size of the dot itself. There is nothing at all inscrutable at least in *this* part of the symbol. It immediately strikes one's eye as the pictorial representation of an ovum and a sperm, with the latter having "overshot" the former.

This, of course, jibes quite nicely with the concepts of chastity and sexual continence contained in Zodiac's allusions to *The Exorcist* and *The Mikado*. It is particularly so, since the sperm is not uniting with the egg, but appears either to have passed it by, or to be disassociated with it altogether. In this context, the meaning behind the second portion of the symbol may be slightly easier to discern. Sperm and ova are microscopic entities, and it would by no means be illogical to impute the same quality to the objects comprising the larger portion of the Zodiac's device. Plainly stated, those objects look like specimens of the single-celled protozoan called *paramecium*, as they appear when viewed beneath the microscope. Like *paramecium*, each object is of oblong shape, pointed at one end and rounded at the other. They are arranged seemingly at random in relationship to one another, mirroring the appearance of the *paramecia* as they swim about; some free, and some colliding or nearly colliding with each another as they go. [See next page]

Although this assessment cannot be other than subjective, certain qualities of the *paramecium* serve to lend it a form of corroboration not obtainable by a visual comparison alone. Like all single-celled organisms, *paramecium* reproduces by the process of division, whereby a single representative of the species produces two identical copies of itself. Yet unlike other one-celled species, *paramecium* also has the unique and fascinating ability to reproduce by a process called *conjugation*.

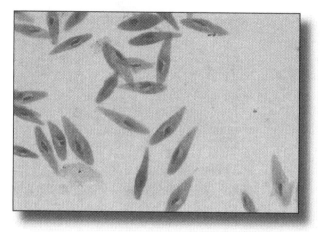

This is a form of sexual reproduction, in which two individual *paramecia* conjoin, or unite, for the purpose of exchanging genetic information. Like sexual reproduction in higher species, the purpose behind this complex pattern of behavior is the creation of diversity within the species. It is a kind of *sexual* reproduction, complementing the *asexual* reproduction most typical of one-celled creatures.

This subject has spawned at least one major work of literary endeavor, in the form of a poem entitled *The Conjugation of the Paramecium*, penned by the radical poet Muriel Rukeyser in 1968:

This has nothing
to do with
propagating

The species
is continued
as so many are
(among the smaller creatures)
by fission

(and this species
is very small
next in order to
the amoeba, the beginning one)

The paramecium
achieves, then,

immortality
by dividing

But when
the paramecium
desires renewal
strength another joy
this is what
the paramecium does:

The paramecium
lies down beside
another paramecium

Slowly inexplicably
the exchange
takes place
in which
some bits
of the nucleus of each
are exchanged

for some bits
of the nucleus

of the other
This is called
the conjugation of the paramecium.[15]

The erotic aspects of this poem are immediately apparent. One can only wonder whether the wealth of knowledge possessed by Zodiac included this work in particular, or whether it is only coincidence that such a work exists, in light of the obvious connections that seem to arise from the inferences contained within the poem, the symbol, and his overt allusions to *The Exorcist* and *The Mikado*. Whatever the case, the symbol appearing at the bottom of the Exorcist Letter, when seen as consisting of two closely-related elements (the sperm and egg on the left-hand side, and the *paramecium* on the right) conforms very closely to the themes of chastity and sexual continence presented in the letter. On the one side, the sperm has not conjoined with the egg, which indicates both sexuality *and* asexuality. On the other side, we see the *Para-*

mecium, with both sexual and asexual components of its own. Given the circumstances, including what we know of his past behavior, Zodiac is using these allusions to offer yet another clue as to his identity: namely, that he lives his life as an asexual, devoid of sexual companionship. Once again, this is patently Kaczynski.

★   ★   ★

We have seen how the Unabomber employed names, both fictitious and otherwise, to offer hints as to his personal identity. Such names as Crist, Smith, Bearnson, Percy, Enoch, Fischer, Ravenswood and Hagenberger all appeared in association with bombs and correspondences sent during the early years of his activities, from 1978 through 1985. We have seen how these names comprised allusions to literary works, particularly the Wagnerian productions of *The Ring* and *Parsifal.* In the same light we must now examine the succession of names appearing on mailed bombs and correspondences beginning in 1985, as well as the *leitmotif* of wood.

Of all the teasing references devised by Kaczynski to bedevil and entice the authorities, none was so readily apparent as his continual allusion to wood. Names such as Leroy *Wood* Bearnson, Percy *Wood,* Raven*swood,* and Frederick Benjamin Isaac *Wood,* combined with the extensive use of wood in the construction of his devices, and even the inclusion of cherry twigs along with those devices, marked the Unabomber as someone possessing a fascination with wood. In his *Harvard and the Unabomber,* Alston Chase opines that, for Kaczynski, the word was actually intended to be translated in its Old English sense, as signifying someone who is crazy, or insane. This may very well be so; and the idea is particularly tempting when seen in the light of Kaczynski's linguistic abilities. (Especially given the existence of the "old Norse" (SLA) letter attributed to the Zodiac.) It seems more likely, however, that for Kaczynski, the original intention was to offer a rather transparent hint concerning his location.

For Kaczynski, woods and forests held a special significance, as sanctuaries to which he could retreat from the storm and stress of civilized existence. "Taking to the woods" is a recurrent theme in Kaczynski's early writing, and it was to the woods that he continually returned, even going so far as to construct a series of "secret shacks," deep within the hidden forests that surrounded his cabin in Montana. Hindsight tells us now what the authorities never guessed about the Unabomber during his many years at large, though the hint had been placed beneath their very noses.

This is borne out by certain names, fictitious and otherwise, employed by Kaczynski as purported senders and receivers of his correspondences from 1985 through the time of his capture in 1996. Among these, eight in particular stand out. The names are, in the order in which they appeared, (1) Weiburg Tool and Supply (fictitious), mailed May 8, 1985; (2) 10 Hagenberger Ct. (fictitious), the return address given for the former; (3) Ralph C. Kloppenburg (fictitious), mailed November, 1985; (4) James Hill (professor, Sacramento State), mailed June, 1993; (5) Mary Jane Lee (professor, Sacramento State), mailed June, 1993; (6) H. C. Wickel (fictitious), mailed December 3, 1994; (7) Closet Dimensions (Oakland, California woodworking company), mailed April 20, 1995; and (8) Manfred Morari (electrical engineer) also mailed April 20, 1995.

The fictitious names of Weiburg and Kloppenburg, appearing six months apart in 1985, each bear the ending "burg." *Burg* is a German word meaning "castle." Almost identical in spelling, and closely related in pronunciation is the German *berg*, translated literally as "mountain." Kaczynski, of course, lived the majority of his life as a denizen of the mountains, in the state of Montana, whose name itself is derived from the Spanish *montaña*, meaning "mountainous."

The name of "Hagenberger," appearing as part of the return address for Weiburg Tool and Supply contains the proper German spelling of the word "berg," for "mountain." And while the variation *per se* does not exist in German, a "berger" could be understood within the context of the language as one who dwells among the mountains.

The next name in the series is James *Hill*, which perpetuates the same motif and comes across as obvious in its intent:

> But I want to die in my home hills in Montana, not here in the city. Death in the city seems so sordid and depressing. Death in those hills — well, if you have to die, that's the place to do it![16]

Clearly these are allusions to the surroundings amongst which Kaczynski lived during the period of time in question — the *hills* and *mountains* of *Montana*. In this context, the name of Mary Jane Lee (used contemporaneously with that of Professor Hill) becomes highly transparent in its significance. *Lee* is a homonym of *lea*, defined as a tract of grassland, or a meadow — yet another defining feature of the landscape surrounding Kaczynski's Montana home.

> The best ones usually grow down in the lower areas which are agricultural areas, actually ranches, and the ranchers presumably don't want you digging up their meadows . . . .[17]

> When I see a motorcyclist tearing up the mountain meadows . . . .[18]

Moreover, "lee" may be used in a geological sense, as a formation "located in or facing the path of an oncoming glacier."[19] The State of Montana is renowned for its Glacier National Park. *Lea* and *lee* would both have borne meaning for Kaczynski in reference to his domicile in Montana.

Consider now the next name in the succession, that of H. C. Wickel. In German, the word *wickeln* means "to wrap" or "to wind." It shares a common origin with the English "wicker," a type of woven wood, which derives from the Scandinavian words "vikker" (willow) and "wika" (to bend). In this sense, "Wickel" becomes associated both with wood *and* winding. Since the name H. C. Wickel was purely a product of Kaczynski's imagination, one may assume that the initials "H. C." stood for something of significance. Interestingly, Kaczynski's home cabin in Montana sat just off a long and winding road called Humbug Contour Road, while his street address was given as *HCR* 30. A look at the map shows the former to be particularly *winding*, doubling back on itself at least twice in its course along the contour of the hills near Kaczynski's cabin. Thus, in H. C. Wickel, we see two further hints alluding to location.

"Closet Dimensions" seems almost self-evident in what, by hindsight, it suggests. Not only was Closet Dimensions an actual business, specializing in custom-made cabinets — ostensibly made with *wood* — but the name itself suggested something peculiar about the Unabomber's own living arrangements at the time, i.e., a small cabin possessing the *dimensions* of a *closet*.

Finally, the name of electrical engineer Manfred Morari evokes an interesting connection with a famous poem by the renowned Lord Byron. Because Manfred Morari was an actual living person, it seems unlikely (though perhaps not impossible) that both names bore significance for Kaczynski. If only one of them bore significance, it seems puzzling as to exactly what could have been intended by the surname "Morari." The word itself is Latin in origin, and signifies a "hindrance," or "delay." It is difficult to see what Kaczynski might have had in mind if his intention was to associate the word with either of those meanings. "Manfred," however, gives us far more material with which to work, especially in the context of the eponymous Byronic poem. In terms of relating to Kaczynski, the poem is of great interest in its thematic content alone. Its protagonist, the noble Manfred, has exhausted the possibilities of human knowledge, and in the process committed an unnamed crime or crimes that have led to the death of his beloved. This is a Faustian theme, and, like all such themes, involves the concept of *hubris*, defined loosely as "defiance against the gods." Summoning the spirits of the earth and air, Manfred importunes them for solace in the form of forgetfulness, or self-oblivion. Told that this is beyond their power, he seeks forgetfulness in death. Climbing to the heights of Jungfrau Mountain, he prepares to fling himself from the cliff upon which he totters, but is rescued by a passing hunter. Later, in his castle at the summit of the Jungfrau, demons arrive to lead Manfred to his death. Defiant to the end, he drives them off, yet succumbs to the inevitable demands of nature, and dies in the presence of a baffled Abbot, who can only look in wonder and exclaim

> He's gone, his soul hath ta'en its earthless flight
> Whither? I dread to think; but he is gone.

The Faustian aspects of *Manfred* would, in and of themselves, have proven relevant to Kaczynski, whose anti-technology worldview perceived the advances of human civilization (particularly in the nineteenth century, when the poem was conceived) as false gods, leading inevitably to disillusionment and discontent. The poem comprises an excellent allegory for Kaczynski and his own particular brand of disaffection. More significant, however, is its setting. For Byron placed his Manfred among the mountains and glaciers of the Alps:

> Mont Blanc is the monarch of *mountains*;
>   They crown'd him long ago
> On a throne of rocks, in a robe of clouds,
>   With a diadem of *snow*.

> Around his waist are *forests* braced,
> The Avalanche in his hand;
> But ere it fall, that thundering ball
> Must pause for my command.
> The *Glacier's* cold and restless mass
> Moves onward day by day;
> But I am he who bids it pass,
> Or with its ice delay.

No less stark is the image of Manfred himself, poised precariously on a snow-covered crag atop the Jungfrau and preparing to take the fatal plunge that will end the torments of a guilt-wracked mind. It is the subject of a famous painting by the English artist Ford Madox Brown, titled *Manfred on the Jungfrau.* The entire poem is bedight with this kind of imagery, which once again refers us back to Kaczynski and his mountain home.

In light of these connections, we must now turn our attention to the strange series of correspondences attributable to Zodiac and dated March 22, 1971, July 13, 1971 and December 27, 1974.

The first of these, the Pines Card, consisted of a picture cut from an advertisement that appeared in the *San Francisco Chronicle.* The ad, for Forest Pines Condominiums at Incline Village, Nevada, featured an artist's rendition of the newly-constructed condominiums, nestled within a wooded area consisting of snow-covered pine trees. It was this rendition that Zodiac used as the basis for his correspondence. Pasted on the card, in cut-out letters taken from the *Chronicle,* appeared the words *Sierra Club, "Peek through the pines,", pass LAKE TAHOE areas, Sought victim 12* and *around in the snow.* [See next page]

References within the Pines Card to a twelfth Zodiac victim, coupled with the mention of Lake Tahoe, led authorities to suspect that a young nurse named Donna Lass had fallen victim to the depredations of the Zodiac. Lass, who worked at the Sahara Hotel in Stateline, was last seen on September 26, 1970. On September 27, an unknown male caller informed her landlord that a family emergency had drawn Lass away, and that she would not be returning to work. The call was later found to have been a hoax, and Donna Lass has not been seen or heard from since. This possible Zodiac connection received a fair amount of newspaper publicity. A reward poster appeared in the early 1970s, showing a photograph of Lass in conjunction with a reproduction of

the 1969 police sketch of the killer and two lines of coded symbols similar to those used by Zodiac in his correspondences.

The second card in the series, the Monticello Card, is known to researchers only by its inclusion in a San Francisco Police document entitled "Suspected Zodiac Correspondence." This document contains a listing of all the extant Zodiac missives in conjunction with attempts to extract DNA from their associated stamps and envelopes. The card is plainly described as

> LETTERS PASTED ON PICTURE "NEAR MONTICELLO
> SHOUGHT VICTIMS 21 ... IN THE WOODS
> DIES APRIL". [Monticello Card]

Currently there is no public knowledge concerning the nature or origin of the picture, the placement of the letters, or whether any other textual material accompanied the phrases described in the report. The card is listed as having been addressed to the *San Francisco Chronicle*, with a date of July 13, 1971, nearly four months after receipt of the Pines Card by the *Chronicle*.

On December 27, 1974, Mrs. Mary Pilker of Sioux Falls, South Dakota, received a Christmas card from an anonymous sender. Pilker was the sister of Donna Lass. The envelope in which the Donna Card was mailed bore two 10-cent stamps of the Currier and Ives series, depicting a male-and-female couple riding across a snow-covered field in a horse-drawn sleigh. On the card's front panel was a lithographed photo depicting a snow-covered hill upon which stood a grove of pine trees blanketed in newly-fallen snow. Inside the front panel, beneath a stock inscription of "Holiday Greetings and Best Wishes for a Happy New Year," the sender had written in a cursive script, "Best Wishes, St. Donna & Guardian of the Pines."[20]

These three cards form a clear continuum, containing a set of identical themes that are easy to discern. Common to all three is the motif of woods and trees, which is repeated at least twice in each of the correspondences. Common to the first two is the motif of mountains. Common to the first and last is the motif of snow in general, and snow-covered trees in particular.

It requires no stretch of the imagination to perceive that, of these three themes, the first two are identical to those employed by Kaczynski in his series of correspondences as the Unabomber. The theme of snow, while not directly attributable to Kaczynski (apart from the *Manfred* poem), nevertheless demonstrates in no uncertain terms the use of a continuing motif by the author of the cards. This, in itself, is an undoubted Kaczynski trait.

The Pines Card displays a picture depicting houses in a *wooded* setting. "Peek through the *pines*," exhorts a single line of text, cut from the ad for Forest *Pines* condominiums, placed by the company Boise/Interlake, whose logo, as it appeared upon the ad itself, was a stylized *tree*. "In the *woods* dies April," proclaims the Monticello Card, while its successor, the Donna Card, visually depicts a stand of *pines* and announces its sender as the "Guardian of the *Pines*." In terms of mountains, the picture that formed the Pines Card was cut from an ad for "*mountain* condominiums," while the "Sierra" of "Sierra Club" is actually the Spanish word for "*mountain* range." Appearing on the Monticello Card, "monticello," is an Italian word which translates into English as "little *mountain*." Finally, the snow motif is presented on the Pines Card as a winter scene bedight with *snow*-covered trees and accompanied by the cut-out words "around in the *snow*." The Donna Card likewise shows *snow* scenes both on the card itself and as part of the Currier and Ives stamps with which it was posted. Like the Pines Card, *snow*-covered trees feature prominently on its front panel.

Additionally, the Monticello card contains an interesting reference in the form of the mysterious statement "in the woods dies April." The

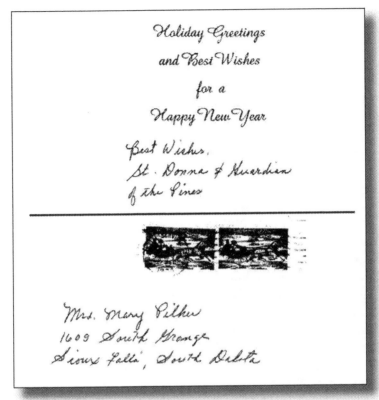

Holiday Greetings
and Best Wishes
for a
Happy New Year

Best Wishes,
St. Donna & Guardian
of the Pines

Mrs. Mary Pilker
1609 South Grange
Sioux Falls, South Dakota

The Donna Card, interior writing and envelope. (Courtesy of Howard Davis.)

words are evocative of an obscure poem titled "Agatha," written by Alfred Austin, the English Poet Laureate from 1892 to 1913:

She wanders in the April woods,
That glisten with the fallen shower;
She leans her face against the buds,
She stops, she stoops, she plucks a flower.
She feels the ferment of the hour:
She broodeth when the ringdove broods;
The sun and flying clouds have power
Upon her cheek and changing moods.
She cannot think she is alone,
As o'er her senses warmly steal
Floods of unrest she fears to own,
And almost dreads to feel.

Among the summer woodlands wide
Anew she roams, no more alone;
The joy she fear'd is at her side,
Spring's blushing secret now is known.
The primrose and its mates have flown,
The thrush's ringing note hath died;
But glancing eye and glowing tone
Fall on her from her god, her guide.
She knows not, asks not, what the goal,
She only feels she moves towards bliss,
And yields her pure unquestioning soul
To touch and fondling kiss.

And still she haunts those woodland ways,
Though all fond fancy finds there now
To mind of spring or summer days,
Are sodden trunk and songless bough.
The past sits widow'd on her brow,
Homeward she wends with wintry gaze,
To walls that house a hollow vow,
To hearth where love hath ceas'd to blaze:
Watches the clammy twilight wane,
With grief too fix'd for woe or tear;
And, with her forehead 'gainst the pane,
Envies the dying year.

A careful reading of this poem discloses a theme of youthful innocence lost to experience and age. The first and last lines relate on
a one-to-one basis with the import of the statement "in the woods
dies April," even employing the same or similar words in the form of
"woods," "April," and "dying." The sylvan setting of the poem, with
its references to woods and woodlands jibes perfectly with the motif of
woods and forests present in all three cards of the Pines, Monticello
and Donna series. As in Kaczynski's reference to the Byronic *Manfred*,
a hint is given that leads convincingly to a nineteenth-century poetic
work whose setting corresponds to the continuing *leitmotif* of mountains, snow, woods and trees. Moreover, its central theme of sexual innocence lost to age and experience corresponds with the motif of sexual
chastity present in the Exorcist Letter of 1974, referring us forward to

the same themes presented by Kaczynski in the Wagnerian allusions within his Unabomber missives.

The reference to "St. Donna" in the Donna Card is an obvious allusion to the missing Donna Lass. While no Saint Donna exists within the Catholic hagiography, the list of saints includes Saint *Agatha*, martyred in the reign of the Roman emperor Decius, *ca.* 250 A.D. Agatha, a wealthy and beautiful young woman, had dedicated her life to virginity and Christ. When Decius issued his infamous edict suppressing Christianity, a local magistrate attempted to extort sexual favors from Agatha by threatening to denounce her as a Christian. Having rejected the magistrate's advances, Agatha was imprisoned and cruelly tortured. Her breasts were cut off and her body rolled over live coals until finally she expired. Here, once again, we see an indirect allusion to the theme of sexual chastity, in the steadfast devotion of St. Agatha to her vows.

The Pines, Monticello and Donna series of correspondences commenced in the spring of 1971, the exact period of time in which Kaczynski was said to have left his parents' house in Lombard, Illinois, and traveled to Great Falls, Montana, for the purpose of buying land and building a cabin in the woods. It is instructive to note that the continuing motif of woods and mountains does not exist in the Zodiac correspondences prior to the spring of 1971. We see, in the one instance, Kaczynski's series of letters commencing in 1985, with their continual and now-transparent allusions to the elements that defined his Montana life, namely woods, trees, hills, mountains and meadows. We see that these are hints pertaining to his location, designed to tease the authorities and satisfy Kaczynski's need to identify himself. In the other instance we perceive a series of missives, attributable to Zodiac, and bearing the exact same themes as those presented by Kaczynski, in the form of mountains, hills, woods and trees. Under this scenario, the "mountain condominiums" of the Forest Pines advertisement may be said to represent Kaczynski's own "mountain condominium," which he already had planned to build when the Pines card was received. The "sierra" of "Sierra Club," are the mountain ranges surrounding his new domicile. "Monticello," represents the "little hills," of his newly-acquired property (already purchased when the Monticello Card was mailed), while woods in general, and snow-covered pines in particular, feature prominently in its landscape. Having fulfilled his desire of purchasing land in the Montana woods, in which he would have his own home, isolated in the wilderness from the stress of civilized life, Kaczynski truly became the "Guardian of the Pines," as alluded to in the Donna Card of 1974. In this context, it should be pointed out that the state tree of *Montana* is the Ponderosa *Pine*.

*   *   *

One caveat must be considered in the context of what has been presented here. High literature, such as that seen in the Wagnerian operas, and even including lighthearted, comedic productions such as *The Mikado*, are complex artistic efforts subject to literally endless variations of human interpretation. We cannot see into the minds of either Kaczynski or the Zodiac, and must rely upon our own logical analysis of what those minds contained, based on the best information at hand. It may very well be that we are not *completely* right in our analyses. In one regard, however, we cannot be wrong. Both the Unabomber and the Zodiac made use of literary allusion as a means of casting hints in the direction of the authorities — hints as to their identities, their locations and their personal peculiarities. Moreover, this was not just any form of literary allusion, but *high* literary allusion, involving works of classical or scholarly literary endeavor. It is a characteristic that links them together as closely as their common psychology and their common criminal signature. Of even more profound significance is the undeniable fact that both killers used *opera* as a means of conveying information about themselves to the authorities and the public. That Zodiac reached for the comic form of opera and Kaczynski for its dramatic form is completely immaterial. In terms of linkage, it is a fact that can neither be underplayed nor overlooked. Smoking guns could not say more.

Chapter 9

Wheels within Wheels

Ye spirits of the unbounded Universe,
Whom I have sought in darkness and in light!
Ye, who do compass earth about, and dwell
In subtler essence! Ye, to whom the tops
Of mountains inaccessible are haunts,
And earth's and ocean's caves familiar things –
I call upon ye by the written charm
Which gives me power upon you – Rise! Appear!

LORD BYRON, *Manfred*

THE CODE KILLER. The Cipher Slayer. Until his self-styled cognomen took hold, these were the names by which the public knew the Zodiac. Surprisingly, only four coded communications have been attributed to the killer, the first of which, the so-called Three-Part Cipher, was fortuitously solved within days of its receipt. The remaining three, styled the 340-Symbol Cipher, the Thirteen-Symbol Cipher and the Mt. Diablo Code (so-named by Zodiac himself), have remained unsolved to this very day.

One might reasonably suppose that any person suspected of complicity in the crimes of Zodiac would possess some clear connection to the creation and use of codes and ciphers. For every major suspect, with the exception of Theodore Kaczynski, such connections have been unsatisfactory and tenuous at best, consisting usually of vague military associations with no indication that the suspect ever created or employed codes and ciphers for his own particular use. Kaczynski, on the other hand, is unique in that he is known to have created elaborate ciphers which he used to conceal information relating to his criminal activities, not only as the Unabomber, but as a local miscreant in and around the environs of his home in Lincoln, Montana.

Kaczynski's ciphers are mathematical in nature, and by the general public they are still not completely understood. Despite the fact that keys to both the codes and ciphers were found by the authorities in Kaczynski's cabin, only a single document, bearing the key to one set of ciphers, has been released, and published in Alston Chase's *Harvard and the Unabomber*.[1] This document contains a list of numerals from 0 through 89 and textual equivalents for the numerals, as illustrated in this example:

0	=	for
1	=	be (all present tense forms, including am, is, are, etc.)
2	=	be (all past tense forms)
3	=	be (all future tense; i.e., will b)
4	=	the
5	=	a or an
6	=	have (all present tense forms)
7	=	have (all past tense forms; i.e. had)
8	=	have (future tense)
9	=	ed, or, when tagged onto the end of any verb, indicates the past tense, even if the past tense of that verb is not indicated by "ed" in ordinary English.
10	=	tagged onto the end of any verb indicates the future tense of that verb.

Numbers eleven through 38 represented common words, articles, certain prepositions, personal pronouns and punctuation marks. Thirty-nine through 71 stood for the letters of the alphabet, with double associations given for the common letters A, E, R, S and T. Seventy-two through 89 offered equivalents for the word fragments OM (as in "bomb"), PLOD (as in "explode"), ILL (as in "kill") and ETONA (as in "detonate").

Under this system, a person might encrypt the words "I like killing people," as

I		L	I	K	E		K	ILL	I
29	32	54	51	53	45	33	53	81	51

N	G		P	E	O	P	L	E
56	40	32	56	46	57	58	54	47

While this would have prevented prying eyes from a casual reading of Kaczynski's secret texts, it most likely would not have been sufficiently strong a system to have withstood professional cryptanalysis. In 1998 the Justice Department released numerous pages of Kaczynski's enciphered journals, yet none of the encryptions appears to be solvable by this particular key. Obviously there exists a second cryptosystem, perhaps more elaborate than the one revealed by Alston Chase. Wrote Chase, "[h]e kept his in codes that an FBI cryptologist told me, 'no one, not even NSA computers, could have broken' had their searchers not found the key in his cabin."[2]

Perhaps in a similar vein, three of the four extant Zodiac ciphers have remained unbroken. Of these three, only one — the 340-Symbol Cipher — contains sufficient data for a truly serious attempt at decryption. Even so, one can only wonder whether the cipher actually contains a message, or whether the device served simply as a means for Zodiac to give the authorities some "busy work" to do. Whatever the case, the experience of more than three decades has shown that efforts to solve these ciphers have been little more than exercises in frustration.

Be that as it may, some evidence exists to suggest that the cryptograms may harbor clues above and beyond what their apparent nature holds. This evidence relates to the distinction between the words "code" and "cipher," and the probability that Zodiac understood the difference between the two. Zodiac, for example, referred to his first productions as "ciphers." Each section of the Three-Part Cipher was accompanied by a note that read, "Here is a . . . *cipher* . . . ." Several days later, however, in his August 3 missive to the *San Francisco Examiner*, the killer wrote, " . . . are the police haveing a good time with the *code*?" Accompanying the 340-Symbol Cipher was a text inquiring whether the *Chronicle* could "print this new *cipher*" on its front page. Five months later, the killer asked whether anyone had "cracked the last *cipher*" he had sent. Yet in the June 26, 1970 Mt. Diablo Letter he remarked that "the Map coupled with this *code*" would tell the authorities where a bomb was set. One month later he referred back to this production, calling it the "Mt. Diablo *Code*."

Though the terms are often used interchangeably, there exists nonetheless a clear difference between codes and ciphers. While both are intended to disguise a communication so that its meaning may be understood only by the parties for whom it is intended, the one is very different in nature from the other. Ciphers are defined generally as communications encrypted by a set of algorithms applied to individual letters of the alphabet. Codes, on the other hand, involve the encryption of entire meanings in the form of whole words, sentences and phrases. Ciphers involve keys, whereby each letter of the original message (the plaintext) is replaced by a corresponding letter of a given key (the ciphertext). In a very simple cipher, the letters of the message ATTACK AT NOON might be replaced with the letters ZCCZTE ZC XHHX, with Z standing for A, C for T, and so on. In a coded message, the same order might be represented by a phrase such as "CUBS 6, SOX 5." Here it is easy to see that, of the two methods of encryption, ciphers are the more versatile option. Using a given cipher system, one may encrypt virtually any message, while in the case of codes a unique encryption must exist for each and every meaning one wishes to convey.

Given his seeming knowledge of this distinction, one is naturally led to wonder whether Zodiac buried some form of coded message — a *meta-code*, if we may call it that — within the ciphers he created.

A logical starting point for such a search would be the Three-Part Cipher which, thanks to the amateur cryptologists Donald and Bettye Harden, has a known solution set. Arranging this solution in a grid of 17 columns by 24 rows (as Zodiac arranged the enciphered text itself) gives the result depicted on the following page:[3]

In examining this production, one is struck by a particular area occurring between the fourteenth and eighteenth rows. There, the word PARADICE appears to be intersected vertically, as on a Scrabble board, by three four-letter words, each building on the larger, horizontal word:

R	T	O	F	I	**T**	I	S	T	H	A	T	W	H	E	N	I
D	I	E	I	**W**	**I**	L	L	**B**	E	R	E	B	O	R	N	I
N	**P**	**A**	**R**	**A**	**D**	**I**	**C**	**E**	A	N	D	A	L	L	T	H
E	I	H	A	**V**	**E**	K	I	**L**	L	E	D	W	I	L	L	B
E	C	O	M	**E**	M	Y	S	**L**	A	V	E	S	I	W	I	L

Moving forward to October 27, 1970, we see a similar pattern, vertically, in Zodiac's Halloween Card [jump to Page 132]:

I	L	I	K	E	K	I	L	L	I	N	G	P	E	O	P	L
E	B	E	C	A	U	S	E	I	T	I	S	S	O	M	U	C
H	F	U	N	I	T	I	S	M	O	R	E	F	U	N	T	H
A	N	K	I	L	L	I	N	G	W	I	L	D	G	A	M	E
I	N	T	H	E	F	O	R	R	E	S	T	B	E	C	A	U
S	E	M	A	N	I	S	T	H	E	M	O	S	T	D	A	N
G	E	R	O	U	E	A	N	A	M	A	L	O	F	A	L	L
T	O	K	I	L	L	S	O	M	E	T	H	I	N	G	G	I
V	E	S	M	E	T	H	E	M	O	S	T	T	H	R	I	L
L	I	N	G	E	X	P	E	R	E	N	C	E	I	T	I	S
E	V	E	N	B	E	T	T	E	R	T	H	A	N	G	E	T
T	I	N	G	Y	O	U	R	R	O	C	K	S	O	F	F	W
I	T	H	A	G	I	R	L	T	H	E	B	E	S	T	P	A
R	T	O	F	I	T	I	S	T	H	A	T	W	H	E	N	I
D	I	E	I	W	I	L	L	B	E	R	E	B	O	R	N	I
N	P	A	R	A	D	I	C	E	A	N	D	A	L	L	T	H
E	I	H	A	V	E	K	I	L	L	E	D	W	I	L	L	B
E	C	O	M	E	M	Y	S	L	A	V	E	S	I	W	I	L
L	N	O	T	G	I	V	E	Y	O	U	M	Y	N	A	M	E
B	E	C	A	U	S	E	Y	O	U	W	I	L	L	T	R	Y
T	O	S	L	O	I	D	O	W	N	O	R	A	T	O	P	M
Y	C	O	L	L	E	C	T	I	N	G	O	F	S	L	A	V
E	S	F	O	R	M	Y	A	F	T	E	R	L	I	F	E	E
B	E	O	R	I	E	T	E	M	E	T	H	H	P	I	T	I

It would appear that the crossed words on the Halloween Card refer back to the similar arrangement within the solution set to the Three Part Cipher. This is certainly an improbable phenomenon, and one that seems unlikely to have happened simply by chance — especially since the words WAVE, TIDE and BELL each bear a relationship to one another in the sense that all three carry nautical associations. Tide and wave are obviously so, while bells, mounted on buoys, have historically been employed to warn ships of dangers to navigation. Historically, too, ships have carried bells that serve as signaling devices.

In fact, these three words appear together in the final paragraphs of a short story by the renowned, though now-obscure English author Frederick Marryat. Titled *The Legend of the Bell Rock*, Marryat's chilling tale relates the story of a young man whose love for a woman leads to acts of desperation that end in his ruin, and the death of his beloved.

A dangerous rock lies in the Firth of Tay, upon which many a vessel has been sunk. The citizens of Perth and Dundee collect money toward the purchase of a bell, which they intend to fix upon the rock. Approaching ships will be warned away by the tolling of the bell. Commissioned by the citizens to purchase a bell, young Andrew M'Clise sets sail for Amsterdam, to the home of Vandermaclin, owner of a large and famous bell, which he offers to M'Clise at a favorable price. The terms are agreed to, and the purchase made. Arriving safely home, M'Clise oversees the installation of the bell. But he has fallen in love with Vandermaclin's daughter Katerina, who has reciprocated his affections, and returns to Holland to ask the merchant for her hand.

The merchant replies that he cannot consent until M'Clise can prove his financial worth to the amount of 12,000 guilders. M'Clise, though not a poor man, has only a quarter of the amount, and the merchant tells him that his quest is hopeless. Crestfallen, he lingers in the city. A message arrives from his beloved. It contains but two short words: "*The Bell.*" The portent of these words is dire, as Marryat relates:

> And Katerina raised her eyes to heaven, and whispered, as she clasped her hands, "The Bell." Alas! That we should invoke Heaven when we would wish to do wrong: but mortals are blind, and none so blind as those who are impelled by passion.

Casting his honesty aside, M'Clise steals the bell from its place upon the rock. Sailing back to Amsterdam, he sells it for the sum of 10,000 guilders, to a man who has coveted it in the past. Complicit in the crime, his shipmates sue for equal shares, to which M'Clise cannot consent. He murders them all with poisoned wine, before returning to Vandermaclin to claim Katerina. The couple set sail for Dundee, but as the ship approaches the Firth of Tay, a terrible storm begins to brew. The vessel is dashed to pieces upon the very rock from which M'Clise removed the bell that would have saved it from destruction:

> M'Clise threw from him her whom he had so madly loved, and *plunged into the wave*. Katerina shrieked, as she dashed after him, and all was over.
>
> When the storm rises, and the screaming sea-gull seeks the land, and the fisherman hastens his bark towards the beach, there is to be seen, descending from the dark clouds with the rapidity of lightning, the form of Andrew M'Clise, the heavy *bell* to which he is attached by the neck, bearing him down to the bottom.
>
> And when all is smooth and calm, when at the ebbing *tide* the *wave* but gently kisses the rock, then by the light of the silver moon the occupants of the vessels which sail from the Firth of Tay have often beheld the form of the beautiful Katerina, waving her white scarf as a signal that they should approach, and take her off from the rock on which she is seated. At times she offers a letter for her father, Vandermaclin; and she mourns and weeps as the wary mariners, with their eyes fixed on her, and with folded arms, pursue their course in silence and in dread. [Author's italics]

Seen in reference to the allusions of tide, wave and bell, this production is quite instructive. For it conveys the prospect of an honest man, impelled to the commission of a frightful series of crimes through the agency of passion — *sexual* passion, to be precise. Not only does it direct us toward what we reasonably believe to have been the criminal motives of the Zodiac; it directs us toward what we strongly suspect to have been the original motivation for the criminal career of Ted Kaczynski. It forms yet another exemplar of literary allusion that is used to make a statement about the *identity* of its employer. Moreover, the imagery presented in the story's final sentences corresponds beautifully with the imagery presented in *The Exorcist, The Mikado,* and *Manfred*; namely, that of a person willfully plunging, diving, or falling to his doom. In fact, "plunged into the wave," is almost identical to the line "he plunged himself into the billowy wave," from *The Mikado.* In terms of the imagery they invoke, the words are identical indeed.

Frederick Marryatt achieved widespread acclaim with the publication of his seafaring novels in the early nineteenth century. So popular were his novels that they influenced several generations of writers, not the least of whom were Herman Melville and the Polish-born Jósef Teodor Konrad Korzeniowski, better known as the English author Joseph Conrad. A seafarer in his prime, Conrad's early novels drew heavily upon their author's nautical experience. It is commonly known that he had read Marryat extensively in youth; perhaps to the point that he was impelled by those readings to go to sea. "[Marryat's] greatness is undeniable," wrote Conrad, whose own renown would be attested by the admiration of someone no less famous — though perhaps not *quite* so credible as the celebrated novelist — namely, Ted Kaczynski.

As we have noted above, Kaczynski's mother exposed him to a wide variety of literary classics, particularly the works of nineteenth century authors such as Thackeray, Melville, Dickens, Dostoyevsky and Conrad. Conrad's influence upon Kaczynski is well-documented and undeniable. It is an influence that appears to have been profound. In a *Washington Post* article outlining the relationship between Kaczynski and Conrad, Serge F. Kovaleski wrote:

> During 26 years in the Montana wilderness, he pored over Conrad's writings. In a 1984 letter to his family, "Ted said he was reading Conrad's novels for about the dozenth time," said Washington attorney Anthony P. Bisceglie, counsel to Kaczynski's brother and mother.[4]

According to the same source, Kaczynski used the aliases "Conrad," or "Konrad" on at least three occasions when traveling incognito as the Unabomber. Further, a collection of Conrad's stories was found among the items in Kaczynski's Montana shack. This anthology comprised the short works *Heart of Darkness*, *Youth* and *Typhoon*, nautical stories all. Given this association between Kaczynski and Conrad, it seems likely that the former would have been aware of those Marryat novels that had influenced the writings of the latter. Any connection between Zodiac and Conrad will not be borne out simply by reference to a Marryat work alone. As we will soon point out, however, that association is both obvious and strong. For now, the link between Conrad and Kaczynski, and the link between Marryat and Conrad, must suffice. At a bare minimum we may declare that (1) the word PARADICE is present in the Halloween Card of 1970, intersected by a second word, which leads us back to the Three-Part Cipher where the same word (PARADICE) is intersected in a similar fashion; (2) the words BELL, TIDE and WAVE are four-letter words, spelled out contiguously, which cut vertically through the key word PARADICE; (3) these words each bear a common, nautical meaning; (4) they are found closely associated with one another in a nautical story by the nineteenth century author Frederick Marryat; (5) Marryatt's writings influenced the works of Joseph Conrad; and (6) Conrad's writings worked a notable influence on the mind of Theodore Kaczynski.

Going back to the solution set of the Three Part Cipher, we can discern a second set of four-letter words, immediately to the right of BELL, and each staggered one row above the other:

I	T	H	A	G	I	R	L	T	H	E	B	E	S	T	P	A
R	T	O	F	I	T	I	S	T	H	A	T	W	H	E	N	I
D	I	E	I	W	I	L	L	B	E	R	E	B	O	R	N	I
N	P	A	R	A	D	I	C	E	A	N	D	A	L	L	T	H
E	I	H	A	V	E	K	I	L	L	E	D	W	I	L	L	B
E	C	O	M	E	M	Y	S	L	A	V	E	S	I	W	I	L

HEAL and EARN follow the same pattern as WAVE, TIDE and BELL, in that they appear both vertically and contiguously, spelling out two words whose relationship to one another is not immediately apparent. That relationship becomes more apparent, however, when seen in the context of a third pattern that terminates just a single row above and one column to the right of the "E" in EARN:

S	E	M	A	N	I	S	T	H	E	**M**	O	S	T	D	A	N
G	E	R	O	U	E	A	N	A	M	**A**	L	O	F	A	L	L
T	O	K	I	L	L	S	O	M	E	**T**	**H**	**I**	N	G	G	I
V	E	S	M	E	T	H	E	M	O	S	T	**T**	H	R	I	L
L	I	N	G	E	X	P	E	R	E	N	**C**	**E**	I	T	I	S
E	V	E	N	B	E	T	T	E	R	T	**H**	**A**	N	G	E	T
T	I	N	G	Y	O	U	R	R	O	C	K	S	O	F	F	W
I	T	H	A	G	I	R	L	T	H	E	**E**	B	E	S	T	P	A
R	T	O	F	I	T	I	S	T	**H**	**A**	T	W	H	E	N	I
D	I	E	I	W	I	L	L	B	E	**R**	B	O	R	N	I
N	P	A	R	A	D	I	C	E	**A**	**N**	D	A	L	L	T	H
E	I	H	A	V	E	K	I	L	**L**	E	D	W	I	L	L	B

Following the characters contiguously, down three spaces, across three, down four, across one and up one, we may see the words MA-THITEACH (MATH I TEACH), with a single anomaly represented by the transposition of the "C" and "H" of TEACH.

Kaczynski, of course, taught advanced courses in mathematics from September of 1967 through June of 1969. Teaching was his career during this period of time, and it would have defined him both personally and professionally. By itself, perhaps, this observation is not impressive. The pattern does, admittedly, involve a certain degree of interpretation, since one must work down and across the grid in order to derive its meaning. It assumes greater significance, and shows far less likelihood of having been arbitrarily wrung from the letters of the grid, by a careful reading of the meaning behind the two words HEAL and EARN. Who *earns* his living by *heal*ing? A doctor, of course, and though not a doctor of the medical variety, Kaczynski *was* a doctor nonetheless; a *doctor* of *mathematics*, whose livelihood reposed in *teaching*.

Carrying on, the reader's eye is directed toward the set of words appearing directly to the right of EARN, and staggered one row down:

I	T	H	A	G	I	R	L	T	H	E	B	E	S	T	P	A
R	T	O	F	I	T	I	S	T	H	A	**T**	W	H	E	N	I
D	I	E	I	W	I	L	L	B	E	R	**E**	B	O	R	N	I
N	P	A	R	A	D	I	C	E	**A**	**N**	**D**	A	L	L	T	H
E	I	H	A	V	E	K	I	L	L	E	**D**	W	I	L	L	B
E	C	O	M	E	M	Y	S	L	**A**	**V**	**E**	S	I	W	I	L

That the word TED should appear by itself in a production such as this is neither surprising nor beyond the realm of simple chance. That it should appear in conjunction with the patterns that have been outlined above, is something else entirely. That it should appear as the pattern TED AND DAVE is more than something else entirely; it is positively chilling. Why the name of Kaczynski's younger brother should be found here forms the basis for an interesting discussion that is best not started at the present time. Undoubtedly the explanation is innocent enough. By his own accounting, Dave served as a disciple and confidant to Ted, sharing both his worldview and his penchant for isolation from society. As detailed earlier in the present work, Dave and Ted lived in close proximity throughout the summer of 1969 (and perhaps the spring of 1969 as well), continuing their relationship for many years thereafter. Whatever the case, inclusion of the words AND DAVE lends the pattern a certain credibility that would not have been inherent in the three letter name of TED alone. Perhaps that is why it was included.[5]

Taken altogether, then, we have: [See next page]

These clues — if such they are — appear together in a very tight pattern within the complete grid of the Three-Part Cipher. With the exception of MATHITEACH, all occur within a small area measuring six rows by eleven columns. HEAL, EARN and TEDANDDAVE appear within a very small block measuring six rows by three columns: fifteen significant letters from a sum total of eighteen. MATHITEACH sits just one row from the topmost character comprising this block, aligning with its last two columns. Subjectively speaking, it is difficult to perceive such occurrences as resulting from chance alone.

I	L	I	K	E	K	I	L	L	I	N	G	P	E	O	P	L
E	B	E	C	A	U	S	E	I	T	I	S	S	O	M	U	C
H	F	U	N	I	T	I	S	M	O	R	E	F	U	N	T	H
A	N	K	I	L	L	I	N	G	W	I	L	D	G	A	M	E
I	N	T	H	E	F	O	R	R	E	S	T	B	E	C	A	U
S	E	M	A	N	I	S	T	H	E	M	O	S	T	D	A	N
G	E	R	O	U	E	A	N	A	M	A	L	O	F	A	L	L
T	O	K	I	L	L	S	O	M	E	T	H	I	N	G	G	I
V	E	S	M	E	T	H	E	M	O	S	T	T	H	R	I	L
L	I	N	G	E	X	P	E	R	E	N	C	E	I	T	I	S
E	V	E	N	B	E	T	T	E	R	T	H	A	N	G	E	T
T	I	N	G	Y	O	U	R	R	O	C	K	S	O	F	F	W
I	T	H	A	G	I	R	L	T	H	E	B	E	S	T	P	A
R	T	O	F	I	T	I	S	T	H	A	T	W	H	E	N	I
D	I	E	I	W	I	L	L	B	E	R	E	B	O	R	N	I
N	P	A	R	A	D	I	C	E	A	N	D	A	L	L	T	H
E	I	H	A	V	E	K	I	L	L	E	D	W	I	L	L	B
E	C	O	M	E	M	Y	S	L	A	V	E	S	I	W	I	L
L	N	O	T	G	I	V	E	Y	O	U	M	Y	N	A	M	E
B	E	C	A	U	S	E	Y	O	U	W	I	L	L	T	R	Y
T	O	S	L	O	I	D	O	W	N	O	R	A	T	O	P	M
Y	C	O	L	L	E	C	T	I	N	G	O	F	S	L	A	V
E	S	F	O	R	M	Y	A	F	T	E	R	L	I	F	E	E
B	E	O	R	I	E	T	E	M	E	T	H	H	P	I	T	I

We must turn our attention now to one final observation regarding the Three Part Cipher and the possible coded messages embedded within its solution set. Zodiac used a number of different symbols to encrypt his original message, among which was a set of regular alphabetic letters written backwards. Those letters were, in the order in which they appeared, K, P, E, Q, F, L, D, R, C, and J. Their plaintext equivalents, as seen in the following chart, are:

Я	ꟼ	Ǝ	Ọ	Ⅎ	⅃	◖	ꓤ	Ɔ	⅃
I	E	C	M	D	A	O	R	V	X

Among the resulting set of plaintext characters, i.e., IECMDAORVX, all but the letter X form an anagram reading "I COMRADE V." While this may seem a purely arbitrary rendering, it is actually nothing of the sort. For its validity as a meta-code hinges upon an interpretation suggested by Zodiac himself, in the Mt. Diablo Letter of June 26, 1970.

The Mt. Diablo Letter comprised both a written missive and a map. The map, a Phillips 66 road map, depicted nearly the entire San Francisco Bay area, from the city of San Jose in the south, to Vallejo in the north, and extending eastward to the city of Pleasanton and beyond. Upon this map Zodiac drew a crossed circle, identical in design to his own trademark device, and placed the center of the circle directly above the summit of Mt. Diablo, sixteen miles due east of Berkeley. At the 12 o'clock, 3 o'clock, six o'clock and nine o'clock positions of the circle, Zodiac placed the labels 0, 3, 6 and 9 respectively. Beside the zero indicator appeared the words "is to be set to Mag. N." i.e., "zero is to be set to magnetic north."

The accompanying letter hinted of a bomb, which the authorities could find by following the clues contained within the map, along with two lines of an encrypted message appearing at the bottom of the letter:

> The Map coupled with this code will tell you where the bomb is set. You have until next Fall to dig it up. [Mt. Diablo Letter]

We have seen something already of the relationship between Theodore Kaczynski and the author Joseph Conrad. By all accounts Kaczynski held the works of Conrad in the highest esteem, having read them more than a dozen times before reaching the age of 42. In the course of a creative lifetime spanning over three decades, Conrad's output was impressively large. Yet of all his works, undoubtedly the one most admired by Kaczynski was *The Secret Agent*, a novel first published in 1907. The significance of *The Secret Agent* in reference to the phenomenon of Ted Kaczynski cannot be overstated. A copy of the novel was found among the effects in his cabin. Kaczynski himself is on record as having advised his family to read *The Secret Agent*. In the words of Donald Foster (the literary attributionist who assisted the FBI with its analysis of Kaczynski's writings), "he seems to have felt that his family could not understand him without reading Conrad."[6] According to Foster, he identified strongly with a character in the novel known only as "the Professor."

> In his activities as the Unabomber, as also in his writings from 1967–96, Ted Kaczynski cultivated a likeness between himself and Conrad's bomb-making Professor — as in a shared preoccupation with finding the perfect detonator (a theme of the Unabom documents), and even in such personal details as taking a smug pride in an unkempt appearance.[7]

Kaczynski's identification with the character of the Professor was premised, no doubt, on the purity of the latter's motives as an anarchist, especially insofar as they jibed with Kaczynski's own attitudes and worldview. Like Kaczynski, Conrad depicts the Professor as a deeply disaffected person, filled with bitter hostility against a world that cannot appreciate and understand him:

> He was a moral agent — that was settled in his mind. By exercising his agency with ruthless defiance he procured for himself the appearances of

power and personal prestige. That was undeniable to his vengeful bitterness. It pacified its unrest; and in their own way the most ardent of revolutionaries are perhaps doing no more but seeking for peace in common with the rest of mankind — the peace of soothed vanity, of satisfied appetites, or perhaps of appeased conscience.

Similar also to Kaczynski's is the Professor's penchant for destruction. A master bomb-maker, and a perfectionist in the art, he spends both his time and scant resources in pursuit of "the perfect detonator." To prevent the possibility of arrest, he carries on his person an explosive device that can be detonated at will, should the authorities attempt to take him.

Based upon an actual event that occurred in 1895, the plot of *The Secret Agent* involves an aborted attempt to blow up the Greenwich Observatory, site of the geographical PRIME MERIDIAN. The eponymous "secret agent" is *Verloc*, purported head of a cell of London anarchists. Verloc himself is a double-agent, who reports the movements of his anarchist associates to superiors in a foreign (ostensibly Russian) embassy. Verloc's employers are unhappy with the permissiveness of the English authorities, whom they accuse of indifference toward the anarchists in their midst.

> "The vigilance of the police — and the severity of the magistrates. The general leniency of the judicial procedure here, and the utter absence of all repressive measures, are a scandal to Europe. What is wished for just now is the accentuation of the unrest — of the fermentation which undoubtedly exists."

Wishing to "stir the pot," they commission Verloc with a task of provocation. He must attack an icon of Western sensibilities. That icon will be Science, as represented by the Prime Meridian.

"The sacrosant fetish of today is science," declares Vladimir, First Secretary of the embassy. "Why don't you get some of your friends to go for that wooden-faced panjandrum — eh?"

> The features of Mr Vladimir, so well known in the best society by their humorous urbanity, beamed with cynical self-satisfaction, which would have astonished the intelligent women his wit entertained so exquisitely. "Yes," he continued, with a contemptuous smile, "the blowing up of the *first meridian* is bound to raise a howl of execration." [Author's italics]

Reluctantly accepting his assignment, Verloc approaches the Professor and solicits him to build a powerful bomb. He then enlists the assistance of a willing dupe, in the person of Stevie, the mentally retarded brother of his wife. Verloc and Stevie travel by train to Greenwich, where Verloc sets a timer and Stevie prepares to plant the bomb near the famous landmark. But he stumbles over a protruding root, and the device prematurely explodes, blowing the young man literally to bits.

The *Prime Meridian* is an imaginary line of longitude which passes through the Royal Greenwich Observatory in Greenwich, England. It is physically represented by a marker set in the courtyard of the Observatory. Its purpose is to provide a common base point for calculating geographical positions in terms of longitude.

Created in 1851, the *Mt. Diablo Meridian* was devised for the purpose of establishing land boundaries in Northern California and Nevada. The meridian and its corresponding baseline form an arbitrary starting point for the establishment of all property boundaries in those geographical areas. The Meridian itself is an imaginary line of longitude. Its point of origin is the 3,840-foot summit of Mt. Diablo, and it is physically represented by a marker beneath the floor of an Interpretive Center which sits atop the peak.

Zodiac's Mt. Diablo correspondence and the plot of *The Secret Agent* each involve an explosive device placed in proximity to a well-known, arbitrary, and clearly demarcated line of longitude. This is especially intriguing in light of the anagram for "I COMRADE V" found in the Three-Part Cipher. "Comrade V" would, of course, be Comrade Verloc — for by that name is Verloc known among his fellow revolutionaries in the Conrad tale.

> He did not go into that question, but attentive not to discourage kind fate surrendering to him the widow of *Comrade Verloc* . . . .
>
> However, Comrade Ossipon was not going to quarrel with his luck for the sake of a dead man. Resolutely he suppressed his sympathy for the ghost of *Comrade Verloc* . . . . [Author's italics]

Perhaps not coincidentally, possible hints in the Three-Part Cipher appearing as "MATH I TEACH," "HEAL," "EARN," and "I COMRADE V" may relate to the Professor (someone who *teaches*; who typically is a *Doctor*) and Comrade Verloc — both central characters in Kaczynski's favorite novel.

An additional connection to the Professor may be seen in Zodiac's bomb threat of November 11, 1969. On page six of the Seven Page Letter he warns, "it won't do to re rout & re schedule the buses because the bomb can be adapted to new conditions." This is tantalizingly similar to the observation of the Professor, that he is trying

> . . . to invent a detonator that would adjust itself to all conditions of action, and even to unexpected changes of conditions.

It is an association perhaps not surprising, considering the identification of Kaczynski with the Professor's role.

The Mt. Diablo map shows the crossed-circle centered directly over a small "x" that marks the summit of the peak, and the origin of the Mt. Diablo Meridian.

Further, the imperative that one is to align the "o" marker on the circle to "Mag. N." serves as an indicator that the Y axis on the circle is aligned to "true" north (the geographical North Pole) — in other words, that this is a true line of longitude, corresponding with the Mt. Diablo Meridian.

This revelation is significant, because it closely associates references in two Zodiac correspondences with a literary production touted by Kaczynski himself as the very essence of his identity. By using the Mt. Diablo Meridian as the focal point for the placement of a bomb, Zodiac cleverly makes allusion to *The Secret Agent* and its plot against the Prime Meridian. Moreover, as in the Conrad tale, his Mt. Diablo correspondence was clearly intended to *agitate* both the authorities and the public. Following the Stine murder, Zodiac confined his activities strictly to a bizarre campaign of letter writing, whose apparent purpose, at least through October of 1970, was to stir up the authorities and terrorize the public.

Kaczynski himself employed this pattern in his campaign as the terrorist "group" FC. It has been demonstrated that his motivation to kill was based upon a deep-seated hostility against the classes of people he envied. Far from admitting this to himself, he employed that hostility in the service of a quest to revolutionize human society, through a campaign of violent agitation and public terror. As spoken to the public through the *New York Times*:

> Our more immediate goal .... is the destruction of the worldwide industrial system. Through our bombings we hope to promote social instability in industrial society, propagate anti-industrial ideas and give encouragement to those who hate the system. [Times II Letter]

Here, Kaczynski is following the model provided by those nineteenth-century anarchists whose activities inspired Conrad to write *The Secret Agent*. His inspiration to follow that lead appears to have originated earlier in life than one might think. The Sally Johnson Psychological Report, released in 1998, relates:

> Mr. Kaczynski claimed in his writing, that during his college years he had fantasies of living a primitive life and fantasized himself as "an agitator, rousing mobs to frenzies of revolutionary violence."[8]

Showing himself thus as an agitator (as opposed to a simple killer) and associating the role with a bomb plot involving Mt. Diablo and its well-known meridian, Zodiac makes yet another literary allusion that hints of his identity. Given this association with *The Secret Agent*, it is not surprising that exactly one month after mailing the Mt. Diablo Letter, Zodiac supplied the authorities with a hint that revealed perhaps more of his intentions than was immediately apparent. To the end of his July 26, 1970 Little List Letter, he appended:

PS. The Mt. Diablo Code concerns Radians & # inches along the radians. [Mt. Diablo Letter]

The reader will note that the first three letters of the words _concerns_ _Radians_ spell _Conrad._

* * *

The Mt. Diablo correspondence yields another likely meta-code that occurs within the 32-character encryption at the bottom of the letter.

Invariably, past attempts at decrypting the unsolved Zodiac ciphers have included the obvious methodology of "plugging in" the known values from the solved Three-Part Cipher of 1969. Logic would seem to dictate that Zodiac might simply have re-used the earlier key. Attempting this technique with the Mt. Diablo encryption produces the following result:

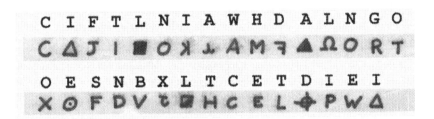

Three arbitrary changes must be effected in order to make this work. The original Three-Part Cipher contained no plaintext equivalents for the letter "C" and the characters for what we presume are the astrological symbols Aries (Λ) and Libra (Ω). For these we may logically substitute "C" for itself, "A" for Aries, and L for Libra. As can be seen in the example, the result does not appear to contain an intelligible solution. A more interesting pattern emerges, however, when one ignores the alphabetic characters in the encryption, and substitutes only for the remaining, non-alphabetic symbols:

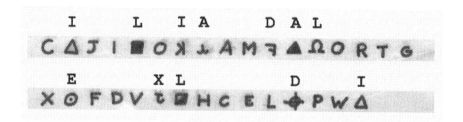

In this case our result — the contiguous letters ILIADALEXLDI — offers a far more cogent and tantalizing clue. It can be divided into three distinct segments, namely, "ILIAD," "ALEX" and "LDI." Of these three, the first two immediately strike the observer as both meaningful and related.

ILIAD, of course, is the Homeric epic which relates the story of the Trojan War — the siege and sack of Troy (Ilium) in ancient times. ALEX is equally meaningful, because it is an abbreviated form of *Alexandros*, otherwise known as Paris of Troy, whose abduction of the beautiful Helen led to the conflict which *The Iliad* relates.

What might these references portend? With its seeming allusion to the Mt. Diablo Meridian, Zodiac's Mt. Diablo Letter appears to offer clues that relate directly to geography. In that sense, ILIAD and ALEX, because they both refer to ancient Troy, might well allude to the tiny town of Troy, California, which lies to the northeast of Mt. Diablo and west of Lake Tahoe, in the Sierra Nevada mountains. Similarly, given the role of Alexandros in the abduction of Helen, one is led instinctively to the city of *Helena*, capital of Montana. In fact, an interesting relationship exists between (1) the Mt. Diablo Meridian and Baseline; (2) the city of Troy, California; and (3) the capital of Montana at Helena. By plotting their geographical coordinates on a grid, one obtains a most curious result. The following chart lists those coordinates, as taken from Microsoft's Terraserver database, available on the public Internet, and rounded to the nearest tenth of a degree:

Mt. Diablo	37.9 degrees north x -122 degrees west
Troy, California	39.3 degrees north x -120.5 degrees west
Helena, Montana	46.6 degrees north x -112 degrees west

A straight line, originating at the coordinates of Mt. Diablo, and passing through the coordinates of Troy, California, will narrowly miss passing through the city of Helena, Montana. The same line will pass *directly* through the city of Deer Lodge, and barely brush the outskirts of Great Falls, both of which are well-known cities in Montana.

The geographical coordinates of the latter cities are as follows:

| Deer Lodge, Montana | 46.3 degrees north x -112.8 degrees west |
| Great Falls, Montana | 47.5 degrees north x -111.3 degrees west |

From which may be produced this graph:

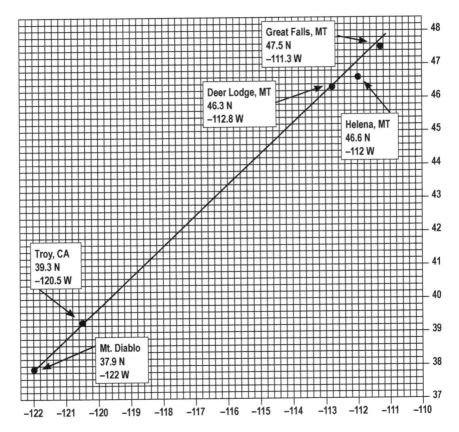

It would appear that by his allusion to Troy and the abduction of Helen, Zodiac has drawn our attention to Montana, and its cities of Deer Lodge and Great Falls. Why this should be significant must be readily apparent to any person having even the most fundamental knowledge of the Zodiac events. Deer Lodge was the name given by Zodiac to victim Bryan Hartnell as the prison from which he had escaped. Though initially confused as to the prison's name, Hartnell confirmed the reference to a Montana prison in the Robertson interview given the day after the event at Berryessa:

> B.H.   And he says, "Nah . . [.] time's running short," he says, "'cause I just got out of . . . ." — some prison in Montana. I don't know what the name of it is. Feathers? Do you know what the name of it is? I'll see if it sounds familiar. Fern or Feathers? It's some double name like Fern Lock or something . . .

> J.R.   It's Lodge . . [.]

> B.H.   Oh yeah, yeah, — Lodge. At least we know we're together on that.

> J.R.   Mountain Lodge Prison, or something of that nature . . .[9]

Constructed in 1895, the Montana State Prison at Deer Lodge was still in use when Zodiac assaulted Hartnell in 1969. Why Zodiac should have referred to Deer Lodge as the prison from which he "escaped" (no recent escapes had, in fact, been made from Deer Lodge) remains a mystery. Numerous California prisons were available to serve as the basis for such a ruse, most notably the notorious San Quentin, just north of San Francisco, and the state facility at Vacaville, approximately twenty five miles from Berryessa itself. No doubt Zodiac had Montana on his mind, and reached for the knowledge that a prison existed at Deer Lodge, when requiring a pretext to intimidate and restrain his victims.

The state of Montana has played a significant part in the life and affairs of Theodore Kaczynski. As detailed earlier, Kaczynski moved to Montana in the spring of 1971, living temporarily with his brother, who had taken a job in Great Falls at some point in the summer of the preceding year. Though one may wonder what particular fascination the state of Montana held for the Kaczynskis, the truth seems obvious on its face, in light of interviews given by David to the *New York Times* and cited in the article "Prisoner of Rage" by Robert D. McFadden in 1996:

> They drove through Saskatchewan, Alberta, British Columbia and the Yukon . . . . at summer's end they went home. *On the way, they drove through Montana, and both were struck by the state's natural beauty.*[10] [Author's italics]

This quote becomes more interesting in light of David's statement to the FBI that the Canada trip commenced when Ted met David in Wyoming and they drove to British Columbia in the elder brother's car.[11] If that is the case, a pass through Deer Lodge might well have been part of their itinerary, because Deer Lodge sits on Interstate 90, the major highway leading from Wyoming, through Montana, and westward to the Pacific Coast states and British Columbia.

Whatever the case, the fact is undeniable that the brothers were impressed by what they had seen of Montana, and must have resolved individually, if not collectively, that it would be an ideal place to live. Postmarked June 26, 1970, the Mt. Diablo Letter corresponds with the period of time in which David, following his graduation from Columbia, left Illinois and took up residence in Great Falls. Clearly, by inserting this meta-code within the Mt. Diablo encryption, Zodiac was drawing the attention of the authorities toward Montana, a place he had already alluded to in his conversation with Bryan Hartnell. The reader should be aware that by using *The Iliad* to point in the direction of Montana, Zodiac indulged in yet another allusion to a famous work of literary art.

In fact, the *Secret Agent* and *Iliad* allusions share a common trait in that each is accompanied (as suggested by the Mt. Diablo map) by a geographical reference. This not only supports their significance as actual meta-codes, but diminishes markedly the possibility that their presence is due to any other factor than deliberate design on the part of the Zodiac.

★ ★ ★

In his July 31, 1969 correspondence to the *San Francisco Chronicle*, Zodiac promised that the accompanying cipher held his "iden[t]ity." Precise to the point of pedantry, Zodiac's promise turned out, in the event, to have been correct. To those who believed "identity" to be a synonym for "name," the decrypted cipher must have proven something of a disappointment, for no name appeared that would have served to point the authorities in the direction of the killer.

Given this penchant for precision, the April 20, 1970 Bus Bomb Letter must have raised eyebrows with its line of thirteen symbols (the Thirteen-Symbol Cipher) preceded by the unambiguous assertion of "My name is —."

$$A \; E \; N \oplus \otimes K \otimes M \otimes \downarrow N \; A \; M$$

Unfortunately, a single line of thirteen characters offers scant material with which to work a solution on a cryptosystem whose nature is totally unknown.

Serendipity is the act of making fortunate discoveries by happenstance or accident. One might perceive the good luck of Donald Harden in solving the Three-Part Cipher as an instance of serendipity, given the fact that he stumbled upon its first three words as part of a wild (though educated) guess. Without that element of fortune, the Three-Part Cipher would probably never have been solved. Similarly one may assume that, barring a circumstance of serendipity at least equal to Donald Harden's, the solution to the Thirteen Symbol Cipher will never see the light of day.

Such a circumstance, however, may already have occurred. Late in 1997, while puzzling over a copy of Theodore Kaczynski's 1966 doctoral dissertation, the author found his interest excited by a single line of mathematical formulation that seemed vaguely, though indefinably, familiar:[12]

$$c \subseteq \bigcap_{n=1}^{\infty} \bigcup_{m=1}^{\infty} \bigcup_{k=1}^{\infty} \bigcup_{\ell=1}^{\infty} A(n, m, k, \ell).$$

What appeared to be most fascinating about this formulation was its uncanny similarity to the Thirteen Symbol Cipher, particularly in reference to the symbols and variables Kaczynski had used in its construction.

$$A \; E \; N \oplus \otimes K \otimes M \otimes \curlyvee N A M$$

$$C \subseteq \bigcap_{n=1}^{\infty} \bigcup_{m=1}^{\infty} \bigcup_{k=1}^{\infty} \bigcup_{\ell=1}^{\infty} A(n, \, m, \, k, \, \ell).$$

Between these two renditions, one from Zodiac and the other from Kaczynski, there exists a remarkable set of similarities. Note the variables within the Kaczynski formula, which, like the cryptogram from Zodiac, include the letter "A," two of the letter "n," two of the letter "m," and at least one "k." Note the lower-case ℓ in the former, which resembles the Aries ($\curlyvee$) symbol in the latter. Note also the circled eights, which match in meaning, if not precisely in appearance, the infinity symbols from the dissertation — not only does the symbol "∞" represent infinity, but the circle does as well, since both are objects that have neither a beginning nor an end.

The large $\cup$ symbol in the Kaczynski formulation represents the union of sets. This concept is a small part of the broad mathematical field involving the theory of *sets*, or collections of objects. Objects comprising sets can be literally anything; they need not be confined to numbers. A set may contain one object, zero objects, or an infinity of objects. Sets are generally denoted by the use of curly brackets. For instance, a set containing the elements red, green and blue would be denoted {red, green, blue}. A set containing only the element pink would by denoted {pink}.

New sets may be created by combining two or more sets through the process of set *union*, or set *addition*. The union of two sets is defined as the set of all objects that are members of one, or the other, or both. Thus, the union of a set containing the elements {red, green, blue} with a second set containing the elements {blue, pink, orange} — written {red, green, blue} $\cup$ {blue, pink, orange} — will produce a third set containing the elements {red, green, blue, pink, orange}. The union of a set containing numerals {2, 6, 8, 9, 10} with a second set containing the numerals {3, 6, 7, 9, 11} will yield a third set containing the numerals {2, 3, 6, 7, 8, 9, 10, 11}.

Given the close similarity between the Thirteen Symbol Cipher and the construction of the Kaczynski formulation, it was naturally wondered whether the simple principle of set addition might have pertained to the Zodiac encryption. The cipher consists of thirteen separate symbols; some of them alphabetic, and some of them abstractions. It was presumed that the alphabetic symbols would most likely have stood for themselves — in other words, an "A" would be an "A," a "K" would be a "K," and so forth. The abstractions themselves would have to be defined. Although the possibility for misinterpretation was real, logic dictated that the crossed-circle should stand for "ZODIAC," the circled eights for "INFINITY," and the Aries symbol for the word it represented, namely, "ARIES." Once these definitions had been decided upon, it was a simple matter to lay out each one as a set, comprising the elements of which it was composed, and add the sets together in the order in which they occurred. The following chart illustrates the result of this experiment: [See next page]

The result is a single set containing the elements {A,E,N,Z,O,D,I, C,F,T,Y,K,M,R,S}. Though it appears a jumble, it is, in fact, a perfect anagram for the three words "FROM TED KACZYNS[K]I" with only the second "k" missing from Kaczynski. This missing "k," however, is consonant with the rule regarding set addition that sets may not contain multiple copies of an element.

This solution is neither illogical, nor forced. Its credibility depends upon three factors: (1) agreement upon the meaning of the non-alphabetic symbols in the cipher; (2) the paradigm of set addition upon which it is based; and (3) the likelihood that the name TED KACZYNS[K]I may result in the final set by chance alone. One circumstance that may work some influence upon the third factor is the curious fact that the word "Zodiac" contains five of the letters found in "Ted Kaczynski." In fact, the name "Theodore Kaczynski" contains all the letters found in the words "the Zodiac," while each and every one of the letters in "the Zodiac," is found in "Theodore Kaczynski." Further, the salutation "the Zodiac speaking" contains every letter in "Ted Kaczynski" with the exception of a "y." Only three letters, "h," "p" and "g" are superfluous. For Zodiac, with his teasing ways, such possibilities might well have proven too tempting to resist.

$\{A\} \cup \{E\}$	$=$	$\{A,E\}$
$\{A,E\} \cup \{N\}$	$=$	$\{A,E,N\}$
$\{A,E,N\} \cup \{Z,O,D,I,A,C\}$	$=$	$\{A,E,N,Z,O,D,I,C\}$
$\{A,E,N,Z,O,D,I,C\} \cup \{I,N,F,I,N,I,T,Y\}$	$=$	$\{A,E,N,Z,O,D,I,C,F,T,Y\}$
$\{A,E,N,Z,O,D,I,C,F,T,Y\} \cup \{K\}$	$=$	$\{A,E,N,Z,O,D,I,C,F,T,Y,K\}$
$\{A,E,N,Z,O,D,I,C,F,T,Y,K\} \cup \{I,N,F,I,N,I,T,Y\}$	$=$	$\{A,E,N,Z,O,D,I,C,F,T,Y,K\}$
$\{A,E,N,Z,O,D,I,C,F,T,Y,K\} \cup \{M\}$	$=$	$\{A,E,N,Z,O,D,I,C,F,T,Y,K,M\}$
$\{A,E,N,Z,O,D,I,C,F,T,Y,K,M\} \cup \{I,N,F,I,N,I,T,Y\}$	$=$	$\{A,E,N,Z,O,D,I,C,F,T,Y,K,M\}$
$\{A,E,N,Z,O,D,I,C,F,T,Y,K,M\} \cup \{A,R,I,E,S\}$	$=$	$\{A,E,N,Z,O,D,I,C,F,T,Y,K,M,R,S\}$
$\{A,E,N,Z,O,D,I,C,F,T,Y,K,M,R,S\} \cup \{N\}$	$=$	$\{A,E,N,Z,O,D,I,C,F,T,Y,K,M,R,S\}$
$\{A,E,N,Z,O,D,I,C,F,T,Y,K,M,R,S\} \cup \{A\}$	$=$	$\{A,E,N,Z,O,D,I,C,F,T,Y,K,M,R,S\}$
$\{A,E,N,Z,O,D,I,C,F,T,Y,K,M,R,S\} \cup \{M\}$	$=$	$\{A,E,N,Z,O,D,I,C,F,T,Y,K,M,R,S\}$

This is a message from the terrorist group FC. To prove its authenticity we give our identifying number (to be kept secret): 553-25-4394.

We blew up Thomas Mosser last December because he was a Burston-Marsteller executive. Among other misdeeds, Burston-Marsteller helped Exxon clean up its public image after the Exxon Valdez incident. But we attacked Burston-Marsteller less for its specific misdeeds than on general principles. Burston-Marsteller is about the biggest organization in the public relations field. This means that its business is the development of techniques for manipulating people's attitudes. It was for this more than for its actions in specific cases that we sent a bomb to an executive of this company.

Some news reports have made the misleading statement that we have been attacking universities or scholars. We have nothing against universities or scholars as such. All the university people whom we have attacked have been specialists in <u>technical fields</u>. (We consider certain areas of applied psychology, such as behavior modification, to be technical fields.) We would not want anyone to think that we have any desire to hurt professors who study archaeology, history, literature or harmless stuff like that. The people we are out to get are the scientists and engineers, especially in critical fields like computers and genetics. As for the bomb planted in the Business School at the U. of Utah, that was a botched operation. We won't say how or why it was botched because we don't want to give the FBI any clues. No one was hurt by that bomb.

In our previous letter to you we called ourselves anarchists. Since "anarchist" is a vague word that has been applied to a variety of attitudes, further explanation is needed. We call ourselves anarchists because we would like, ideally, to break down all society into very small, completely autonomous units. Regrettably, we don't see any clear road to this goal, so we leave it to the indefinite future. Our more immediate goal, which we think may be attainable at some time during the next several decades, is the destruction of the worldwide industrial system. Through our bombings we hope to promote social instability in industrial society, propagate anti-industrial ideas and give encouragement to those who hate the industrial system.

The FBI has tried to portray these bombings as the work of an isolated nut. We won't waste our time arguing about whether we are nuts, but we certainly are not isolated. For security reasons we won't reveal the number of members of our group, but anyone who will read the anarchist and radical environmentalist journals will see that opposition to the industrial-technological system is widespread and growing.

Why do we announce our ~~goals~~ goals only now, though we made our first bomb some seventeen years ago? Our early bombs were too ineffectual to attract much public attention or give encouragement to those who hate the system. We found by experience that gunpowder bombs, if small enough to be carried inconspicuously, were too feeble to do much damage, so we took a couple of years off to do some experimenting. We learned how to make pipe bombs that were powerful enough, and we used these in a couple of successful bombings as well as in some unsuccessful ones. Unfortunately we discovered that these bombs would not detonate <u>consistently</u> when made with three-quarter inch steel water pipe. They did seem to detonate consistently when made with massively reinforced one inch steel water pipe, but a bomb of this type made a long, heavy package, too conspicuous and suspicious looking for our liking.

So we went back to work, and after a long period of experimentation we developed a type of bomb that does not require a pipe, but is set off by a detonating cap that consists of a chlorate explosive packed into a piece of small diameter copper tubing. (The detonating cap is a miniature pipe bomb.) We used bombs of this type to blow up the genetic engineer Charles Epstein and the computer specialist David Gelernter. We did use a chlorate pipe bomb to blow up Thomas Mosser because we happened to have a piece of lightweight aluminum pipe that was just right for the job. The Gelernter and Epstein bombings were not fatal, but the Mosser bombing was fatal even though a smaller amount of explosive was used. We think this was because the type of fragmentation material that we used in the Mosser bombing is more effective ~~than~~ than what we've used previously.

Since we no longer have to confine the explosive in a pipe, we are now

Draft of the Times II Letter, found by authorities in Kaczynski's Montana shack.

Chapter 10

The Elements of Style

Give me thy glove, soldier: look, here is the fellow of it.

SHAKESPEARE, *Henry V*

PERHAPS THE MOST illustrative comparisons between the Unabomber and the Zodiac may be found among the voluminous writings of the former and the handful of correspondences attributable to the latter. Comparisons of tone and style, as they are presented here, must not be taken as examples of formal linguistic analysis or forensic literary attribution. They are given as examples of similarities that immediately strike the eye as singular in the closeness of their wording and the meanings which their authors are attempting to convey. Naturally, the most compelling of these will be found between correspondences whose context is the same — namely, in letters presented by their authors as communications to the media in furtherance of their criminal schemes. In the case of Zodiac, these are the only examples with which we have to work. Because he is a known quantity, the same cannot be said of Kaczynski, whose written works are both numerous and widely-available, though only a small fraction are accessible to the public. In reference to the following examples, it should be noted that effort was made to confine the comparisons to samples taken from writings attributable to Kaczynski *as the Unabomber*. In some cases, however, this was neither possible nor desirable.

None of the examples presented here are exclusive to their authors. It is a common mistake to believe that comparisons of this nature become invalid if it can be shown that the usages in question have been employed by persons other than the suspected individual — even in instances where the usages are relatively rare. For example, the defense in *United States* v. *Kaczynski* were prepared to contend that Kaczynski's use of the proverb "eat your cake and have it too" (a variant of the more customary "have your cake and eat it too") was not admissible as grounds for having placed their client under suspicion because other people, among them historical figures, had used the same construction. This line of reasoning was disingenuous, to say the least. It was disingenuous because the comparison was not between Kaczynski and the entire English-speaking population of the world, but rather, between Kaczynski and a small subset of that population comprising individuals who not only spent their time producing bombs, and visiting the areas where the Unabomber had plied his trade, but kept elaborate coded journals containing detailed accounts relating to the bombs and crimes — a very tiny subset to be sure.

"What you are saying," sneered a critic who had seen the comparisons presented below, "is that Kaczynski is the Zodiac because he started a sentence with the word 'so.'" Of course this is not the case at all. What is being implied is that such a usage is sufficiently unusual among the set of individuals who (1) have murdered; (2) bear a common emotional pathology based on sexual frustration; (3) accompanied their criminal acts with correspondences to major news media demanding publicity for themselves on pain of further killing; and (4) used the credibility fostered by their murders to commit large-scale acts of public terrorism, to narrow that set into an even smaller subset. If even as many as 75 percent of individuals in the general population were known to begin their sentences with "so," it would shrink the existing subset of sexually frustrated, publicity-seeking, terror-inducing killers by 25 percent — a not-inconsiderable figure, considering the relatively small size of the set comprised merely of those who kill.

With that in mind, the following comparisons are presented:

Zodiac
- *To prove* this I shall state *some facts* which only I & the police know. [Times-Herald Letter]

- *To prove* I killed them I shall state *some facts* which only I & the police know. [Chronicle Letter]

- . . . *to prove* this here is a *blood stained piece of his shirt*. [Stine Letter]

- *To prove* that I am the Zodiac, Ask the Vallejo cop about my *electric gun sight* . . . . [Seven-Page Letter]

Kaczynski
- *To prove* that we are the ones who planted the bomb at U. Of Cal. last May we will mention *a few details* that could be known only to us and the FBI who investigated the incident. [1985 Examiner Letter]

- This is a message from the terrorist group FC. *To prove* its authenticity we give our *identifying number* . . . . [Times III Letter]

- *To prove* that the writer of this letter knows something about FC, the first two digits of their *identifying number* are 55. [Chronicle Threat Letter]

- To prove that this letter does come from FC, we quote below the *entire fourth paragraph of a letter* that we are sending to the New York Times. [Scientific American Letter]

Remarks: Both killers are anxious *to prove* their bona fides to the authorities and offer objective proof of their complicity in the crimes, consisting of facts, details, identifying numbers and, in the Stine case, an actual piece of the victim's shirt. *To prove* is a formulation common to both authors.

Zodiac
- I am the killer of the 2 teenagers last christmass at Lake Herman & the girl last 4th of July. *To prove* this *I shall state some facts which only I & the police know.* [Examiner I Letter]

Kaczynski
- *To prove* that we are the ones who planted the bomb at U. Of Cal. last May *we will mention a few details that could be known only to us and the FBI who investigated the incident.* [1985 Examiner Letter]

Remarks: The formulation here is that *to prove* [the commission of a crime], the killer will relate information known only to [himself] and [the authorities]. Note the placement of the personal pronoun *before* the proper noun, i.e., "us and the FBI," and "I and the police." Both these quotes were contained in the first correspondences sent by the respective killers. Each letter was mailed to the *San Francisco Examiner.*

Zodiac
- Here is a cyipher or *that is* part of one. [Times-Herald Letter]

- Here is a cipher or *that is* part of one. [Examiner I Letter]

Kaczynski
- When I was living in the woods, there was sort of an undertone, an underlying feeling that things were basically right with my life. *That is,* I might have a bad day, I might screw something up, I might break my ax handle and do something else and everything would go wrong.[1]

- But we think that for the majority of people an activity whose main goal is fulfillment (*that is,* a surrogate activity) does not bring completely satisfactory fulfillment. [Manifesto]

- A new kind of society cannot be designed on paper. *That is,* you cannot plan out a new form of society in advance, then set it up and expect it to function as it was designed to. [Manifesto]

- By that time it will have to have solved, or at least brought under control, the principal problems that confront it, in particular that of "socializing" human beings; *that is,* making people sufficiently docile so that their behavior no longer threatens the system. [Manifesto]

- As we explained in paragraphs 87–90, technicians and scientists carry on their work largely as a surrogate activity; *that is,* they satisfy their need for power by solving technical problems. [Manifesto]

- The positive ideal that we propose is Nature. *That is,* WILD nature . . . . [Manifesto]

Remarks: Kaczynski's repeated use of the term *that is* in lieu of the more formal "i.e." Zodiac uses the same construction twice.

Zodiac
- In that *epasode* the police were wondering as to how I could shoot & hit my victims in the dark. [Examiner II Letter]

Kaczynski
- So the whole thing was an embarrassing farce, and I think I left her imagining that I was going to die or something. Well, never mind that stupid *episode* anyway. [Exhibits]

Remarks: Use of the word *episode* to describe an extraordinary event.

Zodiac
- *This is* the murderer of the 2 teenagers last Christmass . . . . [Chronicle Letter]

- *This is* the Zodiac speaking. [Most correspondences]

Kaczynski
- *This is* a message from the terrorist group FC. [Times II Letter]

- *This is* a message from FC. [Tyler Letter]

- *This is* a letter from FC, 553-25-4394. [Times II Letter]

Remarks: The authors introduce themselves and their correspondences by a formal announcement beginning with the words *"this is."*

Zodiac
- I shall (*on top of* every thing else) torture all 13 of my slaves that I have wateing for me in Paradice. [Mikado Letter]

Kaczynski
- *On top of* these, I attached on the side of the pipe with strapping tape a layer of small nails. *On top of* everything I wrapped the pipe with friction tape . . . . [Exhibits]

Remarks: *On top of* meaning "in addition to."

Zodiac
- I hope you enjoy your selves when I have my *Blast*. [Dragon Card]

- If you dont want me to have this *blast* . . . . [Dragon Card]

- . . . & will positivily ventalate any thing that should be in the way of the *Blast*. [Seven-Page Letter]

Kaczynski
- For these reasons, I want to get my revenge in one big *blast*. [Exhibits]

Remarks: Reference to a bombing event as a *blast*.

Zodiac
- At the moment the children are safe from the bomb because it is so massive to dig in & the *triger mech* requires much work to get it adjusted just right. [Belli Letter]

Kaczynski
- Its no fun having to spend all your evenings and weekends preparing dangerous mixtures, filing *trigger mechanisms* out of scraps of metal . . . . [Times II Letter]

Remarks: Bomb components described as *triger mech* or *mechanisms*. In each case the author complains about the difficulties involved in working with the trigger mechanism.

Zodiac
- I gave the cops som *bussy work* to do to keep them happy. [Seven-Page Letter]

Kaczynski
- This seems to us a thoroughly contemptible way for the human race to end up, and we doubt that many people would find fulfilling lives in such pointless *busy-work*. [Manifesto]

Remarks: None.

Zodiac
- It is more fun than killing wild game in the forrest because man is the most *dangerou[s] anamal* of all. To kill something gives me the *most thrilling* exper[i]ence. [Three-Part Cipher]

Kaczynski
- I drove up to Humboldt county for deer hunting . . . . deer hunting is *very exciting*. [Turchie]

- He knew how to protect himself from heat, cold, rain, *dangerous animals*, etc. [Manifesto]

Remarks: Association of hunting with emotional excitement or satisfaction. Use of the term "dangerous animals." The "Humboldt" quote is from the period 1967–1969.

Zodiac
- What you do not know is whether the death machiene is at the sight or whether it is being stored *in my basement* for future use. [Seven-Page Letter]

Kaczynski
- For example, it will not be physically possible for everyone to have his own full-scale computer *in his basement* to which he can link his brain. [1971 Essay]

Remarks: Use of *in [his] basement* as an abstraction signifying a storage place where one can place a large object. In both these instances, use of the term is superfluous — unneeded to convey the meaning of the sentence.

Zodiac
- I want you *to print* this cipher . . . . [Chronicle Letter]

- PS could you *print* this new cipher . . . ? [Dripping Pen Card]

- *Be shure to print* the part I marked out on page 3 . . . . [Seven-Page Letter]

Kaczynski
- We encourage you to *print* this letter. [Times II Letter]
- Our promise to desist will not take effect until all parts of our article or book have appeared in *print*. [Times II Letter]
- *Be sure* to tell us where and how our material will be published and how long it will take to appear in *print* . . . . [Times II Letter]
- This letter which we invite you to *print* in Scientific American . . . . [Scientific American Letter]

Remarks: Use of the word *print* in conjunction with a demand for publication in the newspaper media. Use of the admonition *be sure* in association with the demand to print.

Zodiac
- The S.F. Police could have caught me last night if they had searched the park properly instead of holding road races with their *motor cicles* seeing who could make the most *noise*. The car drivers should have just parked their cars & sat there *quietly* waiting for me to come out of cover. [Stine Letter]

Kaczynski
- For example, a variety of *noise-making* devices: power mowers, radios, *motorcycles*, etc. If the use of these devices is unrestricted, people who want *peace and quiet* are frustrated by the *noise*. [Manifesto]
- When I see a *motorcyclist* tearing up the mountain meadows . . . I want to kick him in the face while he is dying. [Exhibits]
- At the end of Summer '75 after the roaring by of *motorcycles* near my camp spoiled a hike for me, I put a piece of wire across a trail where cycle-tracks were visible, at about neck height for a *motorcyclist*.[2]

Remarks: Kaczynski's hatred of *noise*, particularly from *motorcycles*, is well-known and documented. In this example, Zodiac not only remarks upon the motorcycles, but feels constrained to register a complaint about their noise in the form of a sardonic jibe.

Zodiac
- I like killing people because it is so much *fun*. [Three-Part Cipher]

- I was in this phone booth haveing some *fun* with the Vallejo cop when he was walking by. [Examiner II Letter]

- Have *fun*!! By the way it could be rather messy if you try to bluff me. [Seven-Page Letter]

- PS I hope you have *fun* trying to figure out who I killed[.] [Cid Letter]

- Yes I shall have great *fun* inflicting the most delicious of pain to my Slaves. [Mikado Letter]

Kaczynski
- At first he will have a lot of *fun*, but by and by he will become acutely bored and demoralized. [Manifesto]

- [I]t's more *fun* to watch the entertainment put out by the media than to read a sober essay. [Manifesto]

- Its no *fun* having to spend all your evenings and weekends preparing dangerous mixtures . . . . [Times II Letter]

Remarks: The concept of *fun* appears to carry great significance for the authors. Kaczynski lamented the pressure put upon individuals, particularly children, to sacrifice natural pursuits in favor of educational conformity. In the *Manifesto* he writes: "It isn't natural for an adolescent human being to spend the bulk of his time sitting at a desk absorbed in study. A normal adolescent wants to spend his time in active contact with the real world . . . . Among the American Indians, for example, boys were trained in active outdoor pursuits — just the sort of things that boys like. But in our society children are pushed into studying technical subjects, which most do grudgingly."

Zodiac
- *So* I shall change the way the collecting of slaves. [Seven-Page Letter]

- *So* as you can see the police don't have much to work on. [Seven-Page Letter]

- *So* I now have a little list . . . . [Little List Letter]

Kaczynski
- *So* we expect to be able to pack deadly bombs into . . . more harmless looking packages. [Times II Letter]

- *So* we offer a bargain. [Times II Letter]

- *So* if you take the trouble to read our manuscript . . . . [Tyler Letter]

- *So* we are left with the question: What kind of legislative program would have a chance of saving freedom? [1971 Essay]
- *So* certain artificial needs have been created . . . . [Manifesto]
- *So* modern man's drive for security tends . . . . [Manifesto]
- *So* they always feel hard-pressed financially . . . . [Manifesto]
- *So* we present these principles . . . . [Manifesto]
- *So* they send him to Sylvan. [Manifesto]

Remarks: Beginning of a sentence with the coordinating conjunction *so.* Not necessarily an anomaly, but Kaczynski was known to have been a pedant grammatically.

Zodiac
- I shall (on top of every thing else) *torture* all 13 of my slaves that I have wateing for me in Paradice. Some I shall tie over ant hills and watch them scream & twich and squirm. Others shall have pine splinters driven under their nails & then burned. Others shall be placed in cages & fed salt beef untill they are gorged then I shall listen to their pleass for water and I shall laugh at them. Others will hang by their thumbs & burn in the sun then I will rub them down deep heat to warm them up. Others I shall skin them alive & let them run around screaming. [Mikado Letter]

Kaczynski
- I hadn't previously been troubled by rats around here, but I just discovered that my pack has been chewed up so badly that it is nearly ruined . . . This means some deadfalls are going to be set. I hope I catch one of those [expletive] alive — I will *torture* it to death in the most fiendish manner I can devise.[3]

Remarks: *Torture* as a means of emotional gratification.

Zodiac
- As of yet I have left no fingerprints behind me *contrary to what the police say.* [Seven-Page Letter]

Kaczynski
- *Contrary to what the FBI has suggested*, our bombing at the California Forestry Association was in no way inspired by the Oklahoma City bombing. [Times III Letter]

- By the way, *contrary to statements made by the FBI,* the[s]e are not pipe bombs (except in the case of the Mosser bombing). [Penthouse Letter]

Remarks: The formulation is that *contrary to* [some statement made by the authorities] the author has not acted in some alleged way.

Zodiac
- All it *is is* 2 coats of airplane cement coated on my finger tips. [Seven-Page Letter]

Kaczynski
- It seems to me that what boredom mostly *is is* that people have to keep themselves entertained . . . .[4]

Remarks: While not incorrect grammatically, the double *is* comprises an unusual construction for an individual with Kaczynski's grammatical abilities.

Zodiac
- *By the way,* are the police haveing a good time with the code? [Examiner II Letter]

- *By the way* it could be rather messy if you try to bluff me. [Seven-Page Letter]

- *By the way* have you cracked the last cipher I sent you? [Dripping Pen Card]

Kaczynski
- *By the way,* contrary to statements made by the FBI, the[s]e are not pipe bombs except in the case of the Mosser bombing. [Times II Letter]

- *By the way,* when we mention depression we do not necessarily mean depression that is severe enough to be treated by a psychiatrist. [Manifesto]

- *By the way,* my reason for keeping these notes separate from the others is the obvious one. [Exhibits]

Remarks: *By the way* as an informal means of introducing a topic.

Zodiac
- At the moment the children are safe from the bomb because it is so *massive* to dig in . . . . [Belli Letter]

Kaczynski
- Any of the foregoing symptoms can occur in any society, but in modern industrial society they are present on a *massive* scale. [Manifesto]

- It would be possible to give other examples of societies in which there has been rapid change and/or lack of close community ties without he kind of *massive* behavioral aberration that is seen in today's industrial society. [Manifesto]

- To the average man the results would appear disastrous: There would be *massive* unemployment, shortages of commodities, etc. [Manifesto]

- . . . accumulating nuclear waste for which a sure method of disposal has not yet been found, the crowding, noise and pollution that have followed industrialization, *massive* extinction of species and so forth. [1971 Essay]

Remarks: *Massive*, meaning large-scale, or unwieldy.

Zodiac
- I promised to *punish* them if they did not comply, by anilating a full School Buss. But now school is out for the summer, so I *punished* them in another way. [Mt. Diablo Letter]

Kaczynski
- The people who are pushing all this growth and progress garbage deserve to be severely *punished*. But our goal is less to *punish* them than to propagate ideas. [Manifesto]

Remarks: These examples express a desire on the part of their authors to *punish* particular classes of individuals who have roused their ire.

Zodiac
- I was *swamped* out by the rain we had a while back. [Cid Letter]

Kaczynski
- . . . but what he has to say will be *swamped* by the vast volume of material put out by the media . . . . [Manifesto]

- . . . such a change either would be a transitory one — soon *swamped* by the tide of history. [Manifesto]

Remarks: None.

Zodiac
- *In answer to* your asking for more details . . . . [Examiner II Letter]

Kaczynski
- *In answer to* your request for information, I am sending you herewith . . . .[5]

Remarks: *In answer to* used as the preface to a specific reply.

Zodiac
- In answer to your asking for more *details* .... [Examiner II Letter]
- Tell every one about the bus bomb, with all the *details*. [Dragon Card]

Kaczynski
- To prove that we are the ones who planted the bomb at U. Of Cal. last May we will mention a few *details* .... [Examiner Letter 1985]

Remarks: *Details* used in the sense of "individual parts."

Zodiac
- ... I shall be very happy to supply even more *material*. [Examiner II Letter]

Kaczynski
- Whoever agrees to publish the *material* will have exclusive rights .... (If *material* is serialized, first instalment becomes public property ....) .... We must have the right to publish ... three thousand words expanding or clarifying our *material* or rebutting criticisms of it .... Be sure to tell us where and how our *material* will be published .... [Times II Letter]
- ... swamped by the vast volume of *material* put out by the media .... [Manifesto]
- ... flooded by the mass of *material* to which the media expose them .... [Manifesto]
- ... implicitly expressed or presupposed in most of the *material* presented to us .... [Manifesto]
- ... Whoever agrees to publish the *material* will have exclusive rights to reproduce it for a period of six months .... (If *material* is serialized, first instalment becomes public property .... [Times II Letter]

Remarks: *Material* used in the sense of "written matter." Four examples occur in two paragraphs of a single Unabomber missive.

Zodiac
- School children make nice targets, I think I shall *wipe out* a school bus some morning .... [Stine Letter]

- I hope you do not think that I was the one who *wiped out* that blue meannie . . . . [Cid Letter]

Kaczynski
- Even if every fast-food chain the world were *wiped out* the techno-industrial system would suffer only minimal harm . . . .[6]

- . . . the continued development of biotechnology will transform their way of life and *wipe out* age-old human values.[7]

Remarks: *Wipe(d) out* in the sense of "to destroy."

Zodiac
- [B]us *goes bang* car passes by ok . . . . [Seven-Page Letter]

Kaczynski
- The rifle *goes BANG.* You're dead . . . .[8]

Remarks: Loud events characterized as "going bang."

Zodiac
- By the way it could be *rather messy* if you try to bluff me. [Seven-Page Letter]

Kaczynski
- The lemma can be proved by using [7, Theorem 113, p. 216], [1, Theorem 2, p. 179], and the methods of [3], but this involves a *messy* construction, so we omit the details.[9]

- A special case of Theorem (b) was proved (in effect) in [6, proof of Theorem 6] by means of a *rather messy* lemma.[10]

Remarks: A peculiar usage for Kaczynski, given the rigidly formal nature of mathematical writing. All three quotes made their appearance in 1969.

Zodiac
- I want you to print this cipher on the frunt page of your paper. In this cipher is my *iden[t]ity.* [Chronicle Letter]

Kaczynski
- Right now we only want to establish our *identity* . . . . [Examiner Letter 1985]

Remarks: *Identity* used in the sense of "the collective aspect of the set of characteristics by which a thing is definitively recognizable or known." Used by both authors in introductions to the media.

Zodiac
- Because the longer they *fiddle* & fart around, the more slaves I will collect for my after life. [L.A. Times Letter]

Kaczynski
- He would go to the blackboard and hem and haw and *fiddle* around . . . .[11]

- He *fiddled* around on the blackboard for a full half an hour before he finally admitted that he didn't know the answer.[12]

Remarks: *Fiddle* is used in the sense of dawdling or wasting time.

Zodiac
- To prove that I am the Zodiac *Ask the Vallejo cop* about my electric gun sight which I used to start my collecting of slaves. [Seven-Page Letter]

Kaczynski
- *Ask the FBI* about FC. They have heard of us. [Times Letter]

- P.S. *Warren Hoge of the New York Times can confirm* that this letter does come from FC. [Gelernter Letter]

- *Warren Hoge of the New York Times can confirm* that this note does come from FC. [Sharp Letter]

- *Warren Hoge of the New York Times can confirm* that this note does come from FC. [Phillips Letter]

Remarks: Both authors refer to a third party for confirmation of their identities. In one case each, a newspaper editor is requested to direct his inquiry to a law enforcement agent ("Vallejo cop") or agency ("the FBI").

Zodiac
- [M]y killing tools have been boughten through the mail order outfits before *the ban* went into efect. [E]xcept one & it was bought out of the state. [Seven-Page Letter]

Kaczynski
- The stricter *gun control laws* recommended by the U.S. Commission on Violence are a case in point. [Turchie]

Remarks: These examples demonstrate an awareness of contemporary gun control legislation on the part of both authors. Both were penned late in 1969. The Gun Control Act of 1968 prohibited direct mail order of firearms by consumers. The Act was an offshoot of recommendations made by President Johnson's National Commission on Violence, cited by Kaczynski in 1969.

Zodiac
- I hope you do not think that I was the one who wiped out that blue meannie with a bomb at the cop station . . . . It

just wouldnt doo to move in on someone elses teritory. [Cid Letter]

Kaczynski
- Contrary to what the FBI has suggested, our bombing at the California Forestry Association was in no way inspired by the Oklahoma City bombing. We strongly deplore the kind of indiscriminate slaughter that occurred in the Oklahoma City event. [Times II Letter]

- We strongly deplore the kind of indiscriminate slaughter that occurred in the Oklahoma City event. [Scientific American Letter]

Remarks: Both authors go out of their way to deny responsibility for a major bombing event. The Unabomber denial refers to the bombing of the Alfred P. Murrah Federal Building on April 20, 1995, which preceded the California Forestry Association bombing by five days. Zodiac's denial refers to the February 16, 1970 bombing of the Golden Gate Park police station, which injured five policemen and killed officer Brian McDonnell.

Zodiac
- Are the police haveing a good time with the code? [Examiner II Letter]

- The S.F. Police could have caught me last night if they had searched the park properly instead of holding road races with their motorcicles. [Stine Letter]

- The police shall never catch me, because I have been too clever for them. [Seven-Page Letter]

- I gave the cops som bussy work to do to keep them happy. [Seven-Page Letter]

- Hey blue pig, I was in the park . . . . [Seven-Page Letter]

- Hey pig, doesn't it rile you up to have you noze rubed in your booboos? [Seven-Page Letter]

- If you cops think Im going to take on a bus the way I stated I was, you deserve to have holes in your heads. [Seven-Page Letter]

- If the Blue Meannies are evere going to catch me they had best get off their fat asses & do something. Because the longer they fiddle & fart around, the more slaves I will collect for my after life. [L.A. Times Letter]

Kaczynski
- Clearly we are in a position to do a great deal of damage. And it doesn't appear that the FBI is going to catch us any time soon. The FBI is a joke. [Times II Letter]

- For an agency that pretends to be the world's greatest law enforcement agency, the FBI seems surprisingly incompetent. They can't even keep elementary facts straight. [Times III Letter]

- The FBI's theory that we have some kind of a fascination with wood is about as silly as it gets. [Times III Letter]

- The FBI must really be getting desperate if they resort to theories as ridiculous as this one about the supposed fascination with wood. [Times III Letter]

- The FBI's so-called experts should have been able to determine this quickly and easily, especially because we indicated in an unpublished part of our last letter to the NY times that the majority of our bombs are no longer pipe bombs. [Times III Letter]

Remarks: These specimens demonstrate the need of both authors to taunt the authorities investigating their respective cases. They rally the authorities on their incompetence, in language that is surprisingly understated, considering that the authors each have undisputed control of the forum — "pig" is the harshest epithet that the Zodiac can find to hurl at the police. Both make statements to the effect that they will not soon be "caught."

Zodiac
- The death machiene is already made. I would have sent you pictures but you would be nasty enough to trace them back to developer & then to me . . . . [Seven-Page Letter]

Kaczynski
- We apologize for sending you such a poor carbon copy of our manuscript. We can't make copies at a public copy machine because people would get suspicious if they saw us handling our copies with gloves.   [Tyler Letter]

Remarks: These two comments are exceedingly similar in tone. Each offers an excuse for an omission which has been occasioned by the need for caution on the author's part. They show each author's awareness of the need to thwart investigation, as well as demonstrating the author's cleverness in avoiding detection. Neither statement is necessary to further its author's goals.

Zodiac   • . . . he has a *serious psychological disorder* . . . . [Count Marco Letter]

Kaczynski   • During the Victorian period many oversocialized people suffered from *serious psychological problems* as a result of repressing or trying to repress their sexual feelings. [Manifesto]

                  • Such a man has power, but he will develop *serious psychological problems*. [Manifesto]

                  • Thus, in order to avoid *serious psychological problems*, a human being needs goals whose attainment requires effort . . . . [Manifesto]

Remarks: Despite his hatred of the psychological professions, Kaczynski spilled much ink in his discussions of the psychological problems suffered by individuals in consequence of modern technology. *Serious psychological disorder* and *serious psychological problems* are virtually identical phrasings. NB: The Count Marco Letter is not a fully authenticated Zodiac correspondence.

Zodiac   • [T]he system checks out from one end to the other in my *tests*. [Seven-Page Letter]

Kaczynski   • . . . searching the Sierras for a place isolated enough to *test* a bomb. [Times II Letter]

Remarks: Both authors feel compelled to imply that their devices have been *tested*. This lends credibility to their threats.

Zodiac   • *Sierra* Club. [Pines Card]

Kaczynski   • . . . searching the *Sierras* . . . . [Times II Letter]

Remarks: Kaczynski's reference to the Sierras appears to have been a red herring, designed to reinforce the authorities' notion that he lived in Northern California. The single line "Sierra Club" from Zodiac's Pines Card might well have served the same purpose. It led many to believe that Donna Lass's body would be found in the Sierras.

Zodiac   • I am the killer of the 2 teenagers last Christmass at Lake Herman and the Girl last 4th of July. [Times-Herald Letter]

- This is the murderer of the 2 teenagers last Christmass at Lake Herman & the girl on the 4th of July near the golf course in Vallejo. [Chronicle Letter]

- I am the killer of the 2 teenagers last Christmass at Lake Herman and the Girl last 4th of July. [Examiner Letter]

- I also killed those kids last year. [Slover Call]

- I want to report a murder. No, a double murder. [Slaight Call]

- I am the murderer of the taxi driver over by Washington St & Maple St last night ... I am the same man who did in the people in the north bay area. [Stine Letter]

Kaczynski

- We blew up Thomas Mosser last December because he was a Burston-Marsteller executive. [Times II Letter]

- The idea was to kill a lot of business people who we assumed would constitute the majority of the passengers .... [Times II Letter]

- We have no regret about the fact that our bomb blew up the "wrong" man .... [Times III Letter]

- The bomb that crippled the right arm of a graduate student in electrical engineering and damaged a computer lab at U. Of Cal. Berkeley last May was planted by a terrorist group called Freedom Club .... [1985 Examiner Letter]

- We are also responsible for some earlier bombing attempts; among others ... the fire bomb planted at the Business School of the U. Of Utah, which never went off. [1985 Examiner Letter]

Remarks: Both authors readily admit to their criminal activities, in plain language, with no attempt to paper over or euphemize the nature of what they have done. Kaczynski's "[w]e are also responsible for some earlier bombing attempts" is similar in tone and purpose to Zodiac's "I also killed those kids last year."

Zodiac

- School children make nice targets, I think I shall wipe out a school bus some morning. Just shoot out the front tire & then pick off the kiddies as they come bouncing out. [Stine Letter]

- If you cops think Im going to take on a bus the way I stated I was, you deserve to have holes in your heads. [Seven-Page Letter]

Kaczynski
- WARNING. The terrorist group FC, called unabomber by the FBI, is planning to blow up an airliner out of Los Angeles International Airport some time during the next six days. [Chronicle Threat Letter]

- Note. Since the public has a short memory we decided to play one last prank to remind them who we are. But no, we haven't tried to plant a bomb on an airliner (recently). [Times IV Letter]

Remarks: Both authors threaten mass murder involving public transportation, before later retracting the threats in a wry, or joking manner. These threats caused great public consternation at the time they were announced, leading to costly, large-scale efforts to protect school children and airline passengers from the depredations of the respective killers. Each threat letter was mailed to the *San Francisco Chronicle*.

Zodiac
- I look like the description passed out *only* when I do my thing . . . . [Seven-Page Letter]

Kaczynski
- Also, our discussion is meant to apply to modern leftism *only*. [Manifesto]

- . . . while oversocialization is characteristic *only* of a certain segment of modern leftism . . . . [Manifesto]

- He can feel strong *only* as a member of a large organization . . . . [Manifesto]

- In other words, it can express itself *only* in superficial matters . . . . [Manifesto]

- We claim *only* to have indicated very roughly the two most important tendencies . . . . [Manifesto]

- Casting a vote requires *only* a casual commitment, not a strenuous application of willpower. [1971 Essay]

Remarks: Correct placement of the word *only*.

Zodiac
- *If you notice*, in the center of the beam of light if you *aim* it at a wall or ceiling *you will see* a black or darck spot in the

center of the circle of light aprox 3 to 6 in. across. [Examiner II Letter]

Kaczynski   • Just *check* a street map of any suburban area *and see how many* of the street names include as a component either the name of some species of tree or a word such as "wood," "forest," "arbor," "grove" etc. [Times II Letter]

Remarks: Both killers instruct their readers to perform a practical exercise in order to demonstrate the points they wish to make. The instructions are highly didactic in tone.

Zodiac   • When I committ my murders, they shall look like routine robberies, killings of anger, & a few fake accidents, *etc.* [Seven-Page Letter]

• Every one else has these buttons like, [peace symbol], black power, melvin eats bluber, *etc.* [Dragon Card]

Kaczynski   • If material is serialized, first instalment becomes public property six months after appearance of first instalment, second instalment, *etc.* [Times III Letter]

• Just check a street map of any suburban area and see how many of the street names include as a component either the name of some species of tree or a word such as "wood," "forest," "arbor," "grove" *etc.* [Times III Letter]

Remarks: Use of *et cetera* to continue a list. Kaczynski does this twice within the Unabomber missives, five times in his 23-page essay of 1971 and 27 times in the 65-page *Industrial Society and its Future.*

Zodiac   • Well, it would cheer me up considerbly if I saw a lot of people wearing my buton. Please no nasty ones like melvin's[.] Thank you [Dragon Card]

Kaczynski   • On my commissary list dated 12/11/01, I ordered tuna and fifty 1¢ stamps. Today I received the tuna, but I did not receive the stamps. Please explain. Thank you.[15]

Remarks: Requests made by both writers in an exaggerated tone of sarcastic politeness. The general tone of the two statements is virtually identical.

Zodiac

- As of yet I have left no fingerprints behind me contrary to what the police say. [I]n my killings I wear transparent finger tip guards. All it is is 2 coats of airplane cement coated on my finger tips — quite unnoticible & very efective. [Seven-Page Letter]

Kaczynski

- Some inside parts were sanded to remove possible fingerprints. Since wood is porous, sweat from the finger probably penetrates the surface a short distance, so we assume that merely wiping wood does not reliably remove fingerprints. Some metal parts also were scrubbed with sandpaper or emery paper for a similar reason. It is well known that old fingerprints on metal can sometimes be brought out by treating with acid, so presumably the sweat affects the surface of the metal chemically and merely wiping is probably not a reliable method of removing prints. [Times III Letter]

Remarks: Both killers, in letters to the media, describe their ingenuity in devising ways to avoid leaving fingerprints.

Zodiac

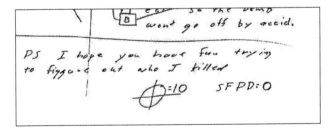

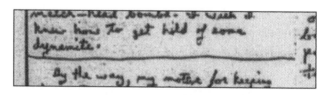

Kaczynski

Remarks: When separating written sections, both Zodiac and Kaczynski employ a single, freehand line that spans the page.

Chapter 11

Prints of Darkness

*Tom lay upon a sofa with an eager auditory about him and told the
history of the wonderful adventure, putting in many striking additions to
adorn it withal; and closed with a description of how he left Becky and
went on an exploring expedition; how he followed two avenues as far as
his kite-line would reach; how he followed a third to the fullest stretch
of the kite-line, and was about to turn back when he glimpsed a far-off
speck that looked like daylight; dropped the line and groped toward it,
pushed his head and shoulders through a small hole, and saw the broad
Mississippi rolling by! And if it had only happened to be night he would
not have seen that speck of daylight and would not have explored that
passage any more!*

MARK TWAIN, *Tom Sawyer*

DESPITE THE LARGE number of tantalizing similarities between the
Unabomber and the Zodiac, a number of circumstances militate against a possible connection between the two. A sense of fair-
ness demands that such circumstances be presented in these pages.
Considerable space has already been devoted to the possible disparities
involving locations, dates and physical descriptions. We must now examine the more serious objections involving fingerprints, handwriting
and the lack of incriminating evidence found within the pages of Kaczynski's journals.

Nearly two months after his arrest, the San Francisco Police Department placed a formal request with the FBI for specimens of Kaczynski's handwriting and fingerprints. Two months later, the results of that
analysis were released. Neither the handwriting nor the fingerprints were
deemed to match the specimens attributed to Zodiac, which effectively
excluded Kaczynski from further consideration as a viable suspect in
the case.

While these revelations may appear to throw a bucket of cold water on the theory that the Zodiac events were authored by Kaczynski, one must refrain from jumping to conclusions and examine the facts surrounding them.

It is assumed, for example, that Kaczynski's fingerprints were compared with those of Zodiac. This assumption is positively correct, only so far as the fingerprints of Kaczynski are concerned. No one is certain of the prints ascribed to Zodiac, least of all the SFPD, who nonetheless have been using them to eliminate or exclude potential suspects for many years. And while SFPD has been somewhat less than forthcoming in revealing the nature and status of the prints they have on file, the public has had the opportunity to view FBI documents related to the case, which offer a much better picture of exactly what it is the authorities have been working with these past three decades and more. One of the early documents, an FBI report dated December 4, 1969 and addressed to the SFPD, offers some detailed information as to the nature of the prints. The document describes them as:

> Remaining unidentified latent fingerprints and a latent impression (fingerprint or palm print) . . . . a latent impression, which is either from the lower joint area of a finger or a palm print . . . .[1]

This is an interesting description, because it appears to support the longstanding belief that one of the prints found on Paul Stine's cab had been made by the killer *in blood*. Such a print would constitute the "impression" described in the FBI report as a latent "impression," as opposed to a simple latent print made by the usual means of sweat and oils from the skin. A second document, however — an intra-departmental memorandum of the SFPD, dated October 19, 1969 — casts doubt upon any such assumption:

> All of the latent prints in our case were obtained from a taxi cab. The latent prints *that show traces of blood* are believed to be prints of the suspect. The latent prints from right front door handle are also believed to be prints of the suspect. These prints are circled with a red pen. The other latent prints many of which are very good prints, may or may not be prints of the suspect in this case.[2] [Author's italics]

This memorandum belies the notion that at least one of the prints recovered from Paul Stine's taxicab was made *in blood*. It shows the existence of two suspected sets of prints from the cab, the one showing "traces of blood," and the other from the right front door handle, which are "believed" to be prints of the suspect. Had the latter been made "in blood," it must be assumed that the memorandum would have qualified them as such, since it remarked upon the "traces" of blood shown upon the former. This is a far cry from prints actually produced by the process of impression with blood as a medium. Had the prints actually been made in blood, such a fact would have supported a belief that they had been left by the suspect himself, assuming that no other person, such as a policeman or a bystander had left them there after contacting the blood-soaked interior of the cab, or overlaying his own prints upon bloody marks left by the *protected* fingers of the killer.

Further FBI documents help clarify the exact nature of the suspect prints, particularly one dated May 12, 1978, in which they are described as:

> One latent fingerprint previously reported as being from tip area of a finger and two latent impressions previously reported as being either fingerprints or portions of palm prints . . . .[3]

What we appear to have then, apart from the "other latent prints" which "may not be prints of the suspect," (see the quote above) are three prints suspected by SFPD of belonging to the Zodiac. The first two of these, per the SFPD report dated October 12, 1969, were taken from the outside rear post of the left front door and consist of "latents" showing "traces of blood." Whether these were the prints of fingers or palms could not be conclusively determined. The second suspected print, per the May 12, 1978 document, consists of "one latent fingerprint previously reported as being from tip area of a finger." No mention is made in any of the official documents that this print was associated with blood, and it is not qualified as such even though the others are.

Based on all the information at hand, documentary and otherwise, the quality of these prints is apparently not good. Copies of the October 12 police report showing all the prints removed from the taxicab are now publicly available, and while the pages appear as nothing more than bad photocopies, it is nonetheless easy to see that the prints ascribed to Zodiac — circled by the SFPD as per the quotation above —

show very few ridge patterns, as opposed to most of the "other" prints, in which the ridge patterns are obvious even to the untrained eye.

Some FBI documents indicated that both the San Francisco and Vallejo police agencies lifted fingerprints from certain of the Zodiac missives. Some of these prints were assumed to have originated with the suspect, since "elimination" prints were supposedly taken of all persons who were positively known to have handled the letters and envelopes prior to their coming into custody of the police. The number and types of such prints remains unknown, although many copies of the Zodiac letters now in circulation show areas where prints have been developed, with some being circled in pencil and initialed by the latent print examiner.[4]

As with the prints developed from Paul Stine's cab, it is impossible to declare with any degree of certainty that these are the prints of Zodiac. Whatever the case, it undoubtedly seems odd that a careful criminal — which by all accounts Zodiac appears to have been — would have been careless enough to handle his materials in such a way as to leave fingerprints behind. This is not to imply that Zodiac represented some idealized species of master criminal who never made mistakes. Yet one must naturally be inclined to wonder why, if sloppiness induced him to leave prints upon his letters, so few of those prints were actually found. Moreover, it seems odd that none of the prints from the letters and the taxicab were found to have matched each other. Early in 1974 a request was made to the FBI relating to the prints developed in the case:

> The FBI Identification Division, Latent Fingerprint Section, is requested to advise how many latent prints believed to be of the "ZODIAC" are available and if there is any possibility of classifying these latent prints to the extent of permitting a search through FBI Fingerprint Files in an effort to identify the "ZODIAC."[5]

Within a mere three weeks the agency had performed the analysis desired. Its response turned out to be anything but encouraging:

> It is not possible to determine which fingers made most of the previously reported Zodiac fingerprints. In this case, therefore, it is not possible to assemble a composite set of prints that could be classified and searched .... Comparable areas of unidentified latent prints previously reported

on items from different crime scenes, as well as latent prints on different envelopes and letters, were compared with each other, but no identifications effected.[6]

The sum total of all the information contained in the documents above may be taken collectively to indicate that the prints associated with Zodiac are of poor quality and cannot be associated with him to any degree of certainty. The police have admitted as much, both in private correspondence with the author, and the media as well. On July 31, 1996, immediately after disclosing the results of Kaczynski's fingerprint analysis, Inspector Vince Repetto was interviwed by the *San Jose Mercury-News*:

> Latent fingerprints on the Zodiac's letters don't match Kaczynski's either, Repetto said, although police don't know whether the prints are Zodiac's. Police technicians are still performing some chemical tests, he said. "We're doing forensic tests in the DNA realm," he said.[7]

Given these factors, it may seem strange that the authorities would still be using fingerprints as the basis for eliminating suspects. In reality, however, there is a simple explanation for the extreme reliance that has been placed upon them over the years, which is, in the words of Zodiac himself, that "the police don't have much to work on." For despite the fondest hopes of theorists and amateur researchers, the role of the authorities in the case is not to promote their particular theories, but to develop evidence against a suspect that can be produced in a courtroom for the purpose of obtaining a conviction. Nothing else will do. At this late date, eyewitness accounts would be tainted by the passage of time and the numerous conflicting statements made by those witnesses in a variety of public forums. A good defense attorney — and in a case of this significance he would be a *very* good attorney indeed — would figuratively tear such witnesses to shreds. A piece of physical evidence, such as a boot whose pattern matches that of the Wing Walker used at Berryessa, or a pistol that can be matched ballistically to one used by the Zodiac, might serve. But the passage of time militates strongly against the existence of such items. Moreover, simply possessing the items would probably not be sufficient cause for a jury to convict. That is why the authorities have relied so heavily upon the supposed prints of Zodiac, and not because they have any high degree of faith in their quality or their provenance.

★ ★ ★

The art of fingerprint analysis is premised on the idea that no two individuals have identical ridge patterns on the surfaces of their palms and fingers. Handwriting analysis makes a similar assumption; namely, that writing styles are sufficiently unique to each and every writer that any individual may be positively identified by the way in which he writes.

Given the number of handprinted correspondences associated with the Zodiac, it can hardly be surprising that the authorities relied quite heavily on the art of forensic handwriting analysis, both to authenticate the letters and as an inclusionary or exclusionary tool in examining potential suspects. The handwriting of most major suspects in the Zodiac case has been forensically analyzed, and that of Theodore Kaczynski is no exception. And, as with every other suspect, the verdict of the examiner was "no match." As related by SFPD's Inspector Repetto to the media:

> The handwriting expert could not absolutely rule out Kaczynski "or any other human being because the samples of Zodiac's writings are not sufficient to exclude a person," Repetto said. But based on a comparison of the Zodiac's handwriting and Kaczynski's, "there's no significant evidence to indicate that Kaczynski wrote any of the Zodiac letters . . . ."[8]

Perhaps the first question that will occur to the mind of a rational inquirer is whether Zodiac made some attempt to disguise his natural writing style. It defies logic to assume that an organized killer, whose crimes exposed him to the possibility of long imprisonment, or even death, would attempt to achieve widespread media publicity by way of letters written in a hand that could easily be recognized by people within the circle of his acquaintances. That is not to say that such an omission could not have taken place, but simply that it would have been highly unlikely for a criminal of Zodiac's obvious intelligence to make no attempt to disguise his writing. This is especially so in light of Zodiac's attempts to conceal or mask nearly every identifiable aspect of himself.

Did Zodiac disguise his writing? The best way to answer this question is to examine the writing itself, and look for factors that are known indicators of disguise. In his fully-authenticated correspondences, Zodiac employed three distinct modes of printing, commonly referred to as the "manic" style, the "Belli" style and a third style that is a composite of the first two. The Belli style, so-called because it first appeared on Zodiac's December 20, 1969 letter to attorney Melvin Belli, forms a definite contrast to the larger collection of the missives, which are represented by the manic style. The manic style is perhaps best typified by one of Zodiac's first correspondences, the Examiner Letter of July 31, 1969:

The first potential aspect of disguise to strike one's eye is the exaggerated slope, or slant, with which the characters have been rendered. So great is this element of slope that certain of the characters, most notably the "d," "t," and "l" appear almost to be toppling over upon their sides. Second, there is a complete lack of connectivity between one character and the next. Each character is drawn distinctively and separately, with none of the connecting lines that are typical of printing that is done in natural, flowing movements of the hand. Third, there is virtually no retracing of lines, a practice that is not typical of a natural handprinting style. Characters such as "P," "p," and "b," are rendered in two distinct strokes, rather than the customary single stroke in which the vertical stem is retraced from the bottom up. Interestingly, the writer attempts to render such characters as "u," "n," "h" and "r" in a single stroke with no retracing, a practice that he cannot consistently sustain throughout the entire body of this, or any other, missive. (Compare additional specimens below.) Fourth, the writer employs a small circle to represent both the period and the i-dot, a quality that is well-known to document examiners as indicative of disguise. Finally, there is use of a felt-tipped pen, which impedes the natural progress of the hand and obscures any fine details present in the writing. Once again, this is a device that is known by document examiners to be used by individuals who wish to disguise their natural writing style.[9]

To further elaborate on these elements, an extant sample of the Stine Letter reveals a number of distinctive areas within the individual characters where ink from the pen has "pooled" at points where the hand has stopped and rested during their formation:

Here one can readily see that the writer has attempted to draw even simple characters such as "d," "e," and "a," with more than one stroke of the pen.

In sharp contrast to the manic style, Zodiac's Belli style is rendered with an exaggerated neatness exemplified by carefully rounded characters, thick, uniform strokes and no significant slant:

> Dear Melvin
>
> This is the Zodiac speaking I wish you a happy Christmass. The one thing I ask of you is this, please help me. I cannot reach out for help because of this thing in me wont let me. I am finding it extreamly difficult to hold it in check I am

These qualities are displayed to an even greater extent in the envelope accompanying the letter, addressed in a hand that is almost "geometrical" in quality:

Especially in the writing on the envelope, one can easily see the painstaking care with which the characters are drawn. This is a classic sign of disguised handwriting, and one of the most frequent methodologies used for such disguise. Of special note are the copybook, two-stroke "a," and the odd construction of the numeral eight, rendered with two distinct circles, the smaller of which sits atop the larger. The i-dots and the t-crosses are both carefully and precisely placed, which forms yet another indicator of disguise.

The Belli Letter was received by attorney Melvin Belli in late December, 1969. The writing style on further Zodiac correspondences gives way to a hybridized manner of composition that comes across as a combination of both the manic and the Belli styles. This "composite" form is best typified by the writing on the April 20, 1970 Dragon Card, which begins with a salutation in the Belli style, but continues with a body that is composed in the composite style:

Of particular interest in this transition is the way in which the writer reverts back to the manic style without retaining all of its peculiarities. He produces, for example, the slant of the manic, along with the cursive "d," and the two-stroke "p" and "b," while abandoning the upward-facing loop of the "e," and the non-retraced renderings of "h," "m," "n," and "r." The characters remain distinctly separate from one another, with no interconnecting lines.

For comparison purposes, Zodiac offers very little in the way of character formation that is either unusual or unique. His letters are drawn almost uniformly in a standard, copybook-like hand that can be best described as "plain vanilla" in appearance. There are no unusual flourishes or clearly individualized characteristics that might be used to furnish precise points of comparison between his hand and that of any other person.

Perhaps it is no coincidence that the handprinted characters of Theodore Kaczynski maintain the same degree of copybook plainness as those we see with Zodiac. It is a fact that Kaczynski is well known for the legibility and straightforwardness of his writing style. One of Kaczynski's thesis advisers, Peter Duren, recalled his "very neat handwriting," while psychologist Gary Greenberg, who corresponded with Kaczynski for a number of months, remarked:

> Kaczynski's evenly spaced block letters are neat and unadorned. His left margin is ruler-straight, his right taken to the edge of the page unless that would disrupt the orderly rhythm of his print. Perhaps Kaczynski's penmanship is his attempt to mimic his impounded typewriter, the one on which he wrote his manifesto. Maybe he misses it.[10]

Numerous examples of Kaczynski's handprinting are available for scrutiny and comparison. In purely qualitative terms, these specimens show almost no variance whatsoever, apart from the relative speed with which they were composed, and whether the writing was rendered on lined or unlined paper. The most significant example of Kaczynski's buttoned-down and formal printing is contained in the faculty biography which he submitted to the University of California along with his 1966 application for employment. [See next page]

This is Kaczynski at his very best; the style he reserved for the most auspicious occasions. More typical of his everyday writing style are the following samples taken from Kaczynski's personal journal, a "cop-out" (complaint) letter to prison authorities, and a personal notation found amongst the effects in Kaczynski's Montana shack:

How to hit an Exxon exec :
Send book-like package preceded → to his home by a letter
saying I am sending him a book I've
written on oil-related environmental concerns
— attacking environmental position — and I'd
like to have his comments on it before
preparing final version of manuscript.

The primary difference between these productions is the degree of
speed with which they are produced. This affects both the shape of the
characters and the degree of connectedness between them. While there
is little or no slant to the writing, Kaczynski's natural tendency is to
draw the ends of most characters slightly toward the right, producing a
curvature to the "t" and "l" and a sort of tailed extension to letters such
as "a," "h," "m," "n," and "u." Often this extension forms a connecting
line to the character immediately after it.

The primary difference between the letterforms produced by
Zodiac, and those produced by Theodore Kaczynski, lies in this visible
curvature and the connections between adjacent characters. Apart from
that, the forms are essentially the same. If we discount the roundedness
of the lower-case characters within the Belli style — a style that is obviously contrived — we see the same degree of angularity associated with
the "pointed" tops of letters such as "m," "n" and "h." We see the same
cursive "d," the same three-stroke "k," the same angularity to the upper
curve of the "f" (with its vertical stroke curving back toward the left),
the same small lowercase "t" that in many cases resembles a plus sign,
and the capital "M" whose inner lines proceed only halfway toward the
center. Moreover (and perhaps most importantly) the overall "color,"
or appearance of the text as a whole, is identical when the printing of
both authors is compared. Each displays a ruler-straight left margin,
writing that is carried out to the extreme edge of the right margin, ir-
regular letterspacing, a "jumping baseline" (except where lined paper
is involved), wide, gappy word spacing, and linespacing in which the
descenders of one line are extended right to the tops of the ascenders on
the succeeding line, but never infringe upon those strokes. This contrast
can perhaps best be visualized by taking one specimen each of Zodiac's

and Kaczynski's printing and blurring the individual words so that only the visual "color" of the specimens is apparent.

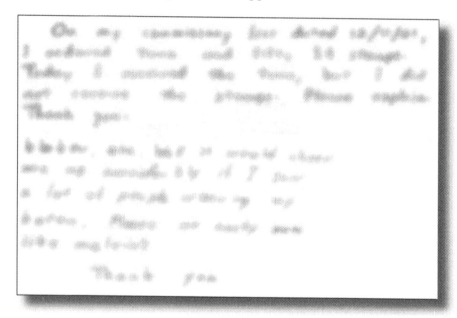

Further, if one has resolved that the handprinting of the Zodiac letters is disguised, it seems logical to ask oneself to what extent Kaczynski (or any other person) would have been obliged to alter his writing in order to achieve the effect produced within those missives. The obvious answer to such a question is that it would not have been difficult at all. One assumes, quite naturally, that individual letterforms must be completely changed in order to effect disguise. In fact, as we have seen, there is very little difference between the letterforms of Kaczynski and the Zodiac. If we begin with the handprinting of the former, and wish to convert it to the latter, we need do nothing more than adjust the slant from Kaczynski's nearly vertical lines to the approximately 30 degrees rightward slant of Zodiac's manic and composite styles. We must then retard the printing speed, assisted by a felt-tipped pen. Finally, we must avoid retracing lines by using multiple pen lifts for characters such as "A," "B," "P," "b," and "p." The more deliberate speed, coupled with the extreme rightward slant, will have the effect of eliminating not only any connecting strokes, but the tendency to produce extreme "tails" on some lowercase characters and the rightward curvature on others as well.

Alternatively, we may do all of the former with the exception of the slant, removing the distinguishing characters by using extreme (and obvious) deliberation in the formation of each letter. This will produce the Belli style.

A subjective assessment can be made by comparing two productions, the first by Kaczynski and the second by Zodiac. The first is a "cop-out" (complaint) letter by Kaczynski to federal prison authorities, while the second is the tail-end of the 1970 Dragon Letter, where the Belli style has begun to slip away into the composite style.

A careful visual comparison of these productions shows how little difference exists between Kaczynski's hand and that of Zodiac. *If the latter was written by the former*, one can see that Kaczynski wasted no special effort attempting to alter the distinguishing characteristics of his letterforms, nor did he attempt to disguise the essential qualities that comprise the "color" of the text as a whole, such as margin alignment, relative character height and spacing between the words. Document examiners universally opine that handwriting disguise is difficult because the individual disguising his writing cannot remember each and every nuance of the proposed disguise and apply the altered characteristics uniformly over the course of a production. In this case, however, alterations in nuance would have been kept to a bare minimum, with the disguise modality consisting primarily of changes in slant, and the use of multiple pen lifts on certain characters. Given the mental abilities of Kaczynski, this modality would not have been difficult to maintain.

Chapter 12

De Profundis

If floods of tears could cleanse my follies past,
And smokes of sighs might sacrifice for sin,
If groaning cries might salve my fault at last,
Or endless moan, for error pardon win,
Then would I cry, weep, sigh and ever moan,
Mine errors, faults, sins, follies past and gone.

JOHN DOWLAND, *The Second Book of Songs or Ayres*

CONVENTIONAL WISDOM holds that Theodore Kaczynski could not have committed the crimes of Zodiac because nowhere within the hundreds of pages of autobiographical accounts and thousands of pages of daily journal entries associated with Kaczynski does there exist so much as a mention of the Zodiac events. Further, Kaczynski's own words (as reflected in the documents) depict an individual restrained from killing by deep-seated inhibitions that took many years to overcome. Not until 1978, when the first Unabomber explosion occurred, did Kaczynski work up "the nerve" to actually kill a fellow human being. Not until 1985 did he actually succeed.

"About a year and a half ago," Kaczynski wrote on Christmas Day of 1972, "I planned to murder a scientist — as a means of revenge against organized society in general and the technological establishment in particular." He continued:

Unfortunately, I chickened out. I couldn't work up the nerve to do it. The experience showed me that propaganda and indoctrination have a much stronger hold on me than I realized. My plan was such that there was very little chance of my getting caught. I had no qualms before I tried to do it, and I thought I would have no difficulty. I had everything well prepared. But when I tried to take the final, irrevocable step, I found myself overwhelmed by an irrational, superstitious fear — not a fear of anything specific, merely a vague but powerful fear of committing the act. I cannot attribute this to a rational fear of being caught. I made my preparations with extreme care, and I figured my chances of being caught were less than, say, my chances of being killed in an automobile accident within the next year. I am not in the least nervous when I get into my car. I can only attribute my fear to the constant flood of anticrime propaganda to which one is subjected. For example, murderers in TV dramas are always caught . . . . [1]

Government documents showed Kaczynski only gradually overcoming the inhibitions that had supposedly restrained him from attempting acts of murder prior to 1975.

As early as 1975, Kaczynski took the first tentative steps on his destructive path. In the summer of that year he engaged in various acts of vandalism, including putting sugar in the gas tanks of various vehicles and vandalizing trailers and camps in Montana. In an act of a more deadly nature, he strung wire at neck height across roads frequented by motorcyclists. These acts continued over several summers and were a prelude to Kaczynski's coming bombing attacks. [2]

Even prior to that date, Kaczynski's journals hint of strong inhibitions fostered by a lifetime of social conditioning, that hindered him in his desire to strike against society:

In Summer '75 I broke into this trailer by unscrewing some screws and prying off a metal window frame, ruining it in the process. (I had a strong psychological inhibition against breaking the window, even though it's very unlikely anyone could have been within earshot.)

Fall '77 I went to some cabins along Dalton Mountain Road. There was one pretentious-looking cabin still not finished on the inside. There was a small house-trailer parked on the lot, immaculately furnished inside. I stole a rusty animal trap I found outside the cabin. Overcoming my earlier inhibition, I smashed out most of the windows in the trailer, then reached inside with my rifle and smashed a coleman lantern and 2 gas-lamp fixtures. I smashed 6 panes on the cabin . . . . As a result of indoctrination since childhood, I had strong inhibitions against doing these things, and it was only at the cost of great effort that I overcame the inhibitions. I think that perhaps I could now kill someone (and I don't mean just set a booby trap having only a fractional chance of success), under circumstances where there was very little chance of getting caught. But I'm not sure if I could, because often one's brainwashing turns out to be stronger than one thought.[3]

Based solely on journal entries such as the foregoing, authorities in the Unabomber case convinced themselves that Kaczynski had never made a serious attempt to kill a human being prior to his first effort at bombing in 1978. They uncritically assumed that the assertions made within the journals were factually correct, and reflected the absolute truth concerning the beliefs, opinions and actions of Kaczynski during the years to which they pertained.

Was this assumption valid? There exists a strong and almost universal presumption that a person will neither prevaricate nor lie to a document intended primarily for himself, such as a diary, or a journal. Grossly speaking, this paradigm is generally correct. Self-deception is a subtle, rather than an overt trait. While a person might have considerable reason to lie to himself about his motivations, it makes absolutely no sense that he should lie to himself about his actions. And that may be taken as a given, so long as he is writing *for himself*, and not for someone else.

Late in the year of 1997, prosecutors in the Unabomber trial approached a forensic psychiatrist by the name of Phillip J. Resnick and requested that he communicate his opinions regarding Kaczynski's refusal to submit to psychiatric evaluation at the hands of government experts. To facilitate this goal, Resnick was supplied with copies of Kaczynski's "voluminous" writings which, among other things, served to inform the opinion he returned to the prosecutors in the case. Resnick tendered that opinion in the form of a three-page document, whose contents are highly enlightening. Among other observations, Resnick concluded:

It is my opinion that Mr. Kaczynski's refusal to submit to a psychiatric examination by government experts is willful, based on his own goals. Specifically, I believe that Mr. Kaczynski does not want to be labeled mentally ill . . . . *Mr. Kaczynski wrote in his journals that one of the reasons he was leaving a written record of his motives for his planned killings was to avoid the possibility that his actions would be explained as those of a "sickie."*[4] [Author's italics]

Resnick then proceeded to quote Kaczynski directly from his journal:

> I intend to start killing people. If I am successful at this, it is possible that, when I am caught (not alive, I fervently hope!) there will be some speculation in the news media as to my motives for killing (as in the case of Charles Whitman, who killed some 13 people in Texas in the '60s). If such speculation occurs, they are bound to make me out to be a sickie, and to ascribe to me motives of a sordid or "sick" type. Of course, the term "sick" in such a context represents a value-judgement. I am not very concerned about the negative value judgements that will be made about me, but it does anger me that the facts of my psychology will be misrepresented. For that reason, I have attempted to give here an account of my own personality and its development that will be as accurate as possible . . . . As I said, if I succeed in killing enough people, the news media may have something to say about me when I am killed or caught. And they are bound to try to analyze my psychology and depict me as "sick." In this connection I would point out that many tame, conformist types seem to have a powerful need to depict the enemy of society as sordid, repulsive, or "sick." This powerful bias should be borne in mind in reading any attempts to analyse my psychology.[5]

Resnick's observations were later recapitulated by Dr. Sally Johnson in her court-ordered psychological survey of Kaczynski:

> Near the end of his autobiography in 1979, Mr. Kaczynski describes his motives for writing, to include that he intended to start killing people and that when caught, he was concerned people would perceive him to be a "sickie." *His writings were an effort to prevent the facts of his psychology from being misrepresented.*[6] [Author's italics]

These quotations are remarkable for the similarity of the conclusions their authors reach. Their mutual finding was that Kaczynski compiled the journals to ensure that his motives for killing would not be misconstrued, and his actions dismissed as the fruit of a lunatic's delusions.

In fact, Kaczynski's conduct throughout the course of his short-lived trial provides abundant evidence that he was perfectly willing to sacrifice his life to avoid the stigma of being labeled "sick." Convinced that his court-appointed defense team would persist over his objections in pursuing an insanity defense, Kaczynski sought to fire them and represent himself, even though to have done so would have guaranteed a guilty verdict and the resultant death sentence sought by the government. Even after pleading guilty to the charges, Kaczynski sought for years to overturn the plea, seeking a new trial whose outcome would not have been in doubt and which most probably would have resulted in his death.

Under these circumstances, and considering the preface to his journals, it requires no stretch of the imagination to understand that Kaczynski's writings were intended primarily for public consumption — to ensure that the *public* would perceive him and his motivations in the best possible light, or the light in which Kaczynski most desired that they should be perceived. As stated by Kaczynski, ". . . it does anger me that the <u>facts</u> of my psychology will be misrepresented. For that reason, I have attempted to give here an account of my own personality and its development that will be as accurate as possible . . . ." When he writes "as accurate as possible," one must not assume that the word "accurate" implies any degree of fidelity to the truth. Rather, it implies a *rendition* of the truth that best fits Kaczynski's image of himself and the worldview he created to accommodate it. For Kaczynski, it is absolutely essential that the public, or rather, the *world* perceive his motivations, not necessarily as "principled," but as rationally conceived. Kaczynski's philosophy cannot sustain his ego (its primary purpose, after all) if the actions he commits in consequence of that philosophy are anything other than under his complete control. Whether his motivation is a deep concern for the welfare of the human race, or simply a desire to achieve a form of vengeance against the scientists and other "bigshots" who promote technology, Kaczynski must act in accordance with the logical conclusions of a clear and reasoning mind. If he does not do this — if his actions are simply a gut reaction to the circumstances of his life — he will be forced to realize that he is at best a failure as a man, and at worst a faceless nobody who lives in a plywood shack with neither plumbing nor electricity because he has not the wherewithal to do better for himself.

Given these circumstances, one can scarcely imagine that Kaczynski's journals would not comprise a curious admixture of truths, half-truths, and calculated lies. Consider his decision to take the assistant professorship at Berkeley. In his autobiography he claims that the only reason he took the job was to earn sufficient money to buy a plot of land.[7] But if that had truly been the case, why did he choose Berkeley?

Given his credentials he could have worked at any of a myriad of smaller colleges or universities where the pay scale would have been the same (or greater), the cost of living less, and the institutional demands of academia not as pressing as they would have been in the high-profile milieu of Berkeley. If hoarding money were his sole consideration, why did he go out of his way in producing three professional papers which were thereafter published in leading mathematical journals — papers whose only purpose would have been to assist him on the path to tenure?

The obvious answer to these questions is that Kaczynski, who composed the autobiography in 1979, could not admit to himself that he had failed in academia, and lied about his motives to cover for his inability to succeed in the field for which he had studied all his life. Kaczynski found it easier to concoct a story about planning for a wilderness existence than admitting to something so unflattering to himself.[8]

Similarly, in his autobiography, we are confronted by curious passages such as these:

> I had no social life at this time and more than ever I made it a principle to be both asocial and amoral . . . .[9]

Based on the entire record of Kaczynski's past, there is little doubt that the first part of this observation is absolutely true, namely, that Kaczynski had no social life during the period of time referred to in the quote (1964–1966). The second part of Kaczynski's observation, however, is suspicious to an extreme degree. By stating that he made it a *principle* to be asocial, Kaczynski is attempting to convey the impression that his lack of a social life was somehow the consequence of an abiding personal precept, rather than any deficiency on his part. This is disingenuous, and tantamount to making a virtue out of a necessity.

Moreover, beginning with the autobiography and continuing on until the year when Kaczynski supposedly first worked up the nerve to kill, the number of allusions made to his supposed inhibitions is small, especially considering the fact that the government purposefully handpicked excerpts from Kaczynski's writings to illuminate their contention that he had spent more than twelve years building up the ability to murder another human being. This buildup was played upon and detailed in the government's sentencing memorandum in United States versus Kaczynski:

Kaczynski's journals also reflect that he worked at overcoming inhibitions against committing crimes, striving to develop what he called "the courage to behave irresponsibly."[10]

The prosecution proceeds to quote the journal entry cited above, regarding Kaczynski's plan to murder a scientist in 1971. It follows with a brief description of the journal entries:

As early as 1975, Kaczynski took the first tentative steps on his destructive path. In the summer of that year he engaged in various acts of vandalism, including putting sugar in the gas tanks of various vehicles and vandalizing trailers and camps in Montana. In an act of a more deadly nature, he strung wire at neck height across roads frequented by motorcyclists. These acts continued over several summers and were a prelude to Kaczynski's coming bombing attacks.

Kaczynski's terrorism began in 1978. The history of his bombings reveal a patient and methodical killer. In May of that year he left Montana and returned to Chicago where he lived and worked for approximately a year. He noted in his journal that his biggest reason for returning to Chicago in 1978 was to "more safely attempt to murder a scientist, businessman, or the like" (Ex. 15) and explained:

> In Montana, if I went to the city to mail a bomb to some big shot, (a Montana neighbor] would doubtless remember that I rode [the] bus that day. In the anonymity of the big city I figured it would be much safer to buy materials for a bomb, and mail it.

Ex. 16. Around the same time, he wrote of his continuing determination to overcome any compunction against committing crimes and realize his "ambition":

> As a result of indoctrination since childhood, I had strong inhibitions against doing these things, and it was only at the cost of great effort that I overcame the inhibitions. I think that perhaps I could now kill someone (and I don't mean just set a booby trap having only a fractional chance of success), under circumstances where there was very little chance of getting caught . . . . My ambition is to kill a scientist, big businessman, government official, or the like. I would also like to kill a Communist.

Kaczynski's writings track his progress in realizing his "ambition." They also reflect his appreciation for the gravity and unlawfulness of his conduct. For example, Kaczynski classified many of his writings by their incriminating nature, and left catalogues designating which writings were the most damning, designating some to be burned and others to be buried. Ex. 18. These entries illustrate how well he grasped the legal significance of his actions, as when he noted that that certain journal passages detailed events "past [the] statute of limitations." Ex. 19. They also reveal his concern for his public image, with Kaczynski describing other passages as "embarrassing, not dangerous," or simply "very bad public relations." Id.

Kaczynski wrote some documents in code, others in Spanish, and concealed carbon copies of his later public "FC" missives deep within a storage container in the loft of his home. many journal entries recount daily activities in plain English text and then revert to coded text, often in Spanish, as the subject matter moves to criminal acts. Some entries explicitly recognize the incriminating nature of the contents, as in this notebook entry where he wrote:

[M]y motive for keeping these notes separate from the others is the obvious one. Some of my other notes contain hints of crime, but no actual accounts of felonies. But these notes must be very carefully kept from everyone's eyes. Kept separate from the other notes they make a small compact packet, easily concealed.[11]

The exhibits mentioned in the memorandum contain a small number of additional references to the supposed "inhibitions" experienced by Kaczynski, beginning with his high school years and continuing up until his return to Chicago in 1978:

However, it is important to understand that, while on the level of the intellect and the conscious will I had completely rejected all morality and all respect for authority, nevertheless on the instinctive animal level I was still the slave of my early conditioning, so that I was very much afraid to act contrary to the precepts of authority.[12]

The reader must realize by now that in high school and college I often became terribly angry at someone, or hated someone, but, as a matter of prudence, I could not express that anger or hatred openly. I would therefore indulge in fantasies of dire revenge. However, I never attempted to put any such fantasies into effect, because I was too thoroughly conditioned, by my early training, against any defiance of authority. To be more precise: I could not have committed a serious crime of revenge, even a relatively minor crime, because my fear of being caught and punished was all out of proportion to the actual danger of being caught. I could have much more easily risked my life in a lawful way, than take an equal risk of spending 30 days in jail for some minor crime.[13]

But I had not actually been liberated from my conditioned inhibitions against defying authority overtly. What I had acquired was the strength and hopefulness to actively fight those inhibitions.[14]

Summer '75 I broke into this trailer by unscrewing some screws and prying off a metal window-frame; ruining it in the process. (I had a strong psychological inhibition against breaking the window, even though it's very unlikely anyone could have been within earshot.)[15]

1977-78 Fall '77 I went to some cabins along Dalton Mountain Road. There was one pretentious-looking cabin still not finished on the inside. Overcoming my earlier inhibition, I smashed most of the windows in the trailer . . . . As a result of indoctrination since childhood, I had strong inhibitions against doing these things, and it was only at the cost of great effort that I overcame the inhibitions. I think that perhaps I could now kill someone (and I don't mean just set a booby trap having only a fractional chance of success), under circumstances where there was very little chance of getting caught. But I'm not sure I could, because often one's brainwashing turns out to be stronger than one thought.[16]

The foregoing quotations constitute the sum total of material employed by the government in support of its contention that Kaczynski had undergone a lengthy psychological metamorphosis by which, over a period of more than two decades, he had overcome the deep-seated inhibitions that prevented him from committing acts of violence or other criminal activities in which he might otherwise have readily indulged. It is not a contention that is well-supported by the evidence. It rests upon the very broad assumption that the veracity of Kaczynski's journal entries is to be taken at face-value, with no consideration given to the fact that they were pointedly intended for public consumption, to afford posterity a particular image of Kaczynski which it was his desire to convey. Furthermore, Kaczynski's repeated allusions to the so-called psychological inhibitions that prevented him from committing crimes do not appear to sit naturally within the context of the quoted material. Rather, they bear the flavor of having been deliberately placed within the narrative for the purpose of leading the reader to an inevitable conclusion.

For example, in the quotation cited above, Kaczynski writes, "[o]vercoming my earlier inhibition, I smashed most of the windows in the trailer . . . ." One might naturally assume that overcoming inhibitions of the power suggested by Kaczynski up to this point would require some transitional experience that would have acted upon his will and rendered him capable of performing an action he had found all but impossible a short time earlier. Since overcoming his inhibitions was evidently a great theme with Kaczynski, one might also assume that the reader would be treated to a description of the events that led to such transcendence. Kaczynski, however, offers no such insight. He simply says that he overcame his earlier inhibition, with no indication as to how that might have come to pass. Unable to offer an adequate explanation for his new-found "nerve," Kaczynski conjures up a sort of *deus ex machina* to resolve the problem of his inhibitions, without resorting to the bothersome elucidations which are not, perhaps, within his ability to give. And in fact, nowhere within the publicly-available entries of his writings does he offer any kind of rational explanation for the phenomenon.

"I had strong inhibitions against doing these things," writes Kaczynski, "and it was only at the cost of great effort that I overcame the inhibitions." That comment is explanatory, but not completely satisfactory. What exactly does he mean by the words "great effort?" Why does "great effort" serve him in 1977, but not in 1971? What has happened in the interval to effect this great alteration in the power of Kaczynski's will? Unfortunately, Kaczynski doesn't say. We are simply expected to take him at his word — the word of a killer whose every action is driven by a personal philosophy that he must promote at any cost.

The Turchie Affidavit offers an interesting quotation in the form of an undated letter written by Kaczynski to his brother:

> As you know, I have no respect for law or morality. Why I never committed any crime? (of course, I'm not talking about something like shooting a grouse out of season now and then. I mean felony type stuff — burglary, arson, murder, etc.) Lack of motive? Hardly. As you know, I have a good deal of anger in me and there are lots of people I'd like to hurt. Risk? In

some cases, yes. But there are other cases in which I can figure out ways of doing naughty things so that the risk would be insignificant. I am forced to the humiliating confession that the reason I've never committed any crime is that I have been successfully brainwashed by society. On an intellectual level I have only contempt for authority, but on an animal level I have all too much respect for it. My training has been quite successful in this regard and the strength of my conditioned inhibitions is such that I don't believe I could ever commit a serious crime. Knowing my attitude toward psychological manipulation of the individual by society, you can imagine how humiliating it is for me to admit to myself that I have been successfully manipulated.[17]

This letter would appear to support the belief that Kaczynski's social inhibitions and conditioned responses to his "brainwashing" by "society" were genuine phenomena against which he struggled throughout the decade of the 1970s. Such a conclusion appears unfounded, however, in light of an undated and coded journal entry in which Kaczynski clarifies the statements made in the selfsame letter to his brother:

I recently wrote a letter to my brother, that the inhibitions that have been trained into me are too strong to permit me ever to commit a serious crime. This may surprize reader considering some things reported in these notes but motive is clear. I want to avoid any possible suspicion on my brother's part.[18]

These quotations clearly show how Kaczynski used the idea of personal inhibitions and social conditioning as an alibi against suspicion. He wants the public — *his* public — to believe that only after suffering the depredations of the technological society was he able to overcome his inhibitions and commit an act of violence. He does this because it would kill his ego to admit that the ugliness of his nature is the direct result of the spite and envy born of his own shortcomings as a man. His writings are the vehicle by which the truth — *Kaczynski's* truth — about his motives will be known. And no lie, however great, will be found too egregious not to serve that truth.

Let us for the moment abandon perfect objectivity, and assume for the sake of argument that the Zodiac's crimes may be attributed to Kaczynski. Granted that connection, can imagination conjure any reason why Kaczynski would not have taken credit for those crimes, as he did the Unabomb events, and the activities leading up to them?

To answer that question, we must return to what Kaczynski wrote in the preamble to his journal. In brief, he feared that his motives would be misconstrued, and his actions ascribed to the psychology of a "sickie." So great was his fear of being pigeonholed and labeled in this manner that Kaczynski exposed himself to the very real possibility of death in order to avoid a defense of mental illness at his trial — something forced upon him not only by the District Court, but by his own attorneys as well.

Whatever might have been their motivation, the crimes of Zodiac cannot be viewed by reasonable people as anything other than the product of a warped and twisted mind. This assessment is obvious on its face. What rational person would dare to justify the wanton and brutal slaying of two minor children as they innocently enjoyed each other's company on a cold December night? By what perverted logic might one defend the gunning-down of a young mother who had never harmed another soul, or the cold-blooded butchery of an attractive college woman, simply because she *was* an attractive college woman, enjoying an outing with her boyfriend? What tangled knots of equivocation must be tied before human thought produces a just and reasonable motive for the assassin's bullet that felled Paul Stine? Who will speak for the nobility of the threat to gun down a school bus full of children, or to blast those children to oblivion with explosive charges, coldly calculated to maim and mutilate the most innocent and helpless members of society? To call such actions *sick* is to understate the case. One seeks in vain, however, for a more descriptive word.

Kaczynski would never; *could* never have *admitted* to the crimes of Zodiac. That is not to say, however, that he could not have *committed* the crimes of Zodiac. Those murders were impulsive actions, driven by an explosive combination of personal envy and sexual frustration. We have seen already how those same qualities festered within Kaczynski's brain in the mid- to later-1960s, and formed the underpinnings of his first resolve to kill. But while personal envy may have formed the least common denominator of *any* provocation Kaczynski might have had, whether as the Unabomber or the Zodiac, the element of sexual frustration would have lent an immediacy to his desire to lash out as the Zodiac. Such a provocation does not appear to exist as part of Kaczynski's pathology from approximately 1970 onward. It does, however, appear to comprise a distinct and driving element from 1966 through 1969, especially considering the fact that Kaczynski's documentation of the circumstance was written more than a decade later, and not at the time of its occurrence.

In fact, it is relatively easy to conjure a scenario in which Kaczynski, as a criminal, progresses through a series of stages that commence with an initial distinct persona and conclude with a second persona that is singular enough to be considered separate from the first.

We begin in 1966, with Kaczynski as a graduate student at the University of Michigan. He is alone, as he has always been. But now, with his coursework at an end, and his doctoral dissertation all but written, he has (perhaps for the first time in his life) leisure to consider things other than the academics that have kept him distracted for so many years. He tries to focus, but in vain. The walls that separate his apartment from the rooms adjoining are thin, and he can hear the din of revelry as clearly as if the walls did not exist. These are the rowdy jocks from the Michigan hockey team, and they are blissfully engaged in the time-honored occupation of enjoying their lives. Overcoming his disdain, he listens, fascinated, at the goings-on of people for whom he has neither empathy nor respect. There is drinking, and vulgarity, and perhaps most fascinating of all, the lusty sounds of sex. They fill his mind with loathing, and simultaneously with longing and despair. His thoughts meander, gratis, and fantasy takes possession of his mind.

For Kaczynski, such events most likely precipitated the month-long episode during the summer of 1966, when he found himself sexually excited nearly all the time, and fantasized obsessively about being a woman. As we have seen, this led directly to his considering a sex change operation, and the personal humiliation arising when he suddenly aborted the attempt — shame and humiliation so strong that they led immediately to a grim and terrible resolve. We must not deceive ourselves that this resolve had anything to do with the evil wrought by encroaching technology, or the effects of the technological society upon human freedom, or any of the other rationalizations by which Kaczynski pretended to act in later years. Kaczynski's problem could be stated in a word, and the word was *sex*. For Kaczynski, especially during the last few years of the 1960s, it must have seemed that the entire universe was having sex — with the solitary exception of himself.

The situation did not improve at Berkeley, where by his brother's accounting Kaczynski advertised unsuccessfully in the newspapers for female companionship. It was at this juncture that his pent-up rage — exacerbated by the almost intolerable immediacy of an unrequited sex drive — would have boiled over in acts of violence against the class of people Kaczynski most resented at the time, because they had the thing that Kaczynski wanted but could not acquire. These were acts of impulse, barely rationalized, perhaps, by the pretext that the victims somehow "had it coming" for the crime of trysting in a public place. A long interval of almost seven months transpired between the first attack at Lake Herman Road and the second attack at Blue Rock Springs. Within that interval Kaczynski resigned from his assistant professorship at Berkeley, effectively abandoning the academic scene for which he had spent his life in preparation. With Blue Rock Springs came the realization that murder might be used as an effective vehicle for publicity. Following the murder of Darlene Ferrin we see the first of two telephone calls to the local authorities, followed shortly thereafter by the first of a long series of missives intended to sow terror and achieve increasing recognition in the press. Nearly two months after his initial letters to the media, and driven perhaps by the bloody notoriety of the Manson murders in southern California, the final, impulsive, rage-driven assault takes place, on the isolated shores of Berryessa. This is the last of the signature lover's lane attacks, and the only murder that is not mentioned in any of the killer's later communications with the press. Two weeks later Paul Stine is gunned down in San Francisco. At that point, the Zodiac murders come to an inexplicable and sudden end. They are followed by a bizarre series of dire threats and strange correspondences that decrease both in frequency and the violence of their tone, until at last they come no more.

Continuing with our assumption that Kaczynski was the perpetrator of these deeds, it seems likely, based upon the evidence at hand, that the impulses driving him in the first three murders had played themselves out with the culmination of the event at Berryessa. Each of the first three killings forms part of a continuum, with thematic elements common to the whole. The Paul Stine murder breaks this pattern, by deviating from the crime scene settings and victimology of the preceding Zodiac events. Moreover, the Presidio Heights event will prove to be the last known murder committed by the Zodiac. At this juncture, a number of factors would have wrought an impact on whatever impulses might have played a role in Kaczynski's urge to kill. Foremost among these would have been the simple fact that he had successfully committed murder on three distinct occasions and consequently had succeeded in assuaging his hostility against the particular class of people he despised. Working in conjunction with that circumstance was the uncomfortable perception that both the authorities and the public had caught on to the truth behind his actions. (Here we may perceive our first intimation of Kaczynski's inordinate fear that his motives will be publicly misconstrued, or, to be more accurate, that his *true* motives will be publicly understood. Following Berryessa, both the authorities and the media began to speculate in terms that could hardly have been flattering to Kaczynski. Variously, both labeled Zodiac as a lunatic, a "crazy man," a sociopath, a homosexual (both practicing and latent) and a cowardly weakling who directed the brunt of his attacks toward the woman but had neither the strength nor resolution to kill another man.) Finally, the near-encounter with police in the immediate aftermath of the Stine slaying would have worked as a powerful inhibitor against continuing to kill in the brazen, up-close manner typified by all four Zodiac events.

By this point, Kaczynski had channeled his energies into dropping out of society and finding a place in the wilderness to live. Nothing remained of the Zodiac but a short-lived and highly sporadic campaign of artificial terror, cryptic teasing, and the need to sustain what must have been a highly-gratifying period of national publicity and attention.

For Kaczynski, impulse now gave way to the self-restraint imposed by reasoned thought. Removed from a milieu that offered constant reminders of his sexual inadequacies and continual stimulation of his rage, he could now stand back and make a rational assessment of what had come to pass. He could not have been pleased with the analysis. For the man who once described himself as a cool-headed logician had succumbed to the ravages of hot-headed compulsion and committed acts to which he could never have confessed, perhaps not even to himself.

It is instructive to note that in the spring of 1971 — the precise moment at which Kaczynski relocated permanently to the state of Montana with plans to construct his mountain home — the Zodiac persona comes abruptly to an end. This is also the period of time during which Kaczynski admits to having first discovered the French philosopher Ellul, with his alarmist works decrying the evils of technology. It is the year in which Kaczynski approached academics with his 23-page essay wherein the creation of an anti-technology organization was proposed.

Only at this juncture is the philosophy of the Unabomber born, while only at this juncture does the Zodiac depart. The Unabomber is born because Kaczynski has discovered a worldview that excuses his deficiencies as a human being and provides a rational justification for his hatred of society. The Zodiac departs because it is now neither practical nor desirable that his persona should continue to exist — not practical because in four separate events he has been seen by witnesses on three occasions and nearly caught by the police; not desirable because his actions have been publicly marked as the one thing Kaczynski dreads more than death itself, namely, the practical manifestations of a sick and sordid mind.

By now, Kaczynski is in the wilderness, his energies diverted toward fulfilling the goal of living a solitary and independent life, isolated from all human society to the extent that his circumstances will allow. His passions are overshadowed by the rigors of this new existence. For now he must struggle for survival, and the struggle itself lends a new meaning and a new sense of purposefulness to his life. This is borne out by Kaczynski himself. Writing in the *Manifesto*, he describes the evils succumbed to by individuals who have no clear sense of purpose, or what he calls the "power process":

> But for most people it is through the power process — having a goal, making an AUTONOMOUS effort and attaining the goal — that self esteem, self confidence and a sense of power are acquired. When one does not have adequate opportunity to go through the power process the consequences are (depending on the individual and on the way the power process is disrupted) boredom, demoralization, low self esteem, inferiority feelings, defeatism, depression, anxiety, guilt, frustration, hostility, spouse or child abuse, insatiable hedonism, abnormal sexual behavior, sleep disorders, eating disorders, etc.[19]

Here, Kaczynski appears to be speaking from experience. For the Manifesto is not, as it appears upon its face, a production calculated to cast light upon the pathologies of society, but rather, a vehicle for Kaczynski to elucidate the problems experienced by himself. When he writes about the so-called "power process" — the process of having a goal whose attainment requires effort, and of making an autonomous effort to achieve that goal — he is referring to his own participation in such an effort, which was his struggle to survive by his own efforts in the wilderness. Similarly, when listing the panoply of ills that arise in the absence of such a process he is speaking of the life he experienced *prior* to his existence in Montana. This suggests, in the strongest possible terms, that whatever demons had driven him prior to 1969 had been effectively exorcised by the move to Montana and the day-to-day preoccupation with survival.

Such "demons" would undoubtedly have been well-represented by the sexual frustration that underpinned Kaczynski's first resolve to kill. Sublimated by what Kaczynski called the "power process," and reinforced by the twin elements of fear and shame, the Zodiac persona would not have survived long past the spring of 1971 when, for Kaczynski, the process could be said to have begun — and indeed, it does not survive at any point past that time.

The final correspondence definitely attributable to Zodiac arrives in late January of 1974, nearly three full years after the cryptic Pines Letter and likewise nearly three full years from the time Kaczynski arrived for the first time at his brother's apartment in Montana. Neither the letter nor the envelope bears any reference to the Zodiac *per se.* Notably missing is the opening line made famous by the earlier correspondences. The signature crosshair circle is nowhere to be seen, supplanted by a simple "Me." Strange literary allusions make reference to the possibility of suicide, as depicted by Father Karras in *The Exorcist* and the lovelorn tom-tit in *The Mikado.* In fact, the missive is "*signed,* yours truley," with the quote pertaining to the latter's self-destruction:

> He plunged himself into
> the billowy wave
> and an echo arose from
> the sucides grave

The inferences are easy to discern. The demons have been chased away. By his own hand, the Zodiac has symbolically met his end. The Zodiac is no more.

Even at this point, a new identity has begun to gestate within the mind of Theodore Kaczynski. As the decade of the seventies progresses and he grows accustomed to his hard, new way of life, fresh outrages to his sensibilities arise as civilization begins its inevitable encroachment upon the habitation he has chosen for his retreat. All around the sacred place that was to have been his sanctuary from the evils and demands of civilization, the bustle of human activity imposes itself with a force to which Kaczynski can offer no response save that of exasperated rage.

The sights and sounds he cannot bear assail his senses with a persistence that will not abate. The cacophony of machinery — of chainsaws, motorcycles, snowmobiles, and airplanes — continually disturbs the tranquility of his mountain hideaway. Finally, he can stand it no longer, and Kaczynski resolves to act.

In this case, however, his action is tempered not only by the circumstances of his discontent, but by personal experience as well. Unlike the Zodiac, his provocation is not bound up with any burning physical desire, but with a well-considered and reasoned worldview to which the cool-headed logician Kaczynski has given considerable thought. His rationalizations convince him that the enemy is now "the system," which comprises the legions of scientists, engineers, airline executives, university professors and other "bigshots" who conspire to perpetuate the technological society that Kaczynski hates because it holds no place for him. In terms of vengeance, however, this poses something of a problem. For, unlike the young couples whom he envied and despised as Zodiac, "the system" is not to be caught out necking in a dark and isolated lover's lane. Its representatives do not present such safe, or easy targets as those who seek the privacy and solitude of trysting places that are naturally concealed. By hard experience Kaczynski has learned that, even under the best of circumstances, close-range killing will expose him to a level of risk that has proven uncomfortably high.

His new class of victim will not make itself an easy mark. But Kaczynski has neither the time, nor the physical resources, nor the reckless disregard for his own personal safety that would be required to stalk and kill a particular representative of the class he seeks to harm. Because of these impediments, weapons and tactics that require proximity to the victim are not an option. Only the bomb will do. He begins his campaign against the "bigshots" of society with a series of package bombs. Too large and unwieldy to yield any real destructive force, he turns to the riskier yet more successful option of hand-placing bombs in areas where they will be unwittingly picked up and detonated by some of the people he is targeting. Finally he is spotted in the act of physically placing a device, and the risk has become too great. Withdrawing from sight, he develops a type of bomb that will travel easily in the mail, and with this device he begins to kill and maim on a scale that brings him directly into the public eye.

The change is now complete. Kaczynski has metamorphosed from a close-proximity criminal who murders couples in lovers' lanes, to a sophisticated bomber who targets his victims at a safe and impersonal distance. It must always be borne in mind, however, that no matter what the disparity in their method, the two killers' madness was the same. Each was driven to kill by a combination of envy and despite. Their varying methodologies, while different, each served practical needs at the times they were employed.

Zodiac killed with guns and knives because that was the only effective method he could have used against the class of victims he wished to harm. Further, there existed an immediacy to the provocation that lent a quality of impetuosity to his deeds. The Unabomber killed with bombs because it would have proven neither practical nor safe to assail his intended class of victims in any other way. Moreover, because his provocation was philosophical in nature, as opposed to sexual, his murders could be planned with a far greater element of careful calculation. His was a provocation uniquely suited to its response.

Certainly it defies the common wisdom to suggest that a multiple killer would alter his means of dealing death from guns and knives to bombs. It must be borne in mind, however, that this paradigm applies specifically to the class of criminal known commonly as sociopathic, sexually-sadistic or, "recreational," as we have elsewhere used the term. With killers of the latter type there is indeed a perverse sexual element derived from proximity to the victim at the time of death, which may also be associated with the particular means by which the death is meted out. Zodiac, however, (as we have illustrated earlier) fails to meet the criteria that would define him as a killer of the recreational variety. Zodiac is essentially a *disaffected* killer, whose crimes were calculated to satisfy his ego, as opposed to his libido. Unlike the recreational killer, no pressing psychological need exists for the disaffected killer to be near his victim at the time of death, nor to deliver death by using a specific methodology. With no inconvenience to his psyche, he may change his modus operandi either to fit his victimology or to obviate the possibility of capture.

While it is said by some authorities that the Zodiac would never have progressed from the use of guns and knives to the hands-off bombing methods of Kaczynski, it should be pointed out that the Zodiac himself passed through a metamorphosis that began with guns and knives and ended, not with bombs, but with the *threat* of bombs. This presents us with the interesting notion — if the paradigm is true

— that not only is the Zodiac not Kaczynski, but that the Zodiac is not the Zodiac.

⋆　⋆　⋆

One final piece of evidence exists to support the contention that not only did Kaczynski use his extensive autobiographical and journal entries as a means of preventing an association between himself and the Zodiac, but that his initial foray into violence occurred much sooner than those writings might suggest. It comes in the form of a quotation from the psychiatric survey of Kaczynski performed by Dr. Sally Johnson and was based upon her reading of journal entries that have yet to be made fully available to the public. We have seen this quotation before, and it bears repeating here:

> He wrote in his journal about him not fitting into organized society and not wanting to fit into it, and seeking avenues of escape from it. In his words *in the early 1970s*, he wrote "True I would not fit into the present society in any case but that is not an intolerable situation. What makes a situation intolerable is the fact that in all probability, the values that I detest, will soon be achieved through science, an utterly complete and permanent victory throughout the whole world, with a total extrication of everything I value. Through super human computers and mind control there simply will be no place for a rebellious person to hide and my kind of people will vanish forever from the earth. It's not merely the fact *that I cannot fit into society* that has induced me to rebel, *as violently as I have*, it is the fact that I can see society made possible by science inexorably imposing on me."[20] [Author's italics]

Key to an understanding of the revelations contained within this passage is the date ascribed to it by Dr. Johnson: the *early* 1970s. By all accounts — by all of Kaczynski's accounts, since there exist no other — his violence did not erupt until the *later* 1970s, by which time Kaczynski had finally succeeded in overcoming the inhibitions that had held his violent tendencies in check. In light of the vast amounts of ink spilled by Kaczynski in his efforts to convince the public of his inability to commit a criminal act of violence prior to the Unabomb campaign, one can only speculate as to what particular acts of violent rebellion he refers to in the passage quoted here. It is noteworthy, too, that Kaczynski qualifies the violence primarily as a consequence of his inability to fit into society, and only secondarily as the result of science and technology and whatever effect they were supposed to have on him.

This provides us with a clear view of Kaczynski's metamorphosis as a criminal that reinforces the hypothetical scenario presented in this chapter. For it suggests, quite strongly, that by the time the passage was constructed, Kaczynski had indeed committed acts of criminal violence that were driven, not by a philosophical worldview, but by his inability to "fit into society" as manifested by sexual frustration so extreme that he referred to it elsewhere as "acute sexual starvation." It shows him acknowledging that fact, yet, at the same time, attempting to transform his motives for the violence by wedding them to a newly-minted way of thought——a perfect picture of the transition and how it came to pass.

Kaczynski journal entry, in which he purports to overcome his "inhibitions."

Chapter 13

A Likely Story

I'm sorry, sir, but those ARE *the figures.*

STANLEY KUBRICK, *Dr. Strangelove*

THE PRIMARY, and ostensible, purpose of this work has been to il-lustrate the incredible similarities between two notorious crimi-nals, the Unabomber and the Zodiac. At the same time, there exists an undeniable inference that the scope of the endeavor goes well beyond that goal, and passes into the realm of argumentation for a substantive connection between the two. Plainly speaking, the sheer number and cogence of the similarities cry out for a forthright answer to the insis-tent questions that arise from them. Could one of the most infamous killers in U.S. history have cast himself in a different mold and gone on to become yet another of the most infamous killers in U.S. history? Was Theodore Kaczynski the Zodiac Killer?

Such questions, unfortunately, are not amenable to a conclusive answer. We have seen the arguments both *pro* and *con*, yet lacking in both is a decisive piece of evidence — *hard* evidence, as it were — to form a fixed, unwavering opinion as to Kaczynski's innocence or guilt. In the eyes of the *law*, his innocence must remain a fact. In the eyes of the *public*, his guilt may be established by circumstance alone, and from any such verdict he will enjoy little or no appeal. If we wish to play fair, and exercise toward Kaczynski an element of the justice which he him-self denied his victims, we must refrain from couching that verdict in terms of a simple yes or no. No consideration, however, should prevent us from forming, within our own minds, a logical conclusion based upon the *probabilities* inherent in the comparison.

Let us recapitulate what we have found. The first, and perhaps most obvious connection is that both Kaczynski and the Zodiac were killers.

That is a broad category, in and of itself. We can go farther, however, by observing that both were of the class described as multiple killers. Even this distinction can be further subdivided by the fact that both killers belonged to a peculiar subset of multiple killers commonly known as mass murderers, or what we have described as *disaffected* killers. Beyond this, we see distinctive similarities in the psychological makeup of the killers. Each is driven by sexual frustration, combined with a need to take symbolic vengeance against a class of victims — a need that is founded on personal envy and resentment. As a secondary element of criminal signature, each uses the notoriety achieved by murder to seek publicity on an increasingly larger scale. Each killer forwards taunting and threatening letters to the media — in some cases the *same* media — demanding some form of publication on pain of further killings. In furtherance of their need for recognition, each assumes a self-styled moniker and uses it in a "trademark" fashion. Each places taunting phone calls to the police, while each leaves outdoor graffiti accompanied by an arcane symbol consisting of lines within a circle. Each mails a letter to the editor of the *San Francisco Chronicle*, threatening mass murder on a horrific scale, then issues a wryly-worded, sneering retraction, after panicked authorities have given the "appropriate" response.

Both killers were known to have moved in key areas during the times of several significant occurrences relating to the Zodiac events. Their physical descriptions bear a number of striking similarities, most notably the heavy structure of their facial features, including the large, square jaw that was captured by forensic artists creating composite sketches rendered years apart. Both used disguises in the commission of their crimes. Both displayed a wide range of intellectual abilities. Both revealed an aptitude for mathematics and the thought processes associated with a mathematical state of mind. Both showed an understanding of bomb-making that would have been at approximately the same level of proficiency in 1969. Both employed elaborate cryptograms of their own devising. Both, in the course of their criminal careers, used literary allusion — *high* literary allusion — as a means of casting hints regarding their personal motivations and the details of their surroundings. Both alluded to *opera*, an artistic genre with which few people have any familiarity. Both show numerous similarities within their compositional tone and style, which in many instances practically mirror one another in their form and content. Both display similarities in handwriting style so close that it is easy to see how one could have been converted to the other with a bare minimum of effort.

Some may find these circumstances convincing in and of themselves. Others, however, might not be so easily impressed. None of the similarities cited, they will say, are peculiar to the Unabomber, or any other man. Many people kill, and their numbers are in the thousands. Multiple murder is a rare phenomenon, but not so rare that its commission can be associated with only a single individual. Millions of people are mathematically inclined, and if only ten percent of the current U.S. population possessed a handwriting style similar to that of Zodiac we would have a total of thirty *million* likely suspects to examine, if that were the only criterion we employed. Clearly, none of the similarities are unique. No culprit will be condemned on the basis of any one of them.

The similarities, however, do not exist as discrete elements, each to be applied individually by itself. There is a synergy between them that renders the whole more significant than its parts.

Consider, for example, a hypothetical case of murder, where the perpetrator is unknown. An eyewitness spots a person fleeing from the scene. This individual is a male Caucasian with noticeably red hair who drives away in a luxury sedan of a particular make and model. At the crime scene, police discover a fresh footprint which they determine to have been made by a well-known brand of running shoe.

Consider, now, that the locality in which the crime occurred contains a population of 50,000 persons at the time of the event. How useful, then, is the evidence at hand? Let us assume that 25 percent of the population is non-Caucasian. This leaves 75 percent of 50,000, or 37,500 individuals who would fit that element of the description. Males make up 50 percent of the human population, but even this fact is of little help because 50 percent of the 50,000 population in question still forms a considerable list of 25,000 suspects. Red hair accounts for only three percent of the U.S. population, but even at that small rate a population of 50,000 people could be expected to yield 1,500 individuals carrying the trait. Likewise, if we assume that the particular make and model of automobile driven by the perpetrator is owned by twenty percent of the general population, and that the shoe print has come from a style of shoe commonly worn by ten percent of the general population, our suspect pool from only those connections becomes 10,000 and 5,000 respectively.

Taken individually, none of these pieces of evidence would seem to be of any help in singling out a suspect. It is a mistake, however, to believe that each connection exists *per se*, with no connection to the others. The crux of the matter, for example, is not that the perpetrator is either a Caucasian *or* a male, but that he is both a Caucasian *and* a male. He is, in fact, a Caucasian *and* a male *and* a redhead *and* the owner of a particular style of shoe *and* the driver of a particular kind of car. The probability that he is all these things together will be the product of all the probabilities for each of the single qualities. Seventy-five percent of the population is Caucasian, which, among our 50,000 population, yields a total of 37,500 Caucasians. Half of those Caucasians can be expected to be male, which leaves us with 18,750 Caucasian males. Of that 18,750 Caucasian males, three percent can be expected to have red hair, which now reduces our suspect population to a sum total of 563 — an unwieldy number, to be sure, but a far cry from the 50,000 we began with. Twenty percent of those Caucasian males with red hair can be expected to drive the type of vehicle spotted by the witness, which brings our pool of likely suspects down to 113. Finally, by our reckoning, ten percent of that 113 redheaded Caucasian males driving the type of car in question can be expected to wear shoes of the style which made the footprint at the crime scene. This takes us down to a very manageable 12 persons, from an initial population of 50,000.

This type of reasoning offers an excellent foundation for the most objective kind of analysis that can be produced from the similarities linking Ted Kaczynski to the Zodiac. Because the latter is an unsubstantiated individual we will focus ourselves upon his peculiarities, while ensuring that only those characteristics equally applicable to Kaczynski are included. We begin, as in the above example, with an established population — in this case, the figure of 221,000,000 (221 million). Based on U.S. census figures, this was the average population of the United States from 1969, the year in which the Zodiac committed the majority of his crimes, through 1985, the year when the Unabomber recorded his first fatality.

Both Kaczynski and the Zodiac belong to that relatively rare class of persons who commit the act of murder. The average homicide rate for all years 1969 through 1985, as determined through statistics maintained by the U.S. Department of Justice, is 8.9 per 100,000 population.[1] This works out to an average of 19,669 homicides per year for the range of years in question. Let us assume for the purposes of this exercise that each of these homicides represents a single murderer. By these figures, the average likelihood that any individual will be a murderer for any of the years from 1969 through 1985, inclusive, is .0089 percent (eighty-nine one-thousandths of one percent)

Eighty-nine one-thousandths of one percent of a population of 221 million returns a figure of 19,669 likely murderers in any of the indicated years. For convenience, let us call this value Z. It will change as we progress.

Trait	Percentage	Original population	New population (Z)
Murderer	0.0089	221,000,000	19,669

Unlike the general population, where males comprise fifty percent of the total population, the ranks of murderers are filled with a preponderance of men — 88.6 percent, to be precise, based upon statistics provided by the U.S. Department of Justice.[2] Obviously, both Kaczynski and the Zodiac were males. The figure of 88.6 percent, applied to Z, returns a new result for Z of 17,427 male killers.

Trait	Percentage	Original population	New population (Z)
Murderer	0.0089	221,000,000	19,669
Male	88.6	19,669	17,427

Further, and equally as obvious, both Kaczynski and the Zodiac belonged to the Caucasian race. From 1969 through 1985, this race comprised approximately 75 percent of the United States population.[3] Among murderers, however, the percentage is somewhat lower at 45.9 percent; let us round this figure to an even 46. Forty-six percent of Z, or 17,427 yields a figure of 8,016 male Caucasian killers.

Trait	Percentage	Original population	New population (Z)
Murderer	0.0089	221,000,000	19,669
Male	88.6	19,669	17,427
Caucasian	46	17,427	8,016

The next most obvious criterion is age. This characteristic presents us with something of a quandary, because the range of ages ascribed to Zodiac by a variety of eyewitnesses varies from a low of 25 to a high of 45. It is tempting, and not completely disingenuous, simply to average the sum of all the ages given in the various accounts to arrive at a firm figure of approximately 28 years. This age group sits within a range of 25 to 29 years listed in the 1970 U.S. Census as representing 6.6 percent of the population as a whole. If accepted, it would immediately reduce our suspect population by an astounding 93 percent. We hesitate, however, to apply an averaging methodology, primarily due to the unreliability of eyewitness accounts. Moreover, statistics show that a preponderance of homicides are committed by individuals within distinctive age groupings that are not representative of the population as a whole. We must therefore confine ourselves both to the numbers associated with homicides and the entire range of ages ascribed to Zodiac. Though this will give us a percentage much higher than we would like, it will ensure that we have included Zodiac's true age in our assessment.

Statistics provided by the Department of Justice for the range of years beginning in 1976 give the percentages of all homicides for all the ages between 25 and 45 years inclusive as 46.9 percent.[4] Both Kaczynski and the Zodiac would fit into this range. Let us round the figure to an even 47. Forty-seven percent of Z, or 8,016, yields a total of 3,768 male Caucasian killers in the range of ages from 25 to 45. Still a large figure, it is nonetheless considerably smaller than the 221 million population we started from.

Trait	Percentage	Original population	New population (Z)
Murderer	0.0089	221,000,000	19,669
Male	88.6	19,669	17,427
Caucasian	46	17,427	8,016
Ages 25–45	47	8,016	3,768

Within the category of murderer there exists a distinctive subset to which both Kaczynski and the Zodiac belong. As we have argued above, each may be grouped within a small association of killers, who meet the psychological criteria ascribed to mass murderers, but whose victim counts do not qualify them to bear the label. Moreover, as we have argued, each gives strong, almost overwhelming evidence of having been motivated by rage and hatred against a classes of individuals whose possessions or attainments were envied by the killer.

This presents us with a problem. Statistics for the designation we have in mind do not exist. No data have been compiled to show the actual percentage of killers who fail to attain the status of mass murderer only because their victim counts fall short. Likewise, there exists no hard data pertaining to the percentages of killers — whose primary motivation is a combination of rage, hatred and envy — that we have labeled as disaffected killers.

While such dearth of information may prevent us from using the figures we prefer — figures that would be sufficiently low to reduce our suspect population to a very tiny level — there is nothing to prevent us from using the available statistics to arrive at a figure broad enough to at least include the classifications we have in mind. There is no doubt that such a percentage will be exceptionally high, and contain a large number of individuals who fall outside the desired range. Nevertheless, for an assessment of this kind, it is better to grossly overestimate the data than even minimally to underestimate it.

The U.S. Department of Justice maintains tables showing the circumstances of all homicides (single and multiple) for the years 1976 and onward.[6] These circumstances are divided into five categories, comprising felonies, arguments, gang-related violence, Other and Unknown. The figures for 1976, the year closest in proximity to the Zodiac events, are given in the following table:

Year	Felony	Argument	Gang	Other	Unknown
1976	3,327	9,106	129	4,630	1,588

Of these categories, the first three are highly unlikely to be associated with the type of homicides in question here, i.e., multiple murder or single murder by disaffected killers. Among the remaining two categories it would be especially pleasing to have the "other" category broken down by circumstance. Since it is not, and consequently we cannot parse the data for circumstances unlikely to be associated with our type of killer, we must include figures for the entire range of both the categories labeled Other and Unknown. By doing so we will virtually guarantee that we have included in the final result all instances of single and multiple murder by disaffected killers.

The sum total of the Other and Unknown categories is 6,218, from a total of 18,780 homicides of all circumstances, or 33 percent of the total. Applying this percentage to Z, or 3,768, returns a new value of 1,243 male Caucasian disaffected killers in the range of ages from 25 to 45.

Trait	Percentage	Original population	New population (Z)
Murderer	0.0089	221,000,000	19,669
Male	88.6	19,669	17,427
Caucasian	46	17,427	8,016
Ages 25–45	47	8,016	3,768
Disaffected	33	3,768	1,243

Undoubtedly the single most significant aspect of the Unabomber and the Zodiac affairs — the one aspect that causes them to stand out among all other criminal cases in United States history — is the use of murder to obtain widespread publicity, terror and public recognition. So unique is this quality that in the entire annals of U.S. crime from 1969 to the present date (excluding organized terrorism) we can conjure no other disaffected killers who used the media to package and publicize themselves in the manner of a Kaczynski or a Zodiac. In no other cases have the perpetrators used the media — along with a credible threat of murder — to terrorize the public and mobilize the authorities in their response, as did these two. Each instance involved the commission of a series of murders, followed by correspondences with the major-market media and a do-it-or-else demand for publication on pain of further killings. Each culminated in a dire threat against a form of public transportation that was later retracted by the killer as an idle jest. From 1969 until the present date, only two such killers were known to have existed, each of whose presence in any of those years would have represented an infinitesimal .005 percent, or five one-thousandths of all the expected killers for that year.

Let us be charitable, however, and for the sake of caution elevate this figure by a factor of 10, to .05 percent. This will assume the existence of ten Kaczynskis or ten Zodiacs in any given year — a preposterous assumption, given our historical knowledge of all murderers for the years in question. Applying this percentage to Z, or 1,243, returns a figure of 0.6215 publicity-seeking male Caucasian disaffected killers in the range of ages from 25 to 45.

Trait	Percentage	Original population	New population (Z)
Murderer	0.0089	221,000,000	19,669
Male	88.6	19,669	17,427
Caucasian	46	17,427	8,016
Ages 25–45	47	8,016	3,768
Disaffected	33	3,768	1,243
Widespread publicity, terror and demand for publication	0.05	1,243	0.6215

We now consider a couple of characteristics shared by both Kaczynski and the Zodiac which are peculiar to the population at large and not dependent upon an individual's status as a killer.

So extreme in their variations were the accounts given by eyewitnesses to the Zodiac crimes that it is difficult to pin down any single characteristic with sufficient confidence to include it in our analysis. One exception, however, does stand out, and that is the heavy facial structure depicted in the Zodiac composites, particularly the large, square chin which forms the most salient aspect of the second rendition. This assessment is reinforced by the observation of Mike Mageau that his assailant had a "large face," and the comment of SFPD Office Fouke that there was "something about the chin" of the suspect he had seen. As we have seen, the heavy facial structure and large prominent chin are key elements of Ted Kaczynski's physical appearance, with the latter an almost-identical match for the same feature as it appears on the second Zodiac composite.

No actual statistics exist regarding the prevalence of a heavy facial structure among the population as a whole. Let us assume, however, an artificially high rate of 80 percent for the incidence of a heavy facial structure and prominent chin as shared by both Kaczynski and the Zodiac. While common reason will dictate that this number is grossly exaggerated, it is at least high enough that we can be absolutely certain to have covered the entire range of population that bears the trait. Eighty percent of Z, or 0.6215 provides us with a figure of 0.4972 publicity-seeking male Caucasian disaffected killers in the range of ages from 25 to 45 bearing a heavy facial structure with a large and prominent chin.

Trait	Percentage	Original population	New population (Z)
Murderer	0.0089	221,000,000	19,669
Male	88.6	19,669	17,427
Caucasian	46	17,427	8,016
Ages 25–45	47	8,016	3,768
Disaffected	33	3,768	1,243
Widespread publicity, terror and demand for publication	0.05	1,243	0.6215
Facial structure	80	0.6215	0.4972

Intellectually, Zodiac exhibited a diverse admixture of abilities, as evidenced both by his method of operation and the contents of his letters. The extent of his intelligence is borne out by what we have related of Zodiac's grammatical abilities, his organizational skills, his understanding of literature, and his implied abilities in the fields of chemistry, electronics, and mathematics. To this range of acquisitions must certainly be added the practical abilities he demonstrates in the application of bomb-making and cryptography. His actual intelligence quotient is impossible to assess, since IQ can be determined only by the use of tests employing clear and consistent standards. Nevertheless, we are not completely blind in terms of objectively ascribing some measure of intelligence to the Zodiac.

For educational assessments, intelligence quotients are commonly classified within one of seven categories, each pertaining to a particular range of IQs as follows:

IQ Range	Classification
Very Superior	130 and above
Superior	120–129
High Average	110–119
Average	90–109
Low Average	80–89
Borderline	70–79
Extremely Low	69 and below

Further classifications are made by the types of occupations typically associated with particular ranges of IQ:[6]

IQ Range	Classification
140	Top Civil Servants; Professors and Research Scientists.
130	Physicians and Surgeons; Lawyers; Engineers (Civil and Mechanical)
120	School Teachers; Pharmacists; Accountants; Nurses; Stenographers; Managers.
110	Foremen; Clerks; Telephone Operators; Salesmen; Policemen; Electricians.
100+	Machine Operators; Shopkeepers; Butchers; Welders; Sheet Metal Workers.
100–	Warehousemen; Carpenters; Cooks and Bakers; Small Farmers; Truck and Van Drivers.
90	Laborers; Gardeners; Upholsterers; Farmhands; Miners; Factory Packers and Sorters.

Based upon what we can deduce of Zodiac's intelligence, the categories of Low Average, Borderline and Extremely Low can readily be dismissed. We would assume, therefore, that his actual IQ lies somewhere *between* the lowest "average" figure of 90 and the topmost levels of intelligence at 130 and above. Within that range lie all of the specific classifications of intelligence by occupation, as depicted in the second chart. Looking subjectively at the specific occupations, we must ask ourselves which of those callings we would hesitate to impute to Zodiac, based on the information at hand, and assuming that any individual with sufficient intelligence at work at one level would have no difficulty in working at the lower levels. The highest levels we would not be willing to impute are those given as 120 and greater, or those listed as school teachers, pharmacists, accountants, nurses, stenographers and managers and the categories above them. We hesitate to do so because most such occupations involve attainments of formal education, typically post-secondary education, that we cannot with certainty say that Zodiac possessed.

On the other hand, we are less hesitant about the occupations given in the 110 category, listed as foremen, clerks, telephone operators, salesmen, policemen and electricians. These are occupations whose intellectual requirements include the kinds of skills that in 1969 were typically associated with high school graduates, including the ability to learn a specific set of job functions, basic mathematical and verbal skills, organizational aptitude, the capability of analyzing a situation, and the ability to make important decisions affecting themselves and others. Through his correspondences and his actions, Zodiac gives evidence of possessing all those skills and more. We know that he was organized because of the way he prepared for each of his attacks. We know that his verbal abilities are sound because of the grammatical and syntactical correctness of his missives. He displays *at least* a foundational knowledge of literature, chemistry, electronics and higher mathematics. The very fact that he evinces all these qualities in combination with one another is evidence of an intellectual capacity that is somewhere above the average.

It would hardly be unreasonable, therefore, to place his IQ *at least* in the 110 to 119 range, with a minimum IQ of 110. Statistically, 25 percent of the population can be credited with IQ scores of 110 or higher.[7] Whatever his actual IQ, Zodiac would have fallen somewhere within this range. That Kaczynski would have fit within this range is not in doubt. Twenty-five percent of Z, or 0.04972, provides us with a figure of 0.1243 publicity-seeking male Caucasian disaffected killers in the range of ages from 25 to 45 bearing a heavy facial structure with a large and prominent chin and possessing an IQ of at least 110.

Trait	Percentage	Original population	New population (Z)
Murderer	0.0089	221,000,000	19,669
Male	88.6	19,669	17,427
Caucasian	46	17,427	8,016
Ages 25–45	47	8,016	3,768
Disaffected	33	3,768	1,243
Widespread publicity, terror and demand for publication	0.05	1,243	0.6215
Facial structure	80	0.6215	0.4972
Intelligence quotient	25	0.4972	0.1243

There is no real need to proceed beyond this point. For illustrative purposes we have performed our task, which is to demonstrate, not only the extremely small probability that any individual might possess the characteristics of a Kaczynski or a Zodiac, but their absolute uniqueness in relationship to one another and the population as a whole. The final figure given for Z, at 0.1243 of one individual from a total population of 221 million, may be rendered in whole numbers as a probability of one in 1,777,956,556, or one in one billion, seven hundred seventy-seven million, nine hundred fifty-six thousand, five hundred fifty-six. That is the approximate likelihood that any single individual bears all the qualities we have ascribed to either criminal. Without presuming to speak as statisticians, we may nonetheless affirm that the likelihood of two such criminals appearing together in the selfsame year must be, at the very best, extremely small.

Nit-pickers and other pedants may argue that some of our statistics are far from accurate, and to this we must reply that they are right. Most of the figures have been highballed — in some instances to an unnatural degree — to account for ambiguities or deficiencies in the available statistics. Many characteristics have been omitted because they cannot be adequately quantified. Not included are the connections to bomb-making and cryptography, the facility with weapons, and the use of a disguise, any one of which would have raised the final odds by anywhere from 25 to 50 percent. Not included are the references to mountains, hills and trees, the connection to Montana, or the revelations of the meta-codes. Not included are the similarities in handwriting, and our lengthy list of stylistic similarities, any one of which might raise the final odds by factors of two or three. Omitted also are the line-in-circle graffiti left by both killers in conjunction with a crime, and the use by both of literary allusion, a trait that is as rare in the general population as it is within the ranks of those who commit murder and follow it up with letters to the press. Had those qualities been included, the final numbers would have proven so egregious as to overload the natural capacities of human incredulity.

Such overkill is hardly necessary. For we have not attempted to create a metaphysical certainty of Kaczynski's complicity in the Zodiac affair. Rather, we have sought to buttress, by the use of hard statistics, what appears to be a very good subjective argument arising from the facts and inferences of each respective case. Yet, it must be distinctly understood that to those facts and inferences neither argumentation nor judgment need be applied. No person will be hanged, electrocuted, or lethally injected on the basis of the data given here. If the undertaking has proceeded as designed, its central goal has been achieved. The reader will have emerged with a clearer understanding of the linkage between two of the most enigmatic killers known to modern times. That the similarities are both numerous and astounding, he will have no doubt. And he may rest assured that, as the mystery of the Zodiac passes into legend, one name will increasingly excite the imaginations of those obsessed by a phenomenon whose truth can never fully be resolved. May they marvel at the story and conclude, that in all the broad annals of human crime, there never was a criminal quite like the one who called himself THE ZODIAC — at least until KACZYNSKI came along.

THE END

APPENDIX A

Correspondences and Common Nomenclature of the Zodiac Killer and the Unabomber

Correspondences of the Zodiac:

Nomenclature:	Slover Call
Date:	July 5, 1969
Remarks:	Anonymous telephone call to Vallejo P.D.

Nomenclature:	Times-Herald Letter
Date:	July 31, 1969
Remarks:	Contained one-third of Three-Part Cipher

Nomenclature:	Chronicle Letter
Date:	July 31, 1969
Remarks:	Contained one-third of Three-Part Cipher

Nomenclature:	Examiner Letter
Date:	July 31, 1969
Remarks:	Contained one-third of Three-Part Cipher

Nomenclature:	Three-Part Cipher
Date:	July 31, 1969
Remarks:	Solved cipher containing plaintext message.

Nomenclature:	Examiner II Letter
Date:	August 7, 1969

Nomenclature:	Berryessa Graffiti
Date:	September 27, 1969
Remarks:	Graffiti in black felt-tipped pen on car door of victim Bryan Hartnell.

Nomenclature:	Slaight Call
Date:	September 27, 1969
Remarks:	Anonymous telephone call to Napa County P.D.

Nomenclature: Stine Letter
Date: October 13, 1969

Nomenclature: Dripping Pen Card
Date: November 8, 1969
Remarks: Contained unsolved 340-symbol cipher.

Nomenclature: Seven-Page Letter
Date: November 9, 1969

Nomenclature: Belli Letter
Date: December 20, 1969
Remarks: Addressed to attorney Melvin Belli.

Nomenclature: Cid Letter
Date: April 20, 1970
Remarks: Contained an unsolved 13-symbol cipher.

Nomenclature: Dragon Card
Date: April 28, 1970

Nomenclature: Mt. Diablo Letter
Date: June 26, 1970
Remarks: Contained an unsolved 32-symbol cipher and Philips 66 road map.

Nomenclature: Mikado Letter
Date: July 24, 1970

Nomenclature: Little List Letter
Date: July 26, 1970

Nomenclature: 13-Hole Card
Date: October 5, 1970
Remarks: Index card with paste-up wording and symbols.

Nomenclature: Halloween Card
Date: October 27, 1970
Remarks: Greeting card with paste-up wording and symbols.

Nomenclature: L.A. Times Letter
Date: March 13, 1971

Nomenclature: Pines Card
Date: March 22, 1971
Remarks: Index card with paste-up wording and symbols.

Nomenclature: Monticello Card
Date: July 13, 1971
Remarks: Described by SFPD as "letters pasted on picture." Included by SFPD in its "Suspected Zodiac Correspondence" document as part of the effort to obtain DNA specimens from stamps and envelopes attributed to the Zodiac.

Nomenclature: Exorcist Letter
Date: January 29, 1974

Nomenclature: SLA Letter
Date: February 14, 1974
Remarks: Not officially authenticated. Presumed authentic by the *San Francisco Chronicle*, in an article dated August 26, 1976.

Nomenclature: Citizen Letter
Date: May 8, 1974

Nomenclature: Count Marco Letter
Date: July 8, 1974

Nomenclature: Donna Card
Date: December 27, 1974
Remarks: Greeting card, received by Mary Pilker, sister of Donna Lass. Not officially authenticated.

Correspondences of the Unabomber:

Nomenclature: Percy Wood Letter
Date: June 10, 1980

Remarks: Preceded the bomb sent to Percy Wood, President of
                    United Airlines.

Nomenclature: Berkeley Bomb Note
Date: June 2, 1982
Remarks: Brief notation contained within a package bomb:
                    "Wu — it works! I told you it would. R.V

Nomenclature: McConnell Letter
Date: November 15, 1985
Remarks: Note enclosed within a package bomb addressed to
                    James McConnell.

Nomenclature: 1985 Examiner Letter
Date: Date December, 1985
Remarks: Letter to San Francisco Examiner following the
                    Scrutton bombing of December 11, 1985. Referenced
                    in Unabomber letter to Penthouse Magazine in 1995.
                    Receipt not acknowledged by *San Francisco Exam-
                    iner*; referenced in Government's Trial Brief of No-
                    vember 12, 1997. According to the Trial Brief, a copy
                    of the original was found in Kaczynski's cabin.

Nomenclature: Times Letter
Date: June 2, 1993
Remarks: Letter addressed to Warren Hoge of the *New York
                    Times*.

Nomenclature: Times II Letter
Date: April 20, 1995
Remarks: Letter addressed to Warren Hoge of the *New York
                    Times*, demanding publication of Unabomber Mani-
                    festo on pain of further bombings.

Nomenclature: Gelernter Letter
Date: April 20, 1995
Remarks: Taunting letter to Dr. David Gelernter, victim of
                    1993 bombing.

Nomenclature: Roberts Letter
Date: April 20, 1995
Remarks: Threat letter to Dr. Richard J. Roberts, 1993 Nobel Prize winner.

Nomenclature: Sharp Letter
Date: April 20, 1995
Remarks: Threat letter to Dr. Phillip A. Sharp, 1993 Nobel Prize winner.

Nomenclature: CFA Call
Date: April 23, 1995
Remarks: Anonymous telephone call picked up by the answering machine at the offices of California Forestry Association. Probably intended for the Sacramento County Sheriff's Office. Caller claimed to be the Unabomber.

Nomenclature: Washington Post Letter
Date: June 24, 1995
Remarks: Letter addressed to Michael Getler of the *Washington Post*, accompanied by a copy of the Unabomber Manifesto.

Nomenclature: Times III Letter
Date: June 24, 1995
Remarks: Letter addressed to Warren Hoge of the *New York Times*, accompanied by a copy of the Unabomber Manifesto.

Nomenclature: Penthouse Letter
Date: June 24, 1995
Remarks: Letter addressed to publisher Bob Guccione of *Penthouse*, accompanied by a copy of the Unabomber Manifesto.

Nomenclature: Chronicle Threat Letter
Date: June 24, 1995

Remarks: Letter addressed to Jerry Roberts of the *San Francisco Chronicle*, threatening to blow up an airliner out of Los Angeles International Airport.

Nomenclature: Scientific American Letter
Date: June 24, 1995
Remarks: Letter to *Scientific American* remarking upon an earlier article, "Strange Matters: Can Advanced Accelerators Initiate Runaway Reaction?"

Nomenclature: Tom Tyler Letter
Date: June 24, 1995
Remarks: Letter to Berkeley professor Tom Tyler, accompanying a copy of the Unabomber Manifesto and requesting a critique of the Unabomber's goals.

Nomenclature: Times IV Letter
Date: June 28, 1995
Remarks: Brief note to the *New York Times*, retracting the threat contained in the Chronicle Threat Letter.

Select Publications of Theodore Kaczynski

Nomenclature: 1971 Essay
Date: Spring, 1971
Remarks: 23-page essay proposing the creation of an organization dedicated to stopping federal aid to scientific research.

Nomenclature: Manifesto
Date: None given
Remarks: 65-page treatise outlining the effects of technology on human civilization.

ENDNOTES

Chapter 1

1. Vernon J. Geberth, "Anatomy of a Lust Murder," *Law and Order Magazine*, 46:5.
2. J. Paul de River, *The Sexual Criminal: a Psychoanalytic Study*, (Burbank, California: Bloat Publishing, 2000), 144.
3. Kevin Waters, "Understanding Society's Most Dangerous Offender: A Typology and Corresponding Dynamic Analysis for the Substantive Theory Formulation of Serial Murder," (Masters Thesis). Florida State University, School of Criminology, 1987.
4. Napa County Sheriff's Department, Case No. 105907, Report of Dave Collins and Ray Land, September 29, 1969, 6.

Chapter 2

1. "Interview with Ted Kaczynski," *Green Anarchist*, No. 57-58, 1999.
2. Theodore John Kaczynski, Industrial Society and its Future (New York: 1996, New York Times), ¶ 96.
3. Exhibits in United States v. Kaczynski. United States District Court for the Eastern District of California, CR No. S-96-0259 GEB. May 4, 1998, GX 18-2003F, 1.
4. John Douglas and Mark Olshaker, *Unabomber: On the Trail of America's Most-Wanted Serial Killer* (New York: Pocket Books, 1996), 132.
5. Stephen J. Dubner, "I Don't Want to Live Long. I Would Rather Get the Death Penalty than Spend the Rest of My Life in Prison." *Time Magazine*, October 18, 1999.
6. Robert D. McFadden, "Prisoner of Rage." *New York Times*, May 26, 1996.
7. Exhibits, GX 18-2003F, 1.
8. Psychiatric Competency Report of Dr. Sally Johnson in United States v. Kaczynski, United States District Court for the Eastern District of California, September 11, 1998.
9. Serge F. Kovaleski, "Family Ties Plagued Kaczynski." *Washington Post*, January 20, 1997.
10. FBI Interview of David Kaczynski, February 24–25, 1996.
11. Exhibits, GX 18-2014C, 11.
12. Psychiatric Competency Report.
13. Ibid.
14. Ibid.
15. Ibid.
16. Exhibits, GX 18-2014F, 4.

17. Psychiatric Competency Report.
18. Ibid.
19. Exhibits, GX18-2014F, 3.
20. Ibid.
21. Ibid., GX18-2003F, p.1.
22. Ibid., GX18-2014F, p.3.
23. Ibid., GX18-2003F, p. 11.

Chapter 3

1. "Classmates Recall Suspect's Bomblets, Wood Connection, Immaturity." Associated Press, April 8, 1996.
2. Jeff Jardine, "Modesto DA Grew Up Near Kaczynski." *Modesto Bee Online,* June 26, 1996.
3. Exhibits, KZ014B.
4. Psychiatric Competency Report.
5. Theodore J. Kaczynski, "The Wave of the Future." *Saturday Review,* June 13, 1970, 4.
6. Martin Levin, "I Edited the Unabomber." *Weekly Standard,* June 12, 2000, 21. (" . . . and, yes — the Unabomber could write funny. Go figure.")
7. Kaczynski, *Industrial Society and Its Future,* ¶ 96.
8. Vallejo Police Department Crime Report, Case No. 243-146. Nancy Slover Report.
9. Napa Police Department, Supplementary Report of Officer D. Slaight. September 29, 1969.
10. Douglas and Olshaker, 34.
11. Nancy Gibbs, et al., *Mad Genius* (New York: Warner Books, 1996), 97–98.
12. Ibid., 92.
13. Douglas Oswell and Michael Rusconi, *Dr. Zodiac* (Dover, Delaware: Carfax Publishing, 1998), 545.
14. The Sacramento State graffiti were removed before their significance became apparent.

Chapter 4

1. Affidavit of Assistant Special Agent in Charge Terrie D. Turchie. United States District Court, District of Montana. April 3, 1996, ¶ 135.
2. Correspondence with the author, August 17 through September 15, 2003. For privacy reasons the correspondent has expressed a desire to remain anonymous.
3. McFadden, "Prisoner of Rage."
4. Kovaleski, "Family Ties Plagued Kaczynski."

5. Psychiatric Competency Report.
6. Ibid.
7. FBI Interview of David Kaczynski, March 12, 1996.
8. Exhibits, GX18-2046C, 10–13; GX18-778F, 33–36 (coded journal).
9. "Blood Bond," *People Weekly*, 50:4, 78.
10. McFadden, "Prisoner of Rage."
11. Turchie, ¶ 141.
12. Psychiatric Competency Report.

Chapter 5

1. Vallejo Police Department Crime Report, Case No. 243-146. Rust Report.
2. Dave Peterson, "Killer's Sole Survivor Talks," *The Vallejo News-Chronicle*, August 19, 1969.
3. Robert Graysmith, *Zodiac* (New York: Berkley Books, 1967), 27–39.
4. Napa County Sheriff's Department, Interview of John Robertson, Det/ Sgt., Napa County Sheriff's Department, with Bryan Calvin Hartnell NSO Case #105907, at Queen of the Valley Hospital on Sunday, September 28, 1969.
5. Graysmith, *Zodiac*, 317.
6. *Crimes of the Century*. See transcript at http://www.zodiackiller.com.
7. "Cabbie Slain in Presidio Heights," *San Francisco Examiner*, October 12, 1969.
8. San Francisco Police Department, Report of Frank Peda and Armond Pelissetti, October 12, 1969.
9. San Francisco Police Department, Intra-Departmental Memorandum, Information re: Stein Murder (submitted by Donald G. Fouke). November 12, 1969.
10. *Crimes of the Century*. See transcript at http://www.zodiackiller.com.
11. ABC News, Harry Phillips Interview of Donald Fouke, October 17, 2002.
12. Mike Rodelli Interview of Donald Fouke. See http://www.mikerodelli. com. May, 2004.
13. "Two Victims Found Lying Beside Road," *Vallejo Times-Herald*, July 5, 1969.
14. "Police Seeking Clues in Vallejo Shootings," *Vallejo Times-Herald*, July 6, 1969.
15. Vallejo Police Department, Slover Report.
16. "Killer Hunted As Coed Dies," *San Jose Mercury News*, September 1969.
17. Napa Police Department, Supplementary Report of Officer D. Slaight. September 29, 1969.

18. Exhibits, GX18-2030, 48.
19. FBI Interview of David Kaczynski, February 21, 1996.
20. Chris Waits and Dave Shors, *Unabomber: The Secret Life of Ted Kaczynski* (Helena, Montana: Helena Independent Record and Montana Magazine, 1999), 42.

Chapter 6

1. "Detecting Mind of Mathematician," Google Groups, archive of sci. math, September 30, 1995.
2. Kaczynski letter to R. Steven Lapham, February 19, 2003.
3. Kaczynski note to Warden Pugh, October 12, 2000. [Labadie Collection]
4. Kaczynski letter to Victor Clintron, February 4, 2003.
5. T.J. Kaczynski, "Boundary Functions and Sets of Curvilinear Convergence for Continuous Functions." *Transactions of the American Mathematical Society*, 141, 107.
6. T.J. Kaczynski, "Boundary Functions for Bounded Harmonic Functions." *Transactions of the American Mathematical Society*, 137, 203.
7. T.J. Kaczynski, "The Set of Curvilinear Convergence of a Continuous Function Defined in the Interior of a Cube." *Proceedings of the American Mathematical Society*, 23:2, 325.
8. Kaczynski, "Bounded Harmonic Functions," 203.

Chapter 7

1. Flesch-Kincaid statistics purport to analyze the difficulty of a particular reading passage. Common indices include reading ease and grade level, which are based on the total syllables, total sentences and total words contained within a given passage. Higher scores upon the former indicate greater ease in reading, while scores upon the latter offer a general indication of the grade level required to read and understand the passage. For these exercises, the author has employed the automated spelling and grammar functionality of Microsoft's Word 2003 word processor.
2. Kaczynski, *Industrial Society*, ¶¶ 1, 2.
3. Kaczynski letter to Joe Visocan, 1974.
4. Kaczynski "cop-out" letter. [Labadie Collection]
5. Gibbs, et al., *Mad Genius*.
6. "Suspect Brilliant with Math and Explosives," *USA Today*, November 13, 1996.
7. Exhibits, GX18-2046A, 43–45.
8. Turchie, ¶ 186.
9. Turchie, ¶ 189.
10. Turchie, ¶¶ 16, 19.

11. Turchie, ¶ 22.

12. United States v. Kaczynski, *Government's Trial Brief*, November 12, 1997.

13. Ibid.

Chapter 8

1. McFadden, "Prisoner of Rage."

2. Alston Chase, *Harvard and the Unabomber: The Education of an American Terrorist*. (New York: W.W. Norton & Company, 2003), 39.

3. Ibid.

4. Cynthia Hubert, "Role in Capture Haunts Kaczynski's Brother." *The Sacramento Bee*, January 19, 1997.

5. McFadden, "Prisoner of Rage."

6. Chase, *Harvard and the Unabomber*, 41.

7. Exhibits, GX18-2003B, 2.

8. Turchie, ¶ 26.

9. "Disruption of the Power Process," Google Groups, archive of alt.fan. unabomber, August 31, 1998.

10. Karl Stampfl, "He Came Ted Kaczynski, He Left the Unabomber." *The Michigan Daily*, April 7, 2006.

11. United States v. Kaczynski, Motion for Decision. United States District Court for the Eastern District of California, August 4, 2003.

12. Ibid.

13. Exhibits, K2014B UNA.

14. Ibid.

15. Muriel Rukeyser, "The Conjugation of the Paramecium." See http://www. famouspoetsandpoems.com.

16. Exhibits, GX18-2003F, p. 11.

17. "Interview with Ted Kaczynski," *Green Anarchist*, No. 57-58, 1999.

18. Exhibits, GX18-2003F, 11.

19. American Heritage Dictionary.

20. See http://www.zodiacmurders.com.

Chapter 9

1. Chase, *Harvard and the Unabomber*.

2. Ibid., 41.

3. Several words within the cipher contain obvious errors not attributable to deliberate misspelling. Among these are row 14, column 12 (THAE for THAT), row 21, column 6 (SLOI for SLOW), and row 21, column 13 (ATOP for STOP). These errors have been corrected in the examples given.

4. Serge F. Kovaleski, "1907 Conrad Novel May Have Inspired Unabomb Suspect," *Washington Post*, July 9, 1996.
5. It should be pointed out that the initial "T" in the construction "TEDANDDAVE" was misapplied as "E" in the original encryption of the cipher (see Note 3, above). While this may render the interpretation irrelevant, it appears obvious, to the author at least, that the "T" was intended and the misspelling of "THAE" for "THAT" was unintentional.
6. Don Foster, "The Fictions of Ted Kaczynski" *Vassar Quarterly*, 95:1, 14-17.
7. Ibid.
8. Psychiatric Competency Report.
9. Napa County Sheriff's Department, Hartnell Interview, September 28, 1969.
10. McFadden, "Prisoner of Rage."
11. Turchie, ¶ 135.
12. Theodore John Kaczynski, "Boundary Functions: A dissertation submitted in partial fulfillment of the requirements for the degree of Doctor of Philosophy in the University of Michigan." The University of Michigan, 1967.

Chapter 10

1. Dubner, "I Don't Want to Live Long." *Time Magazine*, October 18, 1999.
2. Waits and Shors, *Unabomber*, 206.
3. Ibid., 40–41.
4. J. Alienus Rychalski, "An Interview with Ted." *Blackfoot Valley Dispatch* (Lincoln, Montana) 19:4, 9.
5. Stampfl, "He Came Ted Kaczynski," April 7, 2006. Letter to Karl Stampfl.
6. Ted Kaczynski, "Hit It Where It Hurts." *Green Anarchy*, Spring 2002.
7. Ibid.
8. Ted Kaczynski, "When Non-Violence is Suicide." *Live Wild or Die*, No. 8, Spring 2002.
9. Kaczynski, "Curvilinear Convergence," 324.
10. Kaczynski, "Boundary Functions and Sets," 124.
11. Stampfl, "He Came Ted Kaczynski." Portion of Kaczynski autobiography.
12. Ibid.
13. Waits and Shors, *Unabomber*, 266.
14. Ibid., 185.
15. Kaczynski "cop-out" letter. [Labadie Collection]

Chapter 11

1. Federal Bureau of Investigation, Report of the Identification Division, Latent Fingerprint Section, Latent Case No. A-10042. December 4, 1969.

2. San Francisco Police Department, Intra-Departmental Memorandum, October 19, 1969.

3. Federal Bureau of Investigation, Report of the Identification Division, Latent Fingerprint Section, Latent Case No. A-10042. May 12, 1975.

4. Improvements in image-enhancement have revealed the presence of a "writer's palm" moving from left to right across the surface of the Zodiac's Exorcist Letter. While the authorities are apparently convinced that this "writer's palm" could have originated only from the hand that wrote the letter, two circumstances militate against that conclusion as an absolute certainty. Perhaps most significant is the fact that no other palm prints of this nature were found on any of the Zodiac correspondences from 1969 through 1971, suggesting that Zodiac understood full well the importance of masking his prints during composition of the letters. Moreover, further enhancements of the letter clearly indicate that the odd-sized sheet of paper had been more-or-less loosely crumpled, then smoothed-out prior to its having been written on. This suggests that the paper had been written on by a third party, crumpled, discarded, and retrieved by the Zodiac for use as a means of confounding the authorities in their investigation. See the author's website at http://unazod.com/essay.html for graphic enhancements of the Exorcist Letter showing both the ridge pattern areas and the obvious crumpling of the paper.

5. Correspondence of California CII (Sacramento) to FBI. February 2, 1974.

6. Federal Bureau of Investigation, Report of the Identification Division, Latent Fingerprint Section, Latent Case No. A-10042. February 21, 1974.

7. Pete Carey, "S.F. Police Discount Theories Pointing to Unabomber Suspect as Zodiac Killer." *San Jose Mercury-News*, July 31, 1996.

8. Ibid.

9. Edwin F. Alford, Jr., "Disguised Handwriting: A Statistical Survey of How Handwriting is Most Frequently Disguised." Journal of Forensic Sciences, October 1970, 486–487.

10. Gary Greenberg, "In the Kingdom of the Unabomber." *McSweeney's Quarterly Concern*.

Chapter 12

1. Exhibits, GX18-2046L, 15–17.

2. Government's Sentencing Memorandum in United States v. Kaczynski. United States District Court for the Eastern District of California, CR No. S-96-0259 GEB, May 4, 1998.
3. Exhibits, GX18-2003B, 1.
4. Declaration of Phillip J. Resnick, M.D. in United States v. Kaczynski. November 19, 1997.
5. Ibid.
6. Psychiatric Competency Report.
7. "Disruption of the Power Process," Google Groups, archive of alt.fan. unabomber, August 31, 1998. Essay by David Buchanan.
8. Ibid.
9. Exhibits, GX18-2014F, 4.
10. Government's Sentencing Memorandum.
11. Ibid.
12. Exhibits, GX18-2014C, 11.
13. Ibid., GX18-2014D, 22.
14. Ibid., GX18-2014F, 4.
15. Ibid., GX18-2003B, 1.
16. Ibid.
17. Turchie, ¶ 185.
18. Chase, *Harvard and the Unabomber*, 352.
19. Kaczynski, *Industrial Society and Its Future*, ¶ 44.
20. Psychiatric Competency Report.

Chapter 13

1. James Alan Fox and Marianne W. Zawitz, "Homicide Trends in the United States." United States Department of Justice, Bureau of Justice Statistics. See http://www.ojp.usdoj.gov/bjs/homicide/homtrnd.htm#contents, revised June 29, 2006.
2. Ibid.
3. Ibid.
4. Ibid.
5. Ibid. Statistics for years earlier than 1976 are not extant.
6. David Wechsler, *The Measurement of Adult Intelligence*.
7. Ibid.